HER DARK LEGION

#5 MESSENGER CHRONICLES

PIPPA DACOSTA

CHAPTER 1

"He that made this knows all the cost,
For he gave all his heart and lost."

\- W.B. Yeats, Old Earthen.

alen

SHINJ'S constant presence hummed at the back of my thoughts, beating in time with her two massive hearts. As those I loved fell apart around me, I wondered what it would have been like to fall into her embrace and bond as her pilot. Eternal life would be so much simpler.

The part of me designed to join with Faerie's enormous warcruisers still yearned for that connection, and always would. Shinj pushed against my mind. She also yearned to keep me and everyone here, in the observation room, safe.

She considered us her family—Kellee, Sota, and perhaps even Sirius, although Shinj remained unconvinced by the guardian. But one of us—our heart—was missing.

"How could you allow him to take Mylana?" Sirius accused Kellee, using Kesh's original name to remind us how the guardian had known her longer than any of us. He leaned over the table, propping himself up on his fists to loom over Kellee, seated opposite. Had there not been a table between them, I might have been forced to intervene.

Kellee stared back, as silent now as he had been since his arrival. He'd sprawled his predatory grace into a chair, and there he remained, face unreadable but for the occasional twitch in his cheek whenever Sirius commented on our failures. A quiet vakaru was a creature best left alone. The guardian was walking a thin line.

"I had her in my care for days, protected against all of Faerie," Sirius continued, straightening to his full fae height. "Cu Sith assassins, vicious Wild Ones, and even King Oberon himself. And you lost her within a few hours? *You* failed her." The guardian flung his tek-hand at Kellee in dismissal, but he wasn't done. The smell of wood smoke and warming spices permeated the air. Sirius was losing control of his magic. In Faerie, Royal Guardians—the oldest and most powerful of Faerie's creations—were known and respected for their composure. Sirius was losing his, but blind rage wasn't pushing him toward lashing out. He cared for Kesh, more than Kellee could fathom.

"You are a disgrace to the vakaru creed," he said, landing his final blow.

Anger lit up my veins, quick as lightning. "That's enough!" Accusations were one thing, but I would not have Kellee's honor called into question, not even by a guardian older than me.

Sirius whirled away in a fan of red hair and russet-colored frock coat, diverting his rage through the obs-window at Faerie's colorful planetary arc, some three hundred miles below our orbit.

Kellee's glare tracked the guardian and then rebounded to me as I approached the table. His eyes, usually green, burned with flecks of red. It wasn't like him to sit in silence. He likely believed Sirius's words to be true. When it came to Kesh, the marshal I'd known for over three centuries made mistakes, but he hadn't *let* Kesh go, as Sirius had accused. Eledan had taken her in her dreams. No one here could have stopped him. My *talents* were chaotic and did not extend to illusion. The Dreamweaver could not be beaten in his own realm.

Kellee dropped his gaze to the table and ground his teeth, his cheek fluttering.

We'd get her back. Eledan was just one fae. Granted, he was particularly good at dancing around us, but together, we, a guardian, a vakaru, and a drone-turned-man, would get her back. Eledan had left us his terms: give him the polestar pieces and he'd let Kesh choose which side she was on in this war. It seemed noble enough, but Kesh had a habit of sacrificing herself for others. Her choice would not be simple.

"He could not take her without her consent," Sota said. His presence, like the ship's, constantly pressed against my senses. Where the ship's touch soothed, however, Sota's created a static tingling. He looked human, but he was further from it than anyone here. Dark hair fell in a messy mop, long enough to obscure his tek-eye—the only outward sign he wasn't what he appeared to be. He looked no older than Kesh, perhaps in his mid-twenties in human years, but inside, his age was indeterminable. Constructed by Kesh's hands and brought to life by a magic she no longer had, Sota had been made to protect her, but in the last cycles, he'd become more than tek-equipment to us.

"He has taken her before." I glanced at Sota and Kellee, two of my most trusted friends and advisors. Kesh loved them. The bond she and I shared broadcasted it every time she favored either with one of her small, rare smiles. "Kellee and I spent months bringing her back from Eledan, and even then, his hold on her remained for months afterward."

"She was weaker then." Sota lifted his head. "Guardian, you spent the most time with her on Faerie. What was her mind like before Eledan took her?"

Sirius didn't turn and remained quiet, likely thinking back on his days with Kesh. Something had happened between them on Faerie. It had shattered the guardian's stoicism and warmed him to Kesh in ways I had thought impossible. "She was focused," he finally said, turning his head. His auburn lashes fluttered, his gaze falling. "Driven. Determined." He turned to address us. "There is something you should all know. The Mad Prince offered her the one thing she could not refuse. She bargained herself into Eledan's ownership for saru freedom."

The truth of his words rocked me on my feet. Shinj's touch reached out to soothe me, and the surrounding lights throbbed a deeper red in response to my distress. I barred the shock from my face and swallowed a sharp knot in my throat.

She had given herself to Eledan for her saru.

A foolish solution, but also a brave one. She believed she had no self-worth—a belief she'd spent her entire life striving to prove wrong—but she always fell into the same trap, and Eledan knew it—knew her. Her people and the past she clung to, believing it shaped her, had always been her weakness.

Sirius mentioned the trade for the polestar, but it took so long for me to regain my runaway thoughts that I missed his words. Bargains on Faerie were binding. Kesh had always escaped before, as a saru so far from home, but Faerie was not so forgiving of oathbreakers, especially now that the Hunt was free. Oathbreakers and those who flouted justice were the Hunt's preferred sustenance.

"Kellee," Sota said, his tone softening. "What do we do?"

Kellee was lost inside his own thoughts. Like this, he was of no use to Kesh. My earlier anger reignited, and this close to Faerie, my restrained and depleted magic crackled awake. This was not the time for Kellee to lose faith in himself or us. None of us had that luxury. Kesh needed us.

If he wouldn't provide any answers, then I would. "We give Eledan the pieces." I said, drawing the weight of everyone's attention. "Once we have Kesh back, we'll have enough power to deal with Eledan."

"That's assuming she chooses to come back," Kellee countered.

"Do you know where the polestar pieces are?" Sirius asked.

"We have—"

"Three pieces," Kellee interrupted. He looked at me, his eyes needle sharp. "Eledan has the last piece. We have three: Kesh is a piece, the acorn, and there's another. Isn't there, Talen?"

Then he knew I'd kept the discovery of Sjora's thimble from him. I hadn't deceived him deliberately, more so out of caution. Kellee's natural desire to be the righteous crusader had convinced me to keep the last piece of the polestar to myself, until I could be sure Kellee wouldn't toss it out an airlock. But seeing how my betrayal cut deep lines into his face, I regretted the decision. Kellee had never trusted easily, and regarding the fae, he didn't trust at all. By concealing

Sjora's thimble, I'd proved the marshal's centuries' old assumptions right.

"I have the thimble," I admitted.

"Were you ever going to tell me?" The scorn in those words cut at a different kind of bond, one of a friendship that had lasted mortal lifetimes.

"Until recently, I was not sure the thimble was a piece."

"Karushit." His sneer revealed the tips of his lengthening fangs.

Sota looked similarly disappointed, while Sirius was as unreadable as all fae who had long ago mastered the art of hiding their emotions.

"For Sjora to have the thimble seemed too convenient," I explained. "I wanted to make sure it was a fragment, but when the events on Hapters revealed my true name and..." Hapters had revealed the monster I'd once been—a powerful killer and everything Kellee despised about the fae. "I feared you would assume I'd kept the thimble for malevolent reasons." Because, as the Nightshade—the unseelie's chosen ruler—I would have kept a piece of Faerie's most dangerous weapon. No matter how many times I said the words—*I am not who I once was*—only Kesh truly believed me. Oberon had wiped out Kellee's people, and he saw that potential in all fae, including me.

Kellee sprang from the chair and marched toward the door. "Take Shinj down to Faerie," he said, coldly. "We don't have a choice. We give Eledan exactly what he wants, or he'll make her sleep forever. I'm not prepared to risk Kesh's mortal lifetime."

He was out of the chamber and gone. If I didn't set this right, he'd assume the worst when we needed to be united.

Sota's soft eyes urged me to go after him. The drone had always known how to fix things between us.

I nodded and followed Kellee, catching sight of him ahead in the corridor. "Wait, Kellee..."

Kellee turned from a solid mass of male into a blur too fast for me to track. His hand locked around my throat, hard fingers squeezing. My back cracked against Shinj's wall. The ship's alarm rang through my thoughts. Kellee's grip tightened. He leaned in, pinning me firmly. Red blazed in his eyes. His fangs extended, and he worked his jaw to accommodate those king-killing weapons. He'd torn out countless throats, and I had no doubt he'd do the same to mine if he believed I'd betrayed him.

"I've warned you repeatedly not to fuck with me, fae." His eyes drilled into mine. "And you kept something as important as that thimble a secret. Why?"

"Because of this..." I croaked. His fingers eased, allowing me to breathe. "Because you still see me as your enemy."

He leaned closer, the threat a living, breathing fire behind his glare. "Then stop making it easy for me."

Now that we were closer to Faerie than I'd been in countless centuries, I had access to power that would make short work of the last vakaru. I could have thrown him off, could easily have fought him, but our clashing wouldn't help either of us. Kesh needed us to work together, not fall apart.

His grip released, and as he backed up a step, I rubbed the ache from my neck.

"The fate of Faerie relies on reuniting those pieces," I wheezed. "I wasn't sure you wouldn't take the thimble and hide it far from us. Tell me you haven't considered it? Tell me you haven't thought of scattering the pieces again for the greater good?"

Kellee dragged his hand across his chin. "I owe Faerie nothing. Scattering the pieces *would* stop anyone from getting their hands on a powerful weapon."

He had considered it. I knew him too well, and that's why I'd kept Sjora's piece from him. As dangerous as the polestar was, we needed it. Faerie needed it. The war wouldn't end without restoring the balance it provided. "You'll do what's right... you always have. I know that, and I don't blame you. Someone needs to stand for good, but it's why I didn't tell you."

"Not me, not this time." His claws retracted. "I'm getting Kesh back at any cost." He ran a hand over his hair and tightened the band holding his hair back. That tightness translated to the rest of him too. Less than a day had passed since he'd killed Oberon. I'd seen him furious, seen him high on victory and low in defeat. In the years he'd acted as my jailor, I'd come to know Marshal Kellee as well as I knew myself, and it wasn't only my keeping secrets tearing him up. He was afraid, just like I was.

"Kellee..." His love was a fierce, wild thing, and one day, it would be ripped from him, as it would be from me. Such was the way of mortals. So brightly they shone, until they extinguished in a blink. "She *is* the polestar," I murmured, creeping the meaning around his anger. "We can't ignore that. Have you thought about what will happen... later?"

He winced and cut me a scorching look to back off. "If she's reunited with all pieces," he said, "they'll cease to exist in their current form." He delivered the fact with all the distance of a lawman doing his work, detaching himself from its reality.

"Not *if*—when."

Kesh would die. He needed to hear it, to understand it. More was at stake than Kesh's life. In many ways, she had been right to bargain for her people; she knew, in the land of immortals, Faerie would resist change for millennia. Kesh was playing the long game. But Kellee... he'd played that game long enough. He'd lost much to it. We both had.

It hurt to hear. By Faerie, I knew it hurt. I was bonded with Kesh. Her death would likely mean my own, but I'd die a thousand times over to save her. "I wanted you to take the pieces and hide them away," I said. "If I gave you that thimble and you threw it away, Kesh would live. I wanted it. I considered having Shinj eject it into space. But what would become of the dark then? It has to end. Kesh knows she can end it. We must reunite the polestar with its fragments. Order must be returned to the light and dark fae. It's inevitable. The longer it goes on, the more lives will be lost—saru, namu, human, and fae alike. Kesh knows even the brightest star must die."

"How can you give up on her, Talen?" His voice cracked, and all the fierce, violent vakaru fell away.

Regret twisted sharply in my chest. "No. No, I haven't... and I never will. We will get her back, and we'll do whatever it takes to keep her safe, but she will fight us. She'll try to give up everything because she believes it's the only way. We have to make her see otherwise. I'm prepared to stand beside you, beside Kesh, no matter the cost, even if it goes against her wishes. I once fought for Faerie, for all the dark fae, but I'm no longer the Nightshade. Faerie doesn't matter to me the way it once did. The polestar, light and dark—those things don't matter to me. They should, and it terrifies me that I'm turning my back on who I was, on who I'm supposed to be, all for a mortal." He looked up, my words finally getting through that vakaru stubbornness. "I'm not your enemy, Kellee. I never was."

Over the years, I'd wondered if he'd suspected how easily I could have escaped him. As I stood with him now, the truth was all over his face. He had known, but as two immortals in a mortal world, where else could either of us have gone?

He extended his hand. "You're with me?"

"I always have been." I gripped his forearm and shook. Together, we were ready to fight for Kesh.

CHAPTER 2

Marshal Kellee

THE OLD ARENA Eledan had chosen to hand over Kesh hadn't seen any gladiator battles in a long time. Terraces that once seated thousands of fae had crumbled, and above us, vines dangled through the broken crystal dome roof. Faerie's thick, tangling flora could consume a structure like this overnight, should they wish to, but there was an age to this place that set my teeth on edge. Everything on this wretched planet was alive. Glowing wisps bobbed in the air like sentient pollen. Pixies chittered and snickered, rustling nearby bushes and irritating my sensitive vakaru hearing with their incessant songs. The huge flowerheads—their black centers like enormous single eyes—tracked us.

I cradled Kesh in my arms, her head resting against my shoulder as she slept. She seemed smaller tucked in close. It always amazed me how someone so small could survive and master everything she had.

Talen walked to my right, Sota to my left. Sirius hung back. Sota had instructions from me to keep an eye on the guardian. I hadn't trusted Sirius before and wouldn't anytime soon, despite Hulia's namu instincts telling her he only had Kesh's wellbeing in mind. My vakaru senses told me to separate his head from his neck at the first opportunity.

Hulia had remained on board Shinj. Our ship hummed above the glass dome like an enormous sea creature. Her lights flowed from stern to bow in colorful ripples. Should the Hunt appear, Shinj would transport us off the planet. Hopefully, it wouldn't come to that. Eledan was more than enough to handle. The Hunt—the creature that had killed Aeon—was off-the-scale dangerous and not something I was ready to encounter. That problem was for another day.

We emerged from the undergrowth to find the Mad Prince sprawled on a lower seated terrace, his head propped on his hand as though he'd been waiting for some time. A crown of bleached twigs sat stark white against his black hair. No royal robes, not for this brat, just simple hunting leathers laced with silver thread. He smirked as we crossed the arena floor. I grinned back, revealing sharp fangs. Such a shame he'd missed his brother's death-by-vakaru. I welcomed the chance to demonstrate his brother's final moments on him.

"The Messenger gang's all here." He jumped to his feet and eyed us in turn, reading our mismatched clothes and lack of visible weapons. Only when his gaze settled on Sota did one fine dark eyebrow arch in surprise. "A fitting upgrade for a unique drone," he said, words bloated with flattery. Sota shifted from one foot to the other. "Your code was a work of genius. I've long admired Kesh's work, and to see you upright and fully functioning..." He touched his fingers to his chest, over where his tek-heart thumped, and beamed like a proud father. "How does it feel to be one of Kesh's males?"

"Fuck you," Sota replied, beating me to it.

Eledan masterfully ignored the insult, unconcerned that Sota could fill him full of holes without warning. Unfortunately, attacking Eledan wouldn't wake Kesh. "The things I could do with your internal processes." The prince's eyes flashed. "Kesh's tek-construction was riddled with flaws. If you like this upgrade"—he flicked his hand at Sota's new body—"what I could do with you would blow your tek-mind. I conceived that body you're wearing. I know every inch of you, *Sota*. I created Arcon. I created the drone you were originally, and I created your current suit. I created *you*. So fitting. I am protofae, after all. From the fae, all life does spring." He winked. "You need only ask for my touch. I'd be more than happy to oblige."

Sota licked his lips and tilted his head toward me in question. "Let me kill him?"

If only Eledan were that easy to destroy. "No."

He held his forefinger and thumb an inch apart. "Just a little bit?"

Eledan spread his arms. "You think you could shoot me and make it stick? On Faerie? Go ahead..."

Sota looked to Talen for a second opinion, but Talen had zeroed in on Eledan as though the rest of us had vanished. They hadn't met before, as far as I knew.

Eledan gave up taunting Sota and methodically appraised our line—skimming over Kesh in my arms. He lifted his chin under Talen's cool glare. "The Nightshade..." the prince purred and something nearby scurried off into the undergrowth. "I witnessed you in battle once. So long ago, you likely don't recall, you commanded Night like the unseelie were your pets. I wasn't sure it was you the Nothing Girl had found until she dreamed you up. The Nightshade, not so dead, as we were led to believe... We have that in common, you and I. We've both survived Oberon. Without my assistance, Kesh would never have known you—the *real* you." He let that gem sink its barb in. "Here, now, you seem... diminished."

Talen glared back, unfazed and immovable, and when Eledan didn't get a rise from the former-Nightshade, he turned his attention to Sirius, now moving into line beside Sota. The guardian's stern face spoke of a history between them. A history Eledan laughed off. "A tek-arm to my tek-heart. Does that make us brothers, Lord of Fire?"

"You are as tiresome now as you've always been. Such a terrible disappointment to your mother."

Eledan instantly lost his smile. "Careful, guardian. How difficult it must have been to live with your unrequited love for so long. To watch my brother torture Kesh day after day and stand by, so helpless and confused by your sordid feelings for a weak saru."

"She was never weak," Sirius replied.

Sirius had loved Kesh... for a long time? I hadn't expected to hear that information, and I had no idea what to do with it, besides burying it deep to examine later. The prince played his games, dropping hints of information to infuriate and undermine. I snagged Talen's knowing gaze. He'd heard it too.

"Eledan, your reign is a farce," Sirius said, raising his voice in true sidhe fashion. "Give up what you do not want. The Wild Ones will protect you from the nightmare of your own making until this is resolved."

Indignation darkened Eledan's face. "I did not give up when my own brother turned against me. I did not give up when Queen Mab neglected me. I did not give up when Faerie forgot me. I shall not give up now." He turned to me. "You have the polestar fragments?"

I considered not answering and telling Sota to fire, Sirius to unleash his flame, and Talen to release his darkness but it would be for nothing. Eledan would still have Kesh in his dream world.

"We hand over the pieces and you wake her?" I asked.

He held out his hand. "Agreed."

"She'll return with us?"

"That's up to Kesh, not you or I." He flicked his fingers toward his palm. "Hand over the pieces, *lawman.*" Sharp intelligence sparkled in his blue eyes, and not for the first time, I wondered who was more dangerous: Oberon or Eledan. Events in the knoll hinted that another force had driven Oberon's actions, but Eledan... his cunning madness was all him.

"Come now, vakaru," he urged. "Kesh's lifetime isn't getting any longer."

"I killed your brother, fae. Don't think I won't kill you too."

Eledan rolled his eyes. "There's so much ignorance in that threat that I'd be wasting my breath in my attempt to enlighten you."

My gums tingled at the memory of tasting Oberon's blood.

"My brother wanted to die," Eledan snapped, *enlightening* me anyway because his ego demanded it. "He *was* weak. You were just the brute standing in front of him with the claws." He likely regretted missing his brother's death. I'd stolen his chance at vengeance. I had that victory over him, at least.

This posturing had already gone on too long. Crouching, I laid Kesh gently on the dirt. Would she hate us for handing Eledan one of Faerie's greatest weapons in exchange for her or agree with our decision? She was still one-quarter of the polestar. Eledan didn't have every piece yet. There was every-thing to play for.

I removed the throbbing acorn from my coat pocket and dropped it into the Mad Prince's palm, then nodded at Talen. Eledan's smile grew as Talen withdrew a glass thimble from his coat. Talen handed it over, and Eledan admired the two trinkets nestled in his palm. So much trouble in such small things.

Eledan poked the thimble. "Now *this* piece has eluded me for a long time. It was stolen when my brother had his flights attempt to kill me during the first war. It's right that it has returned to me now."

"You *stole* it from Valand," I said.

He looked up, his blue eyes as cutting and multifaceted as crystal. "You're so quick to hate, Marshal Kellee, but you and I? We're on the same side."

"We are not on the same side, *prince*."

Both pieces went into his pocket. "No? You don't recall the dreams? Our deal?" He laughed it out, knowing how his games infuriated. "Never mind, it will come back to you as time dictates." He stepped back, brought his hands together, closed his eyes, and bowed his head. His smile however, inched into a grin.

What dream? What deal? "You're lying. I made no deal with you."

"Lying?" He chuckled, eyes still closed. "Today is a dangerous day to lie on Faerie. The time for lies is long over."

Kesh gasped awake.

The ground shuddered. Thunder rolled, but not from above. From *below*. Rock cracked apart, sounding like pistol shots. From my left, a chasm opened like a hungry mouth yawning in the earth. Its edges rushed toward Kesh.

esh

I WAS FALLING, my body weightless.

Weren't you supposed to wake after falling in a dream?

A jolt snapped up my back, yanking me to a stop and dousing me in reality.

"Kesh!"

The world spun. Rocks and earth rained from above. I tasted dirt on my lips, grit on my tongue. My coat's seams cut under my arms, holding me over the darkness below. *No, don't look down...* Too late. A void yawned beneath me, like the yawning darkness that had killed Aeon and was now hunting me. But this was a dead darkness, an emptiness, a hole with no bottom.

"Kesh, reach up!" The words flew at me like bullets.

Sota. Lifting my head, I blinked into dust and dirt.

I was still dreaming, wasn't I? Nothing made any sense.

"Kesh, take my hand!" Sirius was here too. If only the dust would stop falling on me, I'd be able to see them both.

And Talen. His power, a flow of life and energy, beat inside my chest, warm and comforting, his entire being feeding through our bond.

They were real. They were here.

A tek-hand glinted among the trembling earth, and behind that hand, Sirius's green eyes glowed through the clouds of dust. *I should reach for his hand.* He had saved me before, but something seemed wrong, like a thin film of a lie coating reality.

"Kesh!" Sota was so close, but I couldn't see him. I couldn't see much of anything. Just Sirius. It didn't matter. They were all here, together. I trusted them.

I reached for Sirius's metal hand, closed my fingers around his cool grip, and held tight. He smiled, but the smile didn't belong to Sirius. The touch turned warm. Inky black hair consumed Sirius's red locks. Green eyes turned icy blue. Eledan. He laughed that wretched laughter. He let go.

I was falling again, falling far from those who loved me, into whatever trap Eledan had sprung below.

ellee

SOTA GRABBED FOR HER, calling her name, and then they were gone, swallowed by a bank of rolling gray clouds. The crack in the earth was gone too.

Illusions. *That piece of royal fae karushit!*

And then Talen and Sirius had vanished inside the churning gray smoke. Only Eledan's sickening laughter haunted the fog.

"You're out of your depth on Faerie, vakaru," the prince crooned from nowhere and everywhere.

Claws out, I spun, raking at the fog, and narrowly missed disemboweling Sirius at the last second. The guardian threw me a look that told me he knew I had wanted to follow through and plunge my claws into him. He read the thought on my face, and in response, liquid fire burst from his outline, setting him ablaze like a beacon in the night. The beast in me read it as a threat. Instincts urged me to kill him before he could kill me, but as the fog burned away and Sirius backed up, reason reined in the madness, clearing my head.

There the pair of fae stood, one made of fire and the other of silver and darkness, his unseelie wings spread wide. More dark than light. More monster than lordly sidhe. Talen, as the Nightshade, made me look tame. This was Faerie, ripe with magic and monsters. I was in their backyard now, and I'd never felt our differences more keenly than when both powerful fae looked at me as though I should be kneeling.

I shook my head to dislodge the crackling insanity. Sirius was a dick, but apparently, he loved Kesh, and I knew Talen better than my senses tried to tell me.

The fog rolled away, revealing the arena floor. No cracks, and no Kesh or Sota either. Turning on the spot revealed no sight of them and no indication as to where they could have gone.

"You son of a sluagh, Eledan!" My shout sailed far into Faerie, carried by unnatural winds. "The Hunt will not be enough to stop me from killing you!"

Behind me, Sirius's fire cooled and Talen's suffocating magic withdrew. "We must leave," Talen said. "Shinj warns that the Hunt is drawing close."

I'd leave, but I wasn't going far. I turned to face the two fae. "Where would he take her?"

"He's building a seat of power," Sirius replied, hanging back, out of my reach. "Hiding is not the sidhe way. Find the gathering fae and we'll find the prince."

I didn't look at him. Couldn't look. The wildest part of me wanted him dead for all of Faerie's wrongs, for who and what he was, for loving Kesh and letting her go. The protofae had taken my people from me, and now their royal brat had stolen Kesh and Sota. I was so out of my depth I was damn well drowning. Fuck Eledan for being right.

Thunder rumbled. Our enormous ship hovered in low, smothering the sky and broken dome. I needed an army, needed to fight. I needed my damn people back and Kesh by my side.

"We'll find them," Talen said. "For now, Kellee... we must leave."

"Did he get the polestar?" I sighed, shuddering out the killing desire. The wildness was too close and had been since I'd killed Oberon. I needed to be better than this, to think more clearly.

Talen held out a glass thimble, pinched between his finger and thumb, and smiled. "Only one piece."

We'd switched the thimble polestar fragment for a dummy, gambling on the fact Eledan wouldn't notice how his cheap trinket didn't throb with power while beside the acorn. It had worked. "Good."

Shinj's bright, hypnotic light flowed over us, bathing the area in a cool blue. Kesh was awake, and we still had a piece of the polestar. All we had to do was trust Kesh to make the right choice. "Let's go find our messenger."

esh

I WOKE with a head full of dream-like images of Faerie swallowing me down, of Sirius's gleaming arm, and of Eledan's urbane laughter. I might have leaped to my feet had the pair of strong arms clamped around me not tightened into a vise-like grip.

A quick visual check for any immediate threats revealed a high-ceilinged bedchamber with gold and silver flourishes, minimal furniture, including the bed I lay on, and no windows. There was nothing like this room on Shinj, and the shape lacked the human-made feel. This had to be Faerie.

"You can let go now, Sota."

"Must I?" Sota asked in my ear. It felt like before, when he'd been a ball of killing tek and used to sit low on my shoulder. "You're so warm. This body molds perfectly to your back. I'm experiencing some interesting sensations. I don't think I ever want to let you go."

Only Sota had the power to summon a smile in the direst of circumstances. I twisted in his arms and looked him in the eyes. A small smile pulled at his soft lips and brightened his honest mock-human eye. The red tek-eye wasn't as cold up close. I flicked a lock of his hair away to admire its sleek, accurate detail. He really was a work of art.

I touched Sota's cheek, finding it warm. Nothing hinted at its synthetic construction. I'd seen mandroids before, although they were more popular in Sol than Halow, but never this close. Less than a day had passed since I'd learned he was my Sota, and it didn't feel real. Maybe it never would.

He smiled, appearing disarmingly real and very male, now that we were eye to eye. When he touched my face in the same manner in which I'd touched his, my heart did a little anxious flutter.

"This feels kinda weird," he said. "Doesn't it?"

"Yeah." It did feel strange, but I couldn't place the sensation. I looked at him as though he were something precious, something to be loved and admired, but not in the way I looked at Kellee or Talen. Sota was family. *My* family. I'd created him.

He withdrew his hand, his smile gentle and honest.

"How long was I out?" I asked.

"Fifteen hours, four minutes, and three seconds." His voice, so smooth now that it was synthesized through more sophisticated filters, held a delightfully humorous purr that perfectly matched his personality.

"What happened?" I asked.

"Sirius is permanently angry. Talen shouted. Kellee is a twitch away from turning feral."

"Oh." I rolled onto my back and blinked at the ceiling. "They tried to negotiate with Eledan, didn't they?" Of course they had. Clearly, negotiations hadn't gone well.

"Yes and no..." He narrowed his eyes and whispered, "The walls are listening."

Then we weren't free to speak. I sat up and waited for my head to stop spinning before rising off the bed. Dressed in my typical leathers and coat, I dropped my hand and found the whip still clipped to my side. I had no memory of anything after I'd fallen asleep in Kellee's arms, but I did recall being naked then, which meant someone had dressed me and left the whip with me.

"Kellee wants me here?" I asked, turning to find Sota on the bed, eyes dancing over me.

"There weren't many options." He swung his legs off the bed, stood, and stretched his arms over his head, his shirt lifting to reveal his lower waist and hips, his pants slung low. Arcon sure knew how to make their mandroids. "Kellee figured you'd be happier armed when you woke." Had Hulia picked out that body or had he chosen it? It was a fine example of a mid-twenties human male. Sota had picked it, for sure.

He placed a hand on his hip and gestured wildly with the other. "What kind of monster puts a bed in the middle of a room? Even I know that's not where beds go. And this decoration is shockingly ostentatious. Is all of Faerie this ridiculous?"

There was no use fighting my smile. "Do you know where we are?"

"No, but there's no tek. I'm blind here." He ran his fingers through his hair in a very *normal* gesture. "I can only see what is in front of me and only hear what is immediately around me. Is this how you live, stuck in a sensory bubble?"

"Yeah, mostly." I touched my chest and felt the warm beat of Talen's bond inside. I'd gone so long without Talen that I'd forgotten what it felt like to have that connection strumming between us. It felt good, felt right, like I wasn't alone. And I wasn't. Not anymore. Sota was here. Kellee would be nearby too.

"I do have fingers to make up for it, though." Sota lifted his hands, wiggled his fingers, and grinned.

The mention of fingers reminded me of how Sirius's metal hand had reached for me. Clearly, it hadn't been Sirius. "Was any of it real? Falling? Sirius...?"

"No." Sota's smile vanished. "Eledan hit everyone with an illusion to make you see things." He shrugged. "Didn't work on me."

"Then how did he catch you?"

He swallowed and looked away. A touch of heat warmed his cheeks. "I don't want to say..."

Sota was embarrassed? Surely not. "Well, now I have to know." I roamed the room and rummaged through a dresser, its drawers empty. Was this place an underground knoll? It did have that same cavernous feel as Sirius's knoll. I touched a wall, and its organic warmth throbbed against my palm. Definitely alive. Eledan's knoll, then, if he had one? I knew so little about him from before his time in Halow, but there was one vital piece of information Oberon had made clear. Eledan had created the Hunt—a nightmare that was free again, and hungry. The Hunt had killed Aeon and would kill us all eventually.

"Kesh?"

"I was remembering Aeon..." Sota's eyes softened with concern. Kellee had said Aeon had wanted to die, but that didn't make enduring the loss any easier. For all his mistakes, he was still my first friend. I should have done more. We all should have done more.

I headed to the door and tested the handle. Locked.

"You can tell me anything, you know," I told Sota, eager to

steer my thoughts away from the past. "Like it used to be during all those nights on Calicto. I'd tell you a fairytale, and we'd watch those silly shows on virtuavision." Those mundane memories seemed like someone else's, but they were mine, and I'd cling to them forever if I could. Memories of the Calicto messenger and her AI drone when things were simple. Even Sota had changed beyond recognition.

"I have an off switch," he blurted. "Not an actual *switch*. Eledan clicked his fingers, and then I was here, rebooting beside you."

Sota had a failsafe. It wasn't surprising. Eledan had probably implemented it when he'd had Sota in his lab at Arcon, future-proofing him. What else had he programmed into Sota? "He's worked with tek longer than I've been alive. I can try to disable it, with the right equipment..." On Faerie, finding tek-equipment was nearly impossible, and Eledan would have crafted his failsafe with a skill I could only dream of. It would not be easy to unpick his work.

Sota wrapped his arms around himself, biceps tensing. "I don't like the way he looks at me. He wants to cut me open and study my insides."

I offered what I hoped was a reassuring smile. "He looks at everyone like that."

"Not you, Kesh." He shook his head. "We're dust to him, but he admires you."

"It's not admiration. It's lust, but not in the way you're thinking." I tugged at the door again, but it didn't budge. "He wants the polestar fragment inside me. It calls to him."

"It's more than that."

Sota, more than any of the others, could read people from the inside out. He knew Eledan's infatuation with me ran deeper than desire. I turned back to face him. "He has a quarter of the polestar in him too."

"His tek-heart?" he correctly guessed.

I nodded.

Loosening his folded arms, Sota came forward. "I knew there was more than madness wrong with him."

"We simultaneously repel and attract each other. Before, I thought... I thought I was so messed up that I was genuinely attracted to him, even after everything he'd done to me. I didn't know all the facts. Now I do."

"How did he get a piece of the polestar to combine with tek to make his heart?"

"His life magic, the same magic as his mother's, the same magic I had for a few years. I used it to make my whip semi-sentient and... to make you."

Sota drew up next to me and settled his hand on my shoulder. "I haven't thanked you for that."

"Yeah, you have." I squeezed his hand. "Every day, not with words."

Sota looked at my hand over his without blinking, perhaps enjoying the sensation of skin on skin. I had no idea how much he could physically feel or how he processed that information.

He beamed and dropped his hand from my shoulder. "Step back. I've got this." The skin on his forearm unzipped and from inside, a compact pistol dropped out on a cantilevered tek. He aimed at the door handle and a single blast crippled the lock and handle. The gun stowed away again, just as cleanly, and the synthetic skin zipped up without a seam.

I offered my fist, and he bumped it. "You are badass, Sota."

"So are you, Kesh."

"Now let's get out of this prison before Eledan shows up." I tugged the broken door open.

Eledan stood in a hallway, his expression tilted toward boredom. He wore a deep purple doublet and matching pants, laced with pure white thread. The same white thread was braided through his black hair. In his arms, he cradled a bundle of similar clothing, made of the same fabric.

Sota's gun port dropped open again with a metallic whir.

"Save it, drone." Eledan clicked his fingers, and Sota collapsed. His head hit the floor with a sickening *thunk*.

"Sota?" I rushed to his side and cradled his head in my hands. He didn't move, didn't breathe. His open eyes stared at nothing. He looked... dead.

I squared up to the prince, nose to nose, and reached for my whip. "Bring him back!"

He gave a disgusted grunt. "Oh, please, Kesh. He'll be fine. Put this on." He shoved the bundle of clothes at my chest.

I shoved it back hard enough to rock him on his feet. "*You* put it on."

"You will wear this." This time, he shoved hard enough to drive me back against the wall and trap my whip hand beneath the clothes. His eyes narrowed to dark slits, like twin obsidian blades. "Or Sota will spend the next few decades right where he is. I know you don't want that for him. Stop being stubborn and do as I command." He eased back. "After all, you agreed to this, remember?"

I had. His dominion over me in exchange for freeing my people. "I don't have to do anything for you. You haven't freed the saru yet." I snatched the clothes off him anyway, to get him out of my space, and tucked the bundle under one arm.

"That's what we're doing."

We were? I shoved at his chest, forcing him backward, and tugged my coat straight. "Why didn't you tell me that?"

Humor crept into his expression, in the twitch of his wicked mouth and shine of his dark eyes. "When, pray tell, should I have told you? Before or after the drone shot me in the chest?"

I hated him more when his arguments were reasonable. "I wear this and you'll wake Sota up?"

His shoulder lifted. "Fine. Yes. Must everything be a bargain with you?"

It wasn't worth fighting him over something so small as clothing. Ignoring his questions, I flicked the clothes out. Trousers and a fitted blouse adorned with delicate lace fili-gree. At least it wasn't a dress.

I arched an eyebrow. "His and hers matching outfits?"

He smiled. "It seemed appropriate, as you're about to address your saru."

"What?"

A hand gesture was all he deigned to give me before saun-tering down the corridor. "You are their queen, are you not, Mylana?"

"But... the Hunt is looking for me—and you. If we're seen in public, won't it come?"

"I'll handle the Hunt. It's important we appear united in these *terrible times*." He spoke those last words like they were a joke. Was everything a game to him? "Oh, and bring the mandroid." A click of his fingers and Sota stirred to life at my feet. "Keep him close, Kesh. Faerie is not kind to tek."

CHAPTER 6

Sota had stayed quiet since the incident in the hallway. I'd tried to tell him I'd keep him safe, but we both knew Eledan had rooted inside an integral part of his mental processes and would be lodged there until we figured out how to remove him. I knew exactly how it felt to have Eledan's hooks inside your mind.

"We'll fix this..." I whispered.

Sota nodded but didn't reply.

Dressed in my new outfit, I threw my familiar coat over the fancy clothes, clipped my whip to my hip, and followed the contingent of fae guards through what had to be a knoll, considering its confusing layout meant to thwart any attempt to escape. It reminded me of the Arcon basement, just more organic and less shiny. That place, although made of metal, glass, and tek, had the same strange feel as this one, like the walls were alive and watching. Maybe Arcon had been a tek-knoll on a tek planet. If any fae could manipulate tek like magic, it was Eledan. He wasn't like other fae. He'd spent too long on Halow. Some of that humanity had rubbed off on him, and not in a good way. What would the fae think of their prince returning with a tek-heart, especially after he'd used his illusions to scare the magic out of them at the crystal palace? Whatever they thought, they had no choice but to follow him, their new king. There were no other fae of royal blood left. If Eledan kept his word and freed the saru, would the sidhe rise against him? Would the guardians? Would Faerie protect him or fight him?

So many questions, so many unknowns, and I was walking right into each one.

Eledan waited in front of a huge arched door ahead. He'd complemented his purple attire with a black cloak inlaid with silver and a bleached ash-wood crown that looked like bone.

He acknowledged me with a curt nod and closed his hand on the door handle. "Wait here, drone."

Sota glared, his red eye thinning to a laser point.

"Are you ready?" Eledan asked me.

"Ready for what, exactly?"

He swung the door open, captured my hand, and pulled me into a blinding glare. After a few blinks, my eyes adjusted to the sight of a sea of people inside a vast underground pillared hall that stretched to infinity. Hundreds and hundreds of faces, sidhe and saru alike, peered up. So many people, they didn't look real. A cheer thundered through their number and crested to a deafening level. Overwhelmed, I clutched Eledan's hand tighter. His fingers squeezed.

We stepped up to the balustrade, and Eledan raised my arm. If the cheer had been loud before, it shattered through me now, rattling my bones, my soul... Saru... so many of them. Their smiling faces and drab clothing outnumbered the glittering, stoic fae eight to one. And they were cheering for... the Messenger. Not Mylana, not Kesh, but the Messenger, just as Eledan had seeded in their heads since my return to Faerie, maybe before then. He must have planned this long ago, but why? What did he get from their freedom and my myth?

Peering out over the thousands of faces, I realized it had nothing to do with me. I'd made a deal: free the saru in exchange for me—one life for countless saru. But the saru still wouldn't be free; they'd follow the Messenger, a myth Eledan would control thanks to my deal.

I'd be his puppet queen. I'd handed him a saru army.

I plucked my hand from his and gripped the rail. A Faerie breeze whispered across my face, sweeping my hair back and bringing with it the sickly scents of magic and power, of all things Faerie. Wisps gathered above the sea of people, suspended between us like a thousand stars. The saru lifted their hands.

"Our Messenger! Our Messenger!"

These were *my* people. The fae had grown us to serve them in every way. They'd shaped and honed us to do their bidding, and we were already in love with our masters when they harvested us.

I'd see them truly free if it was the last thing I did. Eledan would not have them. I could not have them. One day, they'd be their own people.

"You feel it, Messenger?" The prince smirked beside me. "The power your presence inspires? You are Faerie's queen now. Together, nothing can stop us."

The sidhe lords didn't think so. They stood still and mute among the saru, each one simmering in their own brands of magic. They looked like orchids in a field of plain daisies, and although the saru vastly outnumbered them, they still believed they had power.

"Sire, your guests have arrived," a male guard said behind me, speaking to Eledan.

"Bring them out."

I half turned as a hush descended over the people, curious as to what game Eledan was playing now.

Guards brought Kellee out, his long, wild hair braided with beads and feathers and his face painted with a green handprint in the ancient style of the vakaru. It took a moment for my thoughts to catch up. What was this?

Not daring to look at Eledan, I fixed Kellee under my glare. He came forward, his eyes intense and expression determined, and when he was close enough for me to touch, he dropped to one knee. "As the last vakaru, I pledge myself and all that I am to the Messenger, for now, and forever."

Why was he doing this? It didn't feel right. An illusion? How could I know for certain?

"Where's Sota?" I asked Eledan. Sota could see through Eledan's tricks. I needed him beside me.

"Do you doubt me, my queen?" His glittering eyes confirmed he knew my fear. He crooked a finger at the door. Sota prowled in, seething from his tek-soul, but when I queried this with a glance—*Illusion?*—he gave his head a small shake. It was real. Kellee really was here, on his knee.

"Do you accept my allegiance?" Kellee lifted his head.

What was I supposed to say? What trap was this? Thousands of people watched on, and the new king stood beside me, *waiting*.

"If you're messing with me, Eledan—"

He laughed his rich, deep laughter. "If you weren't so full of lies, it would be easier to see the truth when it kneels before you."

"Kellee?"

He blinked green eyes. No lies. "I'm with you. Always."

"You don't have to do this." I didn't want him to do this. I had never asked or needed him to kneel before me.

His cheek fluttered. "Do you accept all that I am to serve under you?"

"Yes, of course I—"

Eledan clapped his hands and barked a gleeful laugh. "Bring out the Nightshade."

Talen!

Kellee rose to his feet.

"What is this?" I whispered to Kellee while Eledan's back was turned. "What's going on?"

"Go with it," he muttered and fell into line beside Sota.

Talen walked, unguarded, through the arched doorway, joining us on the balcony. He wore his regal clothing, the silver and gray from his time at court, as though he were a winter storm frozen in fae form, but his eyes were violet and true. He outshone Eledan and regarded the prince with icy disdain. The entire crowd fell silent at the return of the Nightshade. All of Faerie held its breath until Talen lifted his chin and appraised those gathered here. Then he fell to one knee before me, just as Kellee had done.

He had done this before, months ago, and practically begged me to free him from a prison I didn't yet understand. *"I will be yours,"* he had told me.

"The Nightshade pledges all that he is to you, for now and forever," Talen said, his words soft and precise but no less heavy for their gentleness. "Do you accept?"

A murmuring sailed through the thousands present. The saru likely didn't understand or know who the Nightshade was—the fae had kept the truth from them—but the sidhe's wide-eyed stillness confirmed they knew. Not only was the Nightshade back, he was kneeling to... a saru? They would be incensed. Did Eledan want them to fight him?

This *was* change, just as Eledan had said. My people saw pillars of Faerie kneel to me, one of their own. They saw change happening right before their eyes. Their Messenger had the fae at her feet. I could never have dreamed this up.

I wanted to settle my hand on Talen's silvery hair. It had always been that way between us—a touch here, a brush there, a stolen kiss that melted my heart—but this moment? Words had power on Faerie. Talen and I were already bonded. This spectacle felt too convenient. I didn't understand any of this. How could I agree when I didn't know what I was agreeing to? It was a trap.

"Kesh?" Talen looked up.

This wasn't fair.

"I can't." He was too important. I needed to understand before I spoke the words.

"Kesh?" Talen's face crumpled.

I whirled on Eledan. "I'm not saying another word until I know what this farce is. You don't control me yet—or them. Why are you making them do this?"

Eledan's lips crawled into a sharp grin. "I knew you'd make this difficult." He nodded at the guards flanking us and ordered, "Hold the Nightshade down."

They rushed Talen before he could rise, and then Eledan was moving, his hand outstretched and the same liquid glow emanating from his fingers as the one he'd used to lock me in a coma for six months. He reached for Talen.

There was no way that bastard was getting his hands on my fae.

I blocked him, hand dropping to my whip, but instead of lunging for Talen, Eledan slammed his hands into *my* chest, and for a single breathless moment, it felt as though he held my heart in his fist. Everything vanished, the people, my friends. Everything but him.

"You're just a single piece of the polestar, Messenger," he sneered.

I didn't understand, but the meaning of his words cracked through me. Light spilled outward over his hand. My light. He couldn't do this. He couldn't take the polestar out of me right here, could he?

The moment stuttered back into motion. Eledan threw me backward. My lower back hit the rail. I tried to rebound, but after one step, the impact of what he'd done ripped the strength from me. I stumbled, and Sota rushed in to hold me up. Kellee was moving for me too, his instinct urging him to protect me, but they should have been watching Eledan, not me. He turned his glowing hand toward Talen.

"Don't touch him!"

He took a sword from one of the guards. A plain weapon, but the moment his hand touched it, light blazed down its length.

Talen struggled against the guards holding him on his knees. His power built, pulling on the shadows and wrapping them around him.

The sword glowed through his dark. It would cut right through it. Eledan wielded more than my polestar essence, but his own. He knew how to access his power and mine.

Eledan lifted the white-flaming sword.

"Talen!"

No, by Faerie, no! Eledan would kill him.

Talen pulled his fists into his chest, yanking the guards off balance. His eyes turned silver, and with a roar, the Nightshade's wings burst from his back, unfurling until their velvety star-touched darkness spilled over the balcony. Night blanketed us all. Talen's eyes shone silver in the dark. That same silver blazed through his clothes and his body, lighting him up, framing the dark creature he was at his core. So beautiful, so terrible, and out of my physical reach.

The bond between us strummed hot and alive.

Eledan's blade came down.

I saw it all in precise detail. Saw the razor-sharp edge sever the Nightshade's left wing and the white fire scorch down Talen's dark outline. The wing burst into a cloud of static silver and ash, blasting us in sparks. Pain was a screeching, clawing thing tearing me apart inside, but it wasn't my pain. Screams I had no control over tore from me. Power snapped through my bones, riding my body too hard.

I flung out a hand to direct this furious, chaotic light inside, using the bond to funnel everything into Talen and save him from the terrible agony. I was on my feet, but not for long. My vessel wasn't strong enough. I wasn't strong enough. It hurt like I was bathed in fire. It hurt in a way I'd never known.

Eledan swung the blade over his head and hacked off the Nightshade's last wing in one smooth slice.

Talen screamed, and an ancient part of me that had nothing to do with being saru, or Mylana, or anyone else awoke. The polestar. Now it was my turn to blaze. Power burst from my skin in a tangle of dark and light, and inside it, I was the heated, beating heart of vengeance. A reservoir of power swelled at my call, and I welcomed it.

Light licked down my back and lifted me off my feet, driving my mortal body toward Eledan.

Eledan pressed the sword to the back of Talen's neck and regarded me as though I were a child. "Kneel, my queen."

"I'm not kneeling to you." My voice held an echo, like it was mine but not mine. An echo like that from the Hunt. It resonated beyond more than just sound, and I knew those words had sailed much farther than this knoll. Faerie had taken them. She'd heard. Everyone had heard me.

"Kneel like we agreed, Mylana, or your silver fae dies and the Hunt will take every one of your saru like it took your doomed gladiator friend. You agreed to this. Now kneel to me and show all of Faerie who their king is."

I looked past Kellee's wide, fearful eyes, ignoring my horror reflected in them, and found the saru looking on, whimpering and fearful alongside the fae.

The bond stuttered, and Talen's head lolled forward, his eyes fluttering closed. The guards held him up. His lips moved, but the words were inside my mind. *"Do. Not. Kneel, Mylana. Do not give... him..."* His voice faded as he lost consciousness.

Eledan had created the Hunt. It was his nightmare. If he wanted it to, the Hunt would take every single saru here and strip them of their souls.

I had freed them and condemned them.

I'd agreed to this.

"I will find a way to kill you," I told Faerie's king. My light faded. I dropped to my knees. "And that monster your putrid mind birthed." The power singing through my veins spluttered and died, leaving my body wretched, panting, and weak.

Eledan tossed the sword to the floor, where it clattered and lost its light. He whirled, raising his arms. "The Nightshade submits. The vakaru submits. And as promised, because I am a fae of my word, saru, *you are henceforth free!* A new reign on Faerie begins today, one that will spread to all four corners of Faerie's worlds."

Slowly, a cheer rose up out of the heavy quiet, but it was a cheer born of fear and suspicion. As well it should be, because as he turned, Eledan caught my gaze and murmured, "Welcome to a new Faerie, my queen."

CHAPTER 7

Talen writhed and clutched at the bedsheets, bleaching his knuckles. His eyes were pinched shut, as though he were fighting not to see. Kellee held him down while Sota reported on Talen's fluctuating life signs.

Hours had passed since Eledan had taken his wings. Talen hadn't woken.

"Kesh, come closer," Kellee said.

I'd already tried that when they'd brought him to this room, and now, as I stood at his bedside, took his hand in mine, and watched him twist and arch in agony, it was almost too much to bear, because I didn't feel a damn thing. The bond—that connection we'd shared for so long, the one that told me I wasn't alone, that he loved me, that I loved him, the one we shared everything through—was gone. Not faded, like when we'd been worlds apart. Gone. Dead. Broken. I knew it, the same way I knew something else, something I had no hope of containing, had shaken loose inside. The polestar. I couldn't think on that yet. On any of it. I'd lost Talen.

Eventually, his body-wracking shudders faded, and he lay still, his chest rising and falling. Occasionally, his brow pinched, but he'd settled into his dreams, where I hoped he might heal. Would the wings grow back? It seemed unlikely. What had losing them done to him?

Sota sat against the wall across the room. He pulled his knees up and draped his forearms over them. Kellee was sprawled in a chair on Talen's other side, looking like a vakaru who'd lost a fight. The green handprint paint had smudged, making him appear fiercer.

"What by Faerie are you doing here, Kellee?"

He blinked a few times, sucked in a breath, and held it until I began to wonder if he would ever breathe again. Finally, he sighed and said, "We had to come. We're stronger together."

"He'll use you against me."

"He won't," the marshal grumbled.

"He just did!"

"Stop it," Sota snapped. "Bickering will not solve this. What *were* you thinking coming here, Kellee? Eledan could just as easily have killed Talen instead of..." He couldn't finish. The memory of what had happened on the balcony stamped itself across my vision. My insides roiled.

"It was the guardian's idea," Kellee grumbled.

I narrowed my eyes. "You never follow fae orders."

"It wasn't an order," he growled. "He said Eledan would have a crowning ceremony to prove his reign. Something public. We figured if we pledged ourselves to your court, we'd get in and get you out. Eledan couldn't refuse us. And then you went and got suspicious—"

"What the hell was I supposed to think? This isn't Calicto, Marshal. You don't kneel on Faerie without meaning it."

His glare hardened. If he'd had hackles, they would have

lifted. "I meant it, and so did Talen. You weren't supposed to reject him."

I scooped up Talen's limp hand and squeezed it. His skin was cool and damp. What if he was dying? "I didn't reject him. I rejected the whole fucking ceremony. It was karushit and you know it. Eledan was preening his peacock feathers in front of the fae. I would have dealt with it, but you showing up made everything a hundred times worse." Eledan had freed the saru, but the victory felt hollow, like I was missing the punchline to his joke.

"Who did you choose, Kesh?"

"What?"

"Your choice. Free the saru and Eledan gets you, right?" He leaned forward in the chair. "Sirius told us. Eledan just freed the saru, so what does that mean for the Messenger?"

"It means I have it under control."

"Karushit."

My jaw ached from grinding my teeth. "You can't free the saru with a few words. Until they stop loving the fae, they won't be free and Eledan will no more own me than you do."

Maybe it was the way I'd worded it, but the fight drained out of Kellee. He fell back into the chair. "I'm sorry..." He blinked up at the ceiling. "Since Oberon, I haven't been thinking clearly."

"I can see that." He'd torn out Oberon's throat—with his teeth. I'd seen his eyes, seen the unseelie in him rejoice. Maybe ancient fae blood didn't do a damn thing to a vakaru, or maybe it did. We hadn't had the time to discuss it.

He rubbed his eyes. "That bastard took his wings, Kesh."

Eledan had taken more than that from Talen. He had taken Talen's identity as the Nightshade and my bond with it. "Eledan knew Talen was the only fae left who could challenge his rule, and you delivered him right to his feet. That was never going to end well. We can't make those mistakes, Kellee, not here. Faerie doesn't allow for fuckups."

"He wanted to be here, with you," Sota said from his spot by the wall. "Kellee couldn't have stopped him. None of us could."

What was I supposed to do with the three of them? This was exactly what I'd been afraid of. "You shouldn't have come. Eledan knows how I feel about you. He's known since this started. To beat him, we have to be smarter than this."

Kellee fell forward and ran his hands through his hair. "I know. You're right." He looked up. "What happened on that balcony... to you?"

"I..." The echo of some other power plastered over me, it hadn't felt good, like when I'd used fae magic in the past. A second longer and it might have torn me open. "I don't know."

"I do," Sota said. "Kesh opened the bond wide, like when Talen broke free of Shinj. You almost died then, Kesh. This time, a part of Talen was dying. Kesh pulled that pain out of him."

"I did what?"

"You didn't see you, but we did. Your eyes were silver, and your whole body was aglow and haloed in darkness, just like Talen is when he goes full Nightshade. You took part of him inside you, or maybe it was always in you since you first bonded and we're just now seeing it."

I looked to Kellee. He nodded. "Sota's right. You looked a whole lot like the Nightshade for a while there, sans wings."

I'd felt it too, the dark reaching outward, but I'd also felt the light. I needed answers. I needed someone to tell me what his polestar could do, what I could do, and how I could control it. And where it all led. Eledan would only tell me if I could convince him it was in his interest, but if that failed, there was another option, one Sirius could help with. "Where's Sirius?"

"On Shinj with Hulia, waiting for our signal." Kellee's gaze fell to Talen. "If we can get him back to the ship, Shinj can help heal him."

Sota stood and approached the end of the bed. "Physically, his body is showing signs of exhaustion, but I don't think what Eledan did was physical. I can't read magic. As he is, he's not strong enough for us to move him. We need to wait until he's conscious."

Still holding his hand, I silently begged his fingers to grip back. He didn't respond.

"He'll recover," Kellee said, sounding surer than the worry on his face suggested.

Before the bond broke, I'd felt Talen's agony. He might recover physically, but mentally? "He didn't deserve this."

He had only ever tried to protect me. I owed him the same. I needed answers.

I shrugged off my coat, laid it over the back of the chair, and climbed onto the bed, gently lying down next to Talen. If the bond was gone, I'd stay close to him this way and hope it was enough.

Sota pulled my abandoned chair close to the bed and settled into it. He nodded at my glance. He wouldn't leave either, and I didn't need to look at Kellee to know the marshal would stay for as long as it took.

"It's not your fault." Talen's fingers brushed my cheek. I leaned into his touch and fell into his sleepy gaze, admiring the way his pale lashes highlighted eyes layered in violet, indigo, and lilac.

He had woken moments ago. Not with a gasp, as I'd expected. He'd simply come around as though he'd just fallen asleep. His arm had wrapped around me, tucking me close against his chest. After what Eledan had done to him, his soft smile pricked my eyes with tears.

"He took your wings," I whispered, bumping my forehead against his.

"It's all right." His knuckles brushed my cheek, then his fingers stroked my hair, setting it right, like he needed everything to be in its place.

Nothing was *all right*. I was so tired of the pain, the endless battle.

His lips brushed my forehead. "He took what he thought was most precious to me..." Talen's warm fingers captured my chin, his gaze fierce. "He was wrong."

I wanted to rest with him, to bury myself against his chest and breathe him in until he became a part of me again.

"I did something to our bond," I whispered. "I broke it."

"I don't need a bond to tell me how much I love you."

I squeezed my eyes closed and buried my face against his shirt so Kellee and Sota wouldn't see the tears. Talen clutched me close. We stayed like that until Kellee rose from his chair, signaling time was not on our side.

"If we leave now, we may get off this planet—"

"We're not leaving Faerie." Reluctantly, I pulled away from Talen's arms and eased him upright. "I need answers. *We* need answers. Leaving solves nothing. We stay on the ground."

"Leaving will keep you alive," Kellee argued.

None of this had ever been about keeping me alive.

Sota rushed in to help Talen, but he waved him off while Talen pushed to his feet, albeit carefully. "I'm fine," he said, noticing how we were ready to catch him if he fell. He swayed and steadied himself on the bed. "I will be fine..."

"If we stay on Faerie, Eledan will try to tear us apart." This came from Sota, and the raw fear on his face almost had my determination wavering. "He'll try to take us from you, Kesh, one at a time, like pulling the legs off a spider."

I frowned at the analogy, but he wasn't wrong. Eledan would try to break us, but he wouldn't succeed. "This spider bites." I tossed him a grin like the ones when I'd scored a valuable delivery back on Calicto. He dragged his own smile onto his lips. "There are fae who know a lot more about the polestar and my place in it. Fae who will speak with me." I adjusted my whip, making sure it was seated home, and breathed in to clear my thoughts. "Signal Sirius here."

Kellee moved in and Talen hooked an arm around his shoulders.

I held the vakaru's doubtful glare. "The dreamweaver and I are going to have a heart-to-heart chat."

"Kesh, if he takes you again..." Gold rimmed the marshal's dark eyes. The unseelie beast within him peered back at me. Sota was right. Kellee was a twitch away from going feral. I'd need to speak with him too—alone. I should take the time to sit with them all and soon, but not here. I had a prince to corner.

"He won't hurt me, Kellee. He needs me to keep the saru in line."

Kellee's gaze skipped from the recovering Talen to Sota and back to me. He flexed his fingers. "I can't keep losing you."

"You won't. Just... trust me? I can handle Eledan."

He nodded curtly. "I'll signal Sirius, but if you're not back in a reasonable time, I'm coming after you."

CHAPTER 8

"*L*et me in there."

Two guards blocked the doorway to Eledan's chambers. Behind them, enormous, ornately decorated doors arched high, their peak ending in unnecessary flourishes. Like the doors, both guards were ridiculously pretty.

"The king is engaged," the guard on the right said.

Engaged? What, by cyn, did that mean?

I dropped a hand to my whip, making sure they got a good look. I didn't want to pull rank, but I would. After what Eledan had done to Talen, he didn't get to hide behind doors. "Let me through, or we'll have a disagreement."

They didn't move. Steely-eyed and righteous in their belief that they were better than me, they reminded me of Sirius, before I understood him.

I freed my whip. Its alien tek-tails licked at the floor near my boots. The guard on my right swallowed, his throat bobbing. They weren't visibly armed, but they'd have tricks up their immaculately tailored sleeves. We all knew they wouldn't throw down with Faerie's new queen. They had to make a stand because they were fae, and that made them pains in my ass.

When it was clear they wouldn't step aside, I looked them both in the eye before settling my glare on the one who had spoken. "Your queen commands you to open the damn door. Don't make me go all Messenger on your asses."

Relenting, they stepped aside, and the door swung open under its own power. A suite full of color, comfort, and elegant design greeted me. A day chamber, like those Oberon had used, only much bigger. Floor-to-ceiling drapes fluttered, disturbed by Faerie's touch on the breeze.

It seemed Eledan wasn't home, but then the breeze found me, carrying his silken voice with it.

"... it is being done, witch. A few more days will not kill you."

I inched toward the drapes, hoping to catch a glimpse of whoever he spoke with.

"Faerie is not how I remember," Eledan said, louder for my benefit. Words too similar to those I'd spoken many times in my head for them to be meant for anyone else.

Peeling back the drapes, I emerged onto a balcony similar to the one that overlooked the grand hall, but instead of looking over a sea of people, this one provided a panoramic view of Faerie's landscape. Blushed by a wash of red light from the nearest binary stars, hills dipped and climbed, sweeping from an emerald ocean to vast, winterlands-tipped mountains. In front of it all, with his back to me, hands grasping the balustrade, stood Eledan. Alone. From behind, he looked so much like Oberon that I deliberately blinked, wiping the comparison clear. The same warrior shoulders and dark hair, only Eledan's tumbled loose down his back. Old instincts tried to drop me to my knees. I snarled them back. The day I voluntarily knelt to Eledan would be the day I died.

Kneeling to save Talen didn't count. I hadn't had a choice, but soon, armed with all the facts, I would.

Slowly, precisely, I coiled my whip and clipped it to my belt.

"It seems so... hollow," Eledan said.

"Maybe it's you who is hollow?" If my words had any impact, he didn't reveal it.

"There's a wasp. They call her *shee het*. She lays her eggs inside Faerie's mighty acorns. The larvae grow, cocooned within a protective shell, and slowly devour the seed until there's nothing left."

His words wove around me, trying to sink in and devour me from the inside, just like his wasp, but they would not find purchase. Hate sizzled beneath my skin, rebuilding unseen armor against all things Eledan. I knew him too well to fall for his spells.

When I didn't reply, he regarded me over his shoulder. His face wore no expression, but it could easily switch to vicious, or kind, or compassionate in a blink. It was impossible to know what was real with him and what was the lie. Right now, he looked through me, like he wasn't sure if I were real or an illusion of his making. He'd spent so long alone, weaving his dreams, that this solid reality must have seemed strange.

"You were no less hollow, Wraithmaker, than my brother's insect, burrowing through human tek to do his bidding."

I let a smile lift my lips. "The Wraithmaker is long dead. Bringing her back here makes you appear weak. Grasping at the past, *my liege?*"

His smile mirrored mine. Bastard. "So proud, you are," he said, facing the vista once more. Leaning forward, he folded up his shirt cuffs and rested his warfae-marked forearms on the balcony rail. Those sweeping marks stood out against his golden skin. "So full of passion and hate." A finger of breeze teased a few errant locks of dark hair against his cheek. "A symptom of mortality. So very saru. I always admired that about your kind."

Maybe I could shove him off the balcony.

"I didn't come to talk wasps—"

He waved a dismissive hand. "Your silver fae will be fine. If anything, by removing his power, I lifted a thousand-year burden off his back. He doesn't want to be the Nightshade and hasn't done for a long time. He should thank me."

Even if he was right, he could have gone about it a different way instead of turning the whole thing into a painful spectacle. "And my saru?"

"What of them?"

"Are they truly free?"

His lips quirked. "How do you free a creature from its nature?"

He believed he'd tricked me, but I already knew the saru could not be so easily freed. Sirius had told me as much when I'd learned he had been trying to free them properly for centuries.

Moving to lean casually against the balustrade, I took a few fleeting moments to admire how the pinkish light stroked his dark hair and lightened his blue eyes. As the human Istvan Larsen, he'd been handsome but unremarkable. All an act he'd played for centuries. Now he looked every part the wicked fae prince. As lean and cruel as a blade, everything about him was cutting, from his smile to his glances. I'd tasted every inch of him in my dreams, and he'd mouthed the most intimate parts of me. I'd once hated him for making me feel those things. Now, I just wanted him, and all the fae like him, dealt with. "What you did to Talen was barbaric."

He snorted. "Says the woman who slaughtered hundreds of her own kind to be *noticed* by Oberon."

I flexed my right hand. "Did it really take Faerie a few thousand years to make you this much of an asshole?"

"Oh no, that's all me." He chuckled. "Faerie has done nothing for me, *my queen*."

Every word out of his mouth grated on my patience, and he knew it. "Still hung up on mommy dearest abandoning you?"

His quick glance revealed a sliver of his dark soul, and for a breathless moment, his eyes narrowed, his lips thinned, and the weight of his rage poured in. I could not forget how powerful he was, and here on Faerie, he was at the height of his power. "I once thought she'd sent you to me as a gift. You were my messenger... I wasn't wrong, but the message was."

Ignoring the flutter of fear tightening my chest, I casually folded my arms. "Why are we here, you and I? What do you want from me?"

"You already know." His smile was back, masking that sudden viciousness. He shifted a step, bringing himself close. His warmth tried to wrap around me like his voice had. He brushed his knuckles down my cheek, easing his thigh against mine. Hard against hard. I didn't stop him, and he came closer, pressing in, filling my head with all things Eledan. His touch trailed lower, running the length of my jaw, sprinkling delicate shivers down my back. Fingers on my chin, he tilted my head up and fell into my eyes. From my dreams, I remembered all too easily how his body had felt undulating beneath my hands. Remembered the powerful contours of a physique, an impossible combination of hard and soft, that belonged to one of Faerie's most deadly predators.

His fingertips brushed my lips, gently parting them, and then he was so close his presence clouded my thoughts. I tasted him on my tongue as he pinned me back against the balustrade with a few hundred feet of nothing below.

His mouth brushed mine, so lightly, but I didn't seal the kiss. He teased, urging me to surrender. I brought my hand up between us and splayed my fingers against his chest, soaking in his warmth until I felt the cool, measured beat of his tek-heart beneath his shirt. His breath stuttered. I sucked that falter in and curled my fingers around his scar. Faerie's new king tensed. He'd been away for so long he no longer recognized his home or his place in it. Which one of us had caught the other? Did he believe I was still the nothing girl he'd held in his thrall for nine long months?

The same ancient power that raced through my veins beat inside the tek-cage inside Eledan's chest. I felt it, that urge to rip his heart free and crush it, but also the beat of two lost pieces brought together for the first time in millennia. Half of me wanted him dead, but the other half, the Faerie part of me, wanted to bury itself inside his veins and wrap around what felt like home. It wasn't me, that need and want, and now that I knew these feelings were alien, I could use them. If I was feeling like I'd ruin worlds to possess Eledan, he surely felt the same toward me.

I danced the fingers of my free hand over his collarbone and around to the nape of his neck, spreading them there to capture him close. "I need answers," I whispered.

His thumb gently stroked below my chin. "You'll have them," he replied, gaze on my lips.

"About the polestar... about us."

He turned his face away. His lashes came down, shuttering his blue eyes. When he opened them again, he lifted a glass thimble between his finger and thumb. Light danced in its construction. I'd seen it before. It had belonged to Sjora. More importantly, I'd learned that trinket was a piece of the polestar. Talen must have given it to Eledan while I was unconscious during the trade that went wrong.

Eledan's fingers spread around my neck. The lust in his eyes hardened.

I still had a hold of his neck too. If he tried anything, I'd fight, and then maybe one of us would discover that drop below.

He smiled, sensing my thoughts, and gently set the thimble on the balustrade rail.

His smile twisted, and with one powerful thump, he shattered the thimble beneath his fist, scattering glass shards.

"Wh—"

His grip locked on my neck, steely fingers clamping shut.

I closed my hand, pulling him close and sinking my fingers in.

"Your messenger men thought to trick me."

They had?

My lungs burned, chest heaving. He pressed in, locking me down. "Do not play me, Messenger. You may not cherish your own life, but they certainly do. They'll do anything and everything to keep you safe, including giving up their lives. You are their weakness, and they are yours. Now they're in my court, trading in lies... Have they forgotten how the Hunt consumed one of their own? Did *you* forget how my creation swallowed your dear friend, Messenger? The Hunt is mine." Tightened. "Faerie is mine." Choked. "You are mine."

Tears leaked from my eyes.

"Get your harem in line, or I will." He released me and pushed away, sweeping back through the drapes.

My vision sharpened, and strength flooded back in. I had my whip out in a step and lifted it up in another. The tails sparked, coming to life as I lassoed them over my head and struck, viper-fast. Eledan knew my mind as though it were his own, and as the whip cut through the drapes, he turned, brought a forearm up, and caught the whip's tails. They snarled around his wrist instead of his neck.

He yanked, tugging me closer, and met my gaze.

The warfae marks on his forearm seemed darker than I remembered, and as I watched, they shied away from my whip's spitting tek.

With a flick, I recalled the whip, freeing his arm. As he lowered his hand to his side, the marks spilled back into place. I hadn't imagined it. They *had* moved.

"I'll never be yours, Eledan. All the stars could fall from Faerie's sky and I'd never be yours. You stole nine months of my mortal lifetime. You mind-fucked me at your whim. You let the fae back into Halow, killing billions." I would never forget the sight of their frozen bodies glistening among the stars. I took a step closer. He lifted his chin, expression locked. "You were just your mother's afterthought when she believed Oberon's mind was too far gone to save. Your tek-heart is the most honest thing about you. Without it, you're just a failed son. Faerie accepts me more than she accepts you. You are nothing to me."

He brought his hand up to strike. I caught his wrist before the blow could land.

"Your only legacy is a nightmare as black and hollow as your soul."

His eyes widened. He tore free from my grip and stalked away. His chamber door slammed closed, rattling the walls.

I stared at the empty room, chest heaving, and then back out at Faerie. I hadn't meant to lose control, to tell him the truth. He was more easily manipulated if he believed he was winning, and now I'd lost any goodwill between us. Huffing, I looked up at Faerie's stars. "So much for getting answers."

CHAPTER 9

"How'd it go with Eledan?" Sota asked, breezing up to me as I approached the chamber.

"It... didn't. Any answers he gave me would have been poison anyway. Where are the others?" I assumed they'd already moved from the room in preparation to leave the knoll.

"Outside. Shinj transported Sirius onto a beach below the knoll. Kellee sent me back up here to find you before he came himself and"—he put on his Marshal Kellee voice —"*tears the place apart looking for you*. Also, Sirius reported that the *Excalibur* crew is getting restless."

I absorbed Sota's words as he led me through the corridors. *I should send Talen back.* We'd hijacked Sol Alliance's *Excalibur* and brought it, cloaked, to Faerie-space after its captain had tried to steal a piece of the polestar from Kellee. Talen's unique ability to control human emotions meant he could keep the human crew subdued, but the thought of being apart from him, from any of them, tightened my chest. We *were* stronger together. Every time we separated, bad shit happened.

Sota and I left the knoll via one of many steep, spiraling staircases and emerged halfway up a cliff face where paths snaked down to a silvery dusk-lit beach. I could just make out the figures of Sirius, Kellee, and Talen on the sands below. Talen leaned heavily against the marshal. His silver-white hair reflected the half-light, while beside him, the marshal's dark hair absorbed it. Sirius, standing apart from them, looked like a flame in fae form.

Gripping a rail, I welcomed the warm breeze trailing across my face. Faerie's green ocean was calm. Night still lingered and would probably stay for weeks, its dark blanket covering Faerie in these troubling times.

"I don't want to see them hurt," I whispered.

Sota joined me at the rail. "They're with you because they choose to be."

His words hit like a punch to the chest. How could I love them all so equally? Was it truly me they loved in return? Not the polestar, not the messenger myth, just the real me beneath all those names? Sirius had somehow admired me from afar for years, and Talen... Talen wanted so badly to be good. And Kellee had made me his messenger long before I agreed to it, but he would never use me, never lie to me. They were all better than me.

Sota's hand settled on my shoulder—the shoulder he'd always preferred to hover over. "They believe in you."

I closed my eyes.

"I believe in you."

I could do this.

I *would* do this.

We would stop Faerie. I'd return the polestar to where it belonged, and this nightmare would end. Forever.

"C'mon." I eased out from Sota's touch and started down

the cliff path. "We should get moving before Eledan realizes we're gone."

Sota followed. "Can you stop him and his nightmare? Can you stop the war?"

"Yes." Not a lie, I hoped. First, I needed those answers from someone who knew Eledan better than anyone else alive.

TALEN APPEARED to be regaining his strength. Some color had returned to his cheeks, and his eyes were no longer hooded or sleepy.

"Are you fit to travel?" I asked, arriving at their side on the beach.

He dipped his chin. "Fit enough."

The wind lashed his long, untethered hair around his shoulders.

All right, so we could make some progress. Kellee nodded, signaling he was ready for anything. His edgy rawness lingered in the way he tapped his fingers against his thigh and in his quick, alert glances.

Sirius stood apart, proud and aloof. The expanse of green ocean offered a startling backdrop to his red coloring. I had to remind myself he wasn't Oberon's tool and likely never had been. He served Faerie, and, apparently, he also served me. That was a revelation we hadn't had time to explore. I'd sparked a wildfire in him with a kiss, but there was no sign of that wildfire now. He looked back at me as restrained and stoic as a soldier awaiting orders.

"Let's get one thing clear so there are no more misunderstandings." All eyes blinked to me. "No more plotting or scheming without consulting one another. We do things together from here on out."

Sota stood at my side, my protector, my friend. Always. "Does that include you, Kesh?" he asked and recoiled under my glare.

"It's a fair question," Kellee added. "You've been known to scheme, on occasion."

Talen huffed a gentle laugh.

"Yes," I conceded, "that includes me."

"Well, all right, then," Kellee drawled.

"With that in mind, are there any more secrets you'd like to tell me or each other?"

Talen flicked his eyes skyward, trying to appear innocent. Kellee immediately noticed his body language, and his humor soured. So something had happened between them while I'd been unconscious.

"What is it?" I asked.

"We have the Valand piece of the polestar," Talen said. "We... I've had it since killing Sjora."

"The thimble?" I asked. Kellee's eyes widened. I'd known. How could I not? I'd wanted to crush that thing or throw it away every time I'd laid eyes on it. I hadn't known what I was looking at, and because I hadn't been seeking it, the polestar had stayed hidden in plain sight. "Eledan crushed your fake. Where's the real one?"

"On Shinj," Talen replied.

"What about the acorn?"

"Eledan has it," Kellee said. "We had to give him something to free you."

Then we were even, Eledan and I. He had two pieces and so did I. Good. But he'd come looking for the thimble as soon as he realized we'd abandoned him.

"Any other revelations?" I asked Talen.

His old-soul eyes said yes. "A millennia's worth, but nothing relevant."

Kellee shook his head. He'd always been honest. And then there was Sirius. The guardian's jaw fluttered under our scrutiny. "I do not believe so, but an immortal's memory is an infinite place where pertinent information can easily be lost," came his typical fae response. It was the best I would get from him.

"As we're sharing," Sota spoke up. "Eledan programmed a failsafe into me. It seems, when he disabled me in Arcon, he added some upgrades. He can render me unconscious with a gesture. There may be more he can do."

Kellee swore. Talen's brow knitted together, and Sirius continued to glare.

"We should leave the drone here," the guardian declared. It was a wise suggestion, and it wasn't ever happening.

"Sota comes with us." I wasn't letting any of them out of my sight, especially Sota.

Sota bowed his head. "He's right. I'm a liability—"

"No." My tone alone shut down any further protests. "We are together, and we will stay together. If any of you have a problem with that, you can walk away."

"I pledged myself to you. I meant it," Kellee said, leaving no room for doubt.

Sirius's brilliant green eyes narrowed. "Sota is a beacon telling Eledan where you are, but Sota's tek-presence could shield you from the Hunt, which is likely why Eledan wanted him close during the ceremony. Perhaps it's worth the risk."

There was no *perhaps*. "Sota stays. We'll deal with whatever fallout comes from it."

Sota toed the sand with a boot, looking so vulnerable that I wanted to throw my arms around him.

"If you want to go, I won't stop you..." It hurt to say, but he had the right to choose. "But know how much I need you, Sota. I don't think I can do this without you."

He looked up and met my eyes. The wild locks of dark hair swept across his forehead and cheek, giving him a boyish appeal, but inside, he was a long way from his naïve exterior. "I'll do my best to protect you."

"I can't do this without any of you," I told them. "You are each a part of me, and while I know we have our differences and it will not always be easy, if we're together, neither Faerie nor Eledan can break us." The wind picked up and whisked my words away, carrying them to any force on Faerie who cared to listen. I'd seen only a small amount of the wonders and horrors Faerie had to offer. That would soon change.

Sirius, Talen, Kellee, Sota. I loved them with a light as bright as any polestar.

"What's our next move?" Kellee asked.

"We visit Ailish and the Wild Ones."

The guardian's glower intensified. "That is... unwise."

"Probably, but she told me more in a few minutes than any other fae has in my entire life, so we're going to her."

"What you saw of her in her home was the good, but she has many faces, Calla. She trades in deception and dark promises."

I smiled. *So do I.* "Of course she does, but we have you and she seemed to like you."

"She fears me. We have our history."

Fear was a potent motivator. "It's time I used all the weapons at my disposal."

"Is that all I am to you? A weapon?" Sirius crafted the question to sound light and careless, but his steady gaze cut through that karushit.

"No, and you well know it." A tension had crept onto the

beach, the kind that would get worse if left to fester. "How might we find Ailish?"

"She will either sense our summons and come to us of her free will, or, more likely, we'll have to seek her at her cavern. If she isn't there, we'll have to travel deeper into Faerie."

"We'll take Shinj there—"

"We cannot. The warcruisers are Oberon's creations. The Wild Ones abhor them. They will not appear in the presence of such a creature."

I glanced at Talen. He nodded in agreement with Sirius. Walking to the cavern would take days—days in which Eledan would delight in hunting us. "I don't suppose you can rustle us up a carriage like you did at the docks?"

Sirius's lips twitched around what might have been a smile if he'd loosened his stoic mask enough to let it slip through. "I can, but I'll need some *items*."

"Items?" Sota echoed.

"Come, let us leave this exposed beach. I'll find the necessary elements along the way." He started toward a section of the cliff that had collapsed onto the beach, providing a gulley through which we could escape the knoll and Eledan. Although, there was likely a reason he hadn't yet raised the alarm.

"One more thing," I called after him. He turned, and they all waited for me to speak. "We can't sleep. Eledan will find us in our dreams. We all know how powerful he is there. He can turn us against each other and make it so we forget his meddling."

"Then we had better hurry," Sirius replied and marched on.

CHAPTER 10

Sirius plucked a pixie nest from a bush as we passed. The nest was no larger than a melon and comprised of twigs, moss, and fluff. I shot Kellee a questioning glance. The marshal shrugged, the look on his face saying, *"How the cyn should I know?"*

Talen would know, but he strode adjacent to Sirius, the two of them discussing something that had Talen chuckling. The pair appeared so utterly different, warm reds and browns against icy silvers and grays, yet they were so very faelike. If I blinked, would they vanish, like in the old human tales?

The strange dusk light never changed. Faerie's stars twinkled as they observed us. On Shinj, Talen had taken me to the navigation room, where the stars hung among us and sang their forever song. I hadn't known then that I was one of those stars, or, more accurately, my blood was. Faerie's stars weren't singing now, but maybe I was just too small to hear them.

Kellee moved in close beside me on the narrow, winding path. "I should have kept you safer."

Kellee blamed himself? "I chose to go to him. I'd made a deal. It had to happen."

He closed his eyes and winced before reopening them, fixing his glare on me. "You should have told me about the deal." He kept his voice low so the fae wouldn't hear, but Sota, walking behind us, heard everything. He always had.

"You would have tried to stop me."

He considered that for a few moments and then tossed me his slick marshal smile. "Yeah, I would have."

"You don't need to protect me."

"I know."

But he always would. We'd come a long way from him tracking me down on Calicto for allegedly murdering a mineworker. The chances of us ever meeting had been slim, yet fate had run me right into him.

We walked some more, enjoying the quiet. Pixies sometimes chirped or something larger would disturb the bushes, prompting Kellee to glare into the shadows. "Some days I regret pushing you into being the messenger," he said.

The words almost tripped me. "You do?"

His gaze found something distant to focus on. "Had I let you go, I might have saved you from all this."

Only Kellee would think he could protect me from Faerie. "You can't shoulder that blame either, Marshal," I said softly. "My destiny was seeded into me before the fae harvested me. This was always going to happen. The only difference is we stopped Oberon before his plans could come to fruition."

He nodded, but a soft melancholy surrounded him. "Have you thought about what comes after?"

"After?"

"When all this is done?"

I looked up and pinned my gaze to Talen's back so Kellee couldn't read the truth in my eyes. The polestar couldn't stay in pieces, and whatever part of it was in me would soon be *removed*. I hoped Ailish would have all the answers, but some I already knew. "Do you think I'll have an after?"

He thought on that a while and glanced ahead at Talen. "I'll make you one."

With your metal-worker hands? If anyone could craft me a life after this mayhem, it was Kellee. I let him see my smile and had to fight the urge to grab him and kiss that smirk off his lips. Here, in the wilds, surrounded by brush, wisps, and creeping things, he seemed more at ease, but that frayed edge lingered in the air around him, his beast so close to the surface I could feel the tension crackling around him.

"Are you all right, Kellee?" My thoughts went back to seeing him tear into Oberon, to seeing him drink down the king's blood. I had no idea if a vakaru had ever killed a fae like Oberon before or what it would do to him. Perhaps nothing. Vakaru could ingest almost any poison and survive.

"No," he finally replied. "But as long as we're together, I'll get by."

I stopped, grabbed his arm, and pulled him close before he could argue. His arm looped around my back and pulled me in so there was nothing between us. His warmth enveloped me. There was no safer place in all four realms.

"Don't ever leave me like that again," he whispered, spilling those words over my lips. It wasn't an ask. His words were a demand, an order, and they sparked a riot of need that urged me to devour him right here.

I threw my arms around his neck, trapping him. "I have no intention of ever letting you go."

Sota cleared his throat. "As much as I'm getting off on watching you, the fae have disappeared through the brush ahead and are moving away. It's best we stay together."

Neither of us moved. I bumped my forehead against

Kellee's and fell into his gold-flecked eyes. Deep inside, he was wild and free and untamable.

His warm, scandalous mouth nudged mine. "Soon," he promised.

Darts of lust scattered low in my stomach at the thought of having him all to myself. It had been a long time coming. Dragging a hand down his chest, I gently pushed. Sota was right. Separating our group out here was a terrible idea.

Kellee didn't budge, so I spread my hand on his shirt, feeling the ridge of pectoral muscle beneath. His marshal's star was missing. I looked up. "Where's your star, Kellee?"

"Right here, in my arms."

The words broke me open, exposing everything I was and had been. He knew me, and still, he loved me. Maybe this was all a dream after all.

"I could call them back here so we can all watch?" Sota suggested.

Kellee's grip eased, but the want in his eyes didn't fade. "Buzz off, Sparky."

I pulled myself from his arms and caught Sota's wide grin. He hadn't lost his kinky humor during his transformation.

Kellee reluctantly hiked farther up the trail. Unlike the fae, who all moved with innate cat-like grace, the play of muscle beneath Kellee's shirt and pants radiated an unforgiving primal strength that demanded to be respected, and admired, and touched.

"He has a very fine ass." Sota made a squeezing gesture and an "oh" expression that suggested he'd like to caress that ass as much as I did. "He's so gonna be worth the wait."

Unexpected laughter tore from me.

Kellee threw a middle-finger salute over his shoulder, indicating he'd heard every word, and plowed on up the path. I laughed harder, looped my arm through Sota's, and followed Kellee into a clearing between tall, leaning trees.

Talen watched Sirius, who was crouched at the center. They'd brushed aside the fallen leaf litter, and as I drew closer, Sirius placed the nest on the ground and four large, round pebbles beside that.

Talen threw me a wild smile that was so unlike him but so filled with delight.

My gut twisted in excitement and apprehension. I folded my arms. "All right, what's happening here?"

"Transportation," Talen said, like that one word explained everything. He backed up toward me, giving Sirius room to work. "You've seen so little of what Faerie is capable of."

"Will it turn into something hideous that'll devour us all?"

"Not quite." The delight in his eyes wasn't exactly comforting. Anything that delighted the fae usually meant others would suffer, but I trusted Talen and, to a lesser extent, Sirius.

The guardian straightened, brushed leaves from his coat, took a few steps back, checked our locations, and bowed his head. He flicked out his hands. The raw tek-hand glittered in Faerie's soft dusk light. The breeze lifted and shifted around the clearing, stirring up a tiny storm of dust and twigs.

Similar storms had blown through the sinks on Calicto, when the fans were down for maintenance, but here, the whirlwinds were probably alive. Funnel after funnel sprung from the ground, no bigger than a man. They danced and spun to music only they heard. Sirius clapped his hands, and the tiny storms became one, blasting a column of air up and yanking all the dust, leaves, and debris out of the clearing. I shielded my face and leaned back against the wind. Sota's fingers steadied my arm, and then the storm collapsed, revealing the impossible at the center of the clearing.

A carriage.

"Holy cyn," Sota blurted.

Talen's richly devious laughter made my toes curl.

"Can you do that?" I asked him.

"No." His lips tilted. "I could have summoned you a dark army, but these days, all I'm good for is a little human mind control. That"—he nodded at the carriage, with its woven wicker-like structure and impossibly shiny marble-like wheels —"is a Wild One's talent."

"Sirius is full of surprises," Kellee drawled. Raising his voice, he asked, "Where are the steeds, fae, or do you intend to pull it too?"

Sirius whistled through his teeth, and for a few minutes, long enough for me to venture closer to the carriage and run my hand over its design, nothing happened. Then a snickering from the trees drew my eye, and from deep within the shadows, a black horse emerged, with fire for its mane, tail, and fetlocks.

Sirius lowered his tek-arm, keeping it out of sight, and approached the stallion, offering his normal hand for the beast to sniff.

Life magic.

Sirius had it too, but not until recently. His powers were returning, just as Ailish had foretold. Faerie approved of his recent choices. Another black fire-tipped horse breached the clearing, this one snorting and kicking, its eyes wide and glassy. Eventually, Sirius got them under control and maneuvered them into the harnesses.

We clambered into the carriage, Kellee wary, Sota in awe, Talen thrilled the more we fell into Faerie's ways. Sirius took up the reins from the outside seat. With his bellowed *"Yah!"* the horses jolted into motion, and we thundered into the dark.

CHAPTER 11

Sota stared out the carriage window, watching the blurred scenery sail by, his eyes absorbing and reflecting the occasional darting ball of light. I spotted enough stars to know we were moving inland, away from the sea.

"How much longer until we're at the cavern, do you think?" I asked, turning my head to find Talen watching me. Somehow, I'd missed him shift across the seat, but with him this close, I could barely think around him. I plucked a twig from his hair. He had others snarled in it, leaves too, but he didn't seem to care. His lips tilted upward, and even his eyes held a more intense sheen than I'd ever seen before. Faerie agreed with him, but of course it would. He'd been away a long time. The Talen I'd met had been starved of Faerie, and while he'd never complained, seeing the changes in him made it clear how much he had suffered.

"Faerie looks good on you," I told him.

"It would be a lie if I said I wasn't glad to be home," he admitted. "But Faerie has changed in my absence. There are oceans where there were none before and dry basins where once there was life. Mountains have split and separated. Great swathes of forest have perished or vanished. I barely recognize it with my eyes, but my soul knows Her."

I'd once had a piece of that old soul, and I'd somehow let it go.

He cupped my face. "Don't grieve the loss of our bond. It was a mistake on my part to offer you such a thing when you did not know who you are. Now you are free to be all you can be without my influence."

His touch warmed my cheek. So gentle. I missed the feel of him inside me, but saying that here, now, with Kellee sitting right opposite, doing his damnedest not to hear every word? How could I? *Soon*, Kellee had told me. I needed that for us all, needed a moment with each of them before the moments were all gone.

"We are together, getting stronger with every passing heartbeat..." Talen's thumb stroked my bottom lip. If I looked into his eyes, I'd want to kiss him—want a whole lot more. These impossible males would not be mine forever, but while I had them captured in my mortal hands, I'd love them wholly and completely. No matter what happened *after*, we would have lived and loved. It would be enough. It had to be enough.

The carriage hit a hole and jolted us free of the moment. Talen reluctantly retreated but stayed close, his presence soothing enough to keep my mind from running over the danger I was charging headlong into.

"What did Eledan say?" Kellee asked. "Did he give you anything?"

"Very little. He and I... He brings out the worst in me. I can't talk to him without trying to kill him."

"What's his endgame? What does he want?"

I thought of how the new king had admired Faerie from

the knoll balcony, thought of his words when he'd spun an illusion at the crystal palace. "He wants Faerie to love him like She never has."

Faerie loves all Her children, Ailish had told me, but Eledan had been away for so long he thought Faerie had forgotten him. His crusade might have begun before that, when he'd created the Hunt to be *seen.* What had he told me? That I'd slaughtered my own kind to be noticed. He understood that need. As the lesser prince, he'd been ignored much of his life.

"I think that's all he's ever wanted, and if Faerie does not favor him, he will not react well."

"He won't stop at Faerie," Talen said solemnly. "His heart is tek. He spent as long pretending to be human as he has as Faerie's prince, and with the Hunt free, he'll send it beyond Faerie."

Silence fell between us as the carriage clattered on.

"He doesn't know what love is." Sota turned away from the window. "He's never known it, not real love. He's searching for something he doesn't understand. He may never know it."

"He believes he loves you, Kesh," Kellee said. "When the Earthens had me restrained, he helped me escape and revealed a few things."

"He helped you escape?" I asked. "Why?"

"I don't know..." Kellee shifted on the bench seat. "Much of it is a blur, but he mentioned a key, and my help. He also said I was to *let you sleep* when the time came." Kellee waved a hand. "We know how that turned out."

"You didn't think to mention this when I asked if anyone had any more secrets to reveal?"

"It wasn't a *secret.* I couldn't remember much of it. Still can't. The pieces are all jumbled in my head. I was drugged."

"He got to you."

Kellee laughed dismissively. "He didn't get to me. He just... We just agreed on some things."

"Some things you don't remember?"

Kellee saw Talen's and Sota's equally unimpressed expressions and sighed. "I had him under control."

Nobody ever had Eledan under control.

"He got to me too," Talen said.

"What?" Eledan had gotten to Talen? "When?"

"I'm not certain." He tilted his head. His silvery hair fell over one shoulder. "Visiting Sol and Earth... I remember little, just the pain, but he was in my dreams."

Kellee closed his eyes and dropped his head back against the carriage. "You were losing your shit on *Excalibur*. I needed Talen, not the Nightshade." When he opened his eyes, he swallowed. "I asked him to keep you asleep, to make you dream so you didn't spook the *Excalibur* crew."

Kellee did what? "You invited him into Talen's head?"

Talen's hand came down on my thigh. "It's all right. It was the better solution."

I'd spent nine months with that sluaghbait in my head. It was not *all right*. "What did he make you dream of, Talen?" I asked.

"You."

I slumped back in the seat. Eledan had touched each of our minds, likely plucked on our motives and desires like a master musician. Damn him, we were all compromised. He knew us better than we knew ourselves. He knew our dreams and our nightmares.

All but Sirius.

I didn't yet know what it meant, or if it meant anything at all, but having Eledan so close couldn't be good. Rubbing away the ache along my forehead, I asked, "You mentioned a key, Kellee?"

"It has something to do with the polestar. One is important to the other, that's all I can remember. He knows where it is, I think."

Of course Eledan did.

"Ailish will know more," I mumbled, looking out of the window at the world rushing by.

"It is dangerous to pin your hopes on a Wild One," Talen offered. "Especially as she is well-known to Eledan. She is likely playing her own game."

Nothing different from dealing with any other fae. Kellee's gaze said he knew it too. Ailish had helped me free Eledan from Oberon's slumber. She knew him, had even spoken fondly of the *foolish prince with a heart full of pride and a head full of dreams* who would visit her cavern.

"What choice do I have?"

Neither Sota, Talen, nor Kellee could answer.

THE CARRIAGE ROCKED to a gentle halt. Sota and I clambered out first, followed by Talen and Kellee.

As soon as I stepped down from the carriage, it was clear Ailish wasn't home. When Sirius and I had approached before, the cave entrance had glowed with life. There was no glowing now, just cold, bare stone.

Sirius turned from the cavern, mouth grimly set. "This makes things more challenging."

"Where do we go from here?" I asked.

He peered over my head, scanning the dense forest. Where wisps had bumbled through the air and illuminated huge oak branches, shadows gathered. The entire place had a sinister feel to it.

"Your hear that?" Kellee asked.

"I don't hear anything," Sota replied.

And that was the problem. Faerie was rarely quiet.

Kellee's claws stretched from his fingers. "We're being watched."

"On Faerie," Sirius said, "you always are." I lowered my hand to my whip. Sirius's gaze followed the movement. "We must travel to Safira," he added, catching my eye before sliding that guarded stare toward Talen.

Something passed between them, some shared knowledge that had Talen straightening and studiously avoiding my pointed look. There was so much the fae said between their words, unheard by the rest of us, that we had no hope of understanding.

"Safira was a seat of power long before the courts reigned," Talen said. "When my unseelie were driven out, the knoll was abandoned."

My unseelie. It was the first time he'd address the dark fae as his, and it reminded me of who I stood beside. The Nightshade. The unseelie's chosen leader. A badass the likes of which Faerie hadn't seen until Oberon had forced Talen and his legions into the dark. *I'm not who I once was.*

"It *was* abandoned," Sirius replied, "but Faerie abhors a vacuum."

That shared knowledge strummed the air with tension. Safira was important, and these two ancient fae were pulling their usual act of speaking only what was necessary so the rest of us had to play catch-up.

"Hey," I barked. "Fewer secrets and more sharing, remember?" They blinked shining secret-filled eyes. "Where is Safira and why are you both acting like this is worse than bad?"

"The Wild Ones are... difficult." Sirius said *difficult* like I'd say *fucking impossible*. "Return to the carriage. Time is not our ally."

Kellee grunted. "How about a please, asshole?"

Something hot and sharp flashed across Sirius's gaze. "You're a visitor here, vakaru. Be careful how you address those to whom this land belongs, lest the land take offense."

I touched Kellee's arm to distract his single-focused glare and draw it away from the departing guardian. He gritted his teeth, cheek tightening.

"If that stick were any farther up his ass, he'd be scaring crows," Sota muttered, sauntering past us, remembering farms and their pests from our time watching Earthen shows on Calicto. Kellee moved away from my touch and followed Sota back to the carriage.

Sirius swung into the driver's seat and took up his fiery horses' reins. After the others had climbed into the carriage, I veered to the front of the carriage and looked up at Sirius. "What aren't you saying?"

His tek-fingers stroked the vine-reins. "There are a great many individuals who would see harm come to you, Calla, and Safira harbors them all."

It was more than that. Sometimes, it had seemed like all of Faerie wanted me dead, and he hadn't been overly concerned then. "You're worried about something else. Is it Ailish?"

"Ailish is more powerful than she seems, and she knows more about you than she should. Enemies often wear friendly faces."

I wanted more time with him. Maybe, if we talked more, I could ease his concerns and make him less prickly. "May I ride shotgun with you?"

"No."

The denial cut.

His hands tightened on the reins, and the vines creaked.

Maybe the library kiss had been an emotional mistake. I

remembered him being full of passion and want, but that was before everything else had happened, and there was none of that truth in him now.

The horses snorted and jostled inside their harnesses, eager to be moving.

"Mylana... *Kesh*... " He waited for me to look up again, and his hard nothing expression softened into understanding. "It is not safe for a mortal to ride to Safira in the open. You'll be protected inside the carriage."

I nodded and climbed inside. Talen's touch looped around my waist, drawing me snug against him. "The guardian will come around, given time."

Maybe, if Kellee didn't gut him first. Kellee and Sota discussed the carriage, arguing over whether it was held together by magic or vines.

With their voices mingling, I breathed out and pulled Talen's arm tighter around me, enjoying the closeness while I could. "What is this Safira place that has you and Sirius so concerned?"

"There have always been those in between, not seelie and not unseelie, just... fae."

"Like you?"

He nodded and brushed my hair from my face. "Safira was my home *before*. It is where we—the fae—would go to feel closer to Faerie."

Why did that set my heart fluttering, like it was a bad thing to go there?

"If Sirius is correct, the Wild Ones have adopted Safira. We'll know more once we arrive."

Talen's home. He'd mentioned it only once, telling me of how he had loved a saru in his household. He'd tried to keep her safe by agreeing to stand beside Oberon. The Hunt had killed the saru at Oberon's command, setting off the chain of events that had turned Talen from a lordly sidhe into the Nightshade.

His fingers danced down my face and lifted my chin. A tickle of his power warmed my jaw and sank into my bones, chasing away my anxiety.

Without the bond between us, he could hurt me, could even control me. He'd turned the entire human crew of the *Excalibur* into puppets eager to do his bidding. It would be easy for him to control me or ravage my mind in the same way.

I swallowed. I didn't want to think these things, but how could I not when I was looking into the eyes of a creature who had once commanded all of Faerie's dark forces?

"I miss the bond as much as you do," he said. "I find your absence startling and cold. You were my light, and the way you're looking at me, I fear you're slipping away. But know this, *I will always be yours*. These words are my bond. Don't leave me, Kesh."

He had said those words long ago, when I'd woken from Eledan's dreams and hadn't yet become the Messenger. He had dropped to his knees and shared his magic with me. We had no bond to make them true, but on Faerie, we didn't need one.

"I won't leave you." I wrapped his hand in mine. "What happened on that balcony, please know it wasn't you I was rejecting. I'll never turn my back on you, Talen."

His eyes fluttered closed, his free hand cupped my face, and he settled the lightest kiss on my forehead. "Come home with me," he whispered, bundling me close against his chest. The warm, heady scents of jasmine and night lily coiled around me too. The feel of him, his magic, all of him—strong yet vulnerable. My heart ached to think of him hurting.

Going home would be difficult after so long away, but he wasn't alone.

Together.

Sirius cracked the reins. The carriage jolted, the horses whinnied, and we were picking up speed at an alarming rate.

"Don't look outside." He nodded at Sota. "You as well, Sota. Keep your gaze inside the carriage."

Sota angled his back to the window. "Where is Safira?"

"Somewhere that cannot be reached by conventional means."

Kellee sat rigidly on the bench opposite me, arms crossed and head back, his gaze fixed on the carriage ceiling as he tried his hardest to appear unaffected by Faerie. Extracting myself from Talen's grip, I crossed to Kellee's side and spread my hand on his thigh. Talen spared the slightest of understanding nods, one Kellee didn't see.

"I'll happily hug you," Sota offered Talen. The fae smiled quickly and looped his arm around Sota's shoulders, reeling him close. Sota tried to pull back. "Unless the tek hurts?"

"It's fine." Talen clamped him closer, and Sota melted against him. It warmed my hardened heart to see them so close.

The carriage rattled and thundered, its wooden seams groaning. Curiosity demanded I look outside to see where we were going so fast. It couldn't be a normal road; we'd have wrecked by now. Faster and faster we traveled, to the sound of galloping hooves. Kellee's thigh was stone beneath my grip. He would never admit to fear, but I knew my vakaru.

I leaned into him and whispered, "You are not ready for what will happen when I finally get you alone." Over the carriage's thunderous sounds, the others wouldn't hear me, but Kellee's sensitive hearing picked up every word.

"You think so, huh?" he whispered back and looked down,

bringing us almost cheek to cheek. I inched my hand higher up his thigh, smiling as he shifted, giving me better access.

"You, me, a bed ... naked except for my whip..." I dug my fingers in and raked them up his thigh to where his pants bunched. He shifted again, adjusting to keep himself comfortable.

"I don't do submissive." His voice had dropped a level, adopting that gravelly maleness he liked to use to seduce. "You'll have to catch me, and maybe then you could persuade me."

Something screamed outside the carriage. One of the horses, perhaps, but it sounded broken, like glass shattering. I'd turned to look for the source when Kellee's hand clamped loosely around my neck and his mouth scorched my skin below my ear. His mouth on my neck ignited a rush of heat. Whatever was outside was quickly forgotten in the feel of having a vakaru's teeth hovering over an artery.

"You like that thought?" he asked.

I liked all the thoughts in my head, but especially the one of him tied to a bed. He'd been around a long time, maybe lived a hundred lifetimes, but in all that time, had he allowed anyone to bind him?

His teeth nipped at my ear. My fingers curled in his shirt. The carriage could have burst into flames and I wouldn't have noticed. Dampness gathered between my legs, where Kellee's free hand roamed toward. As a distraction, it had worked, for both of us, but now I wanted to straddle his legs, tear his clothes off, and fuck my vakaru, and I didn't care that we weren't alone.

His dirty chuckle worsened my raging desire. His fingers found the sweet spot, stroking over my pant seam, his rough touch infuriatingly close. "You don't have the patience for games, Kesh," he purred against my jaw.

"Oh, don't I?"

I gently planted a hand on his chest and pushed him back, delighting in the golden burn haloing his dark pupils and wanting nothing more than to grab him. But the carriage was slowing, and I was in charge of this game. He let me twist out of his grip and rested back into his position, the only difference being his knowing smile.

Talen's gaze had fallen to the window, where strange, dappled lights washed in and over the carriage floor.

"Is it safe to look?"

"It is," he whispered, not taking his eyes off whatever awaited outside. I'd seen that look on his face before, one of need and want, but also of fear.

The Nightshade was home, but what kind of home was it?

The carriage jolted to a halt, and in the quiet that followed, I heard the whistles, chirps, and song of countless pixies. Light danced outside, so bright my light-sensitive eyes couldn't make out anything solid or recognizable.

Sota straightened, on alert, as Talen threw the door open. He hesitated, chest stuttering, before offering me his hand. "Come with me."

I folded my hand in his and stepped out of the carriage.

CHAPTER 12

Alone, as a messenger on Calicto, I'd built a personal safety drone by repurposing an Arcon wardrone and mixing it with borrowed fae magic. I had many reasons for making Sota, but none had been to make a friend. I hadn't known I needed one, until he was there, by my side, filling the silences and chasing away bad memories. Night after night, after I'd finished delivering my messages for the day and earned my fresh water or food rations, I'd tell Sota tales of the fae. Stories like the bucca, for whom human fishermen always left a fish from their catch on the shore. Or how the bucca was used as a threat to quiet noisy children. The changelings that the fae left in place of stolen babies—who the fae took to check up on their human experiment—could be found out by mixing a brew of crushed eggshells. The tatter-foal could take the shape of any creature, not just wolves, like the Cu Sith. On and on I told Sota those human folktales, marveling at many myself. The truth of the fae was kept from saru as it was from humans, but humanity had woven their existence into their myths. I'd often wondered how many of these myths were true. The Faerie I'd been raised in was poised and sedate compared to the colorful Faerie from those tales.

Humans had been right.

When Talen led me from the carriage and the bright light lessened, I found my mind reaching for those fairytales to make sense of the sight. Little people, no taller than my knee, sat in the branches of gnarled trees. Enormous foxgloves, twice as tall as me, swayed in a nonexistent breeze, colored bright red and soft cream. Sidhe fae, like Sirius and Talen, milled about, but some had tails, or cloven hooves where their feet should be, or horns, or hair like manes, or no hair at all, their skin shimmering like fish scales.

"They're real..." Sota whispered. "They were always real."

When Talen finally spoke, his voice was full of awe but undermined by a touch of regret. "Before Oberon's cleansing, before the courts of unseelie and seelie formed, the Wild Ones populated Faerie."

A virtually naked female with tawny, velvety skin sauntered by, singing to herself or the glittering pixies nesting in her dreadlocked hair. Her tail swished around her ankles, and her eyes were like Hulia's, with double eyelids. She was namu, or part namu, perhaps the origin of Oberon's namu creations. There was no mistaking the power of her voice as it urged me to follow her in dance.

Oberon would have hated this riot of beasts and color and the chaos of their construction. To me, they were beautiful, each and every one of them. These were Sirius and Talen's people. They were chaos and mayhem and noise and dance.

"Be careful, calla," Sirius murmured behind my left shoulder. "Remember the docks."

Ah, yes, the docks, when one of these people had tried to lure me away from Sirius. The tales of the messing with humans had been true too. I was close enough to human and susceptible here.

"Ailish will be here," Sirius said. "Do not dally or the earth will root your feet and keep you forever."

Sota huffed a laugh, then lost his smile when he looked down to see how a string of vines had tangled around his boots. He plucked himself free and shuddered. "That's just rude."

Meandering paths crisscrossed the mossy earth and around different-sized earthy mounds propped up by little doors. Homes, I assumed. Some were stores displaying their wares of clothes and fabrics. Above, wisps clung to strings of ivy like the lights slung across the sinks back home on Old Calicto, only here the lights were alive.

I didn't see a sky, just layers of dark on dark with no stars. We were underground, then? A knoll, but much, much bigger, like a small underground town. I moved after the others, trying and failing not to stare. *C'mon, Kesh, nothing down here should be surprising.* Where did I think Oberon had gotten the DNA for all his experiments?

We came to a junction of paths.

"Find Ailish," Talen told Sirius. "I'll take them home."

Sirius veered off one way, toward where the domes grew larger and more closely packed together. Talen nodded at us to follow a less worn path that snaked away from the "town" center toward a copse that looked a lot like Kellee's blood-hungry vakaru trees. I checked Kellee. He nodded. They were those trees. Best not bleed on them.

"Did you know this place was real?" Sota asked, dropping back from Talen.

"No, I had no idea. I thought it was all silly human stories. I knew some of these people lived in the wilds, but not like this, in these numbers."

"Did you see the man-horse?"

"A púca?" I'd missed that.

His gaze had already wandered. "It must be very impractical to have a horse's ass."

"Don't let the pretty fool you," Kellee said. He had stayed close behind, scanning our surroundings for threats. "Anything here will kill you as readily as any sidhe." His claws were out. Here, those claws were normal. He even looked like he belonged, with his wild hair and multicolored eyes. Oberon's idea for the vakaru had come from here too.

I wasn't sure where I'd expected Talen to live. In a palace, like Oberon, maybe? He'd been the Nightshade, so surely that required a fortress? I'd been wrong. We entered the gardens first, and I knew it had to be his from the enormous sprawling patches of lilies and flowering jasmine tumbling over terraces that led up to a single-story cave-house, the type carved from rock, but this was Faerie, so his house had grown this way, spreading outward through the rockface, peppered with doors and windows. Veins of silver flowed through the gray stone. Now that I'd seen his home, I couldn't imagine him living anywhere else.

Roots snapped from the ground ahead of him and scurried out of the way. Trees leaned their branches out of his path. Plants peeled back to expose the polished stone beneath, and ahead, the honeysuckle lifted from the dwelling, like a curtain revealing its showpiece. Talen strode on as if this were all perfectly normal.

We'd reached the front deck when a cloud of enormous moths burst from a few windows, dusting us all with glitter.

Sota sneezed. Kellee pulled his hand across his mouth and sighed, already tired of the drama. He caught me looking at him and narrowed his eyes. Only, how could he appear threatening with glitter in his hair? My lips twitched. I swallowed the laugh.

He lifted a finger, and I rolled my lips together, locking the laughter away, but he saw it in my eyes and smiled coyly.

Talen's home had been empty for a long time, and little bugaboo creatures had made it their home. Talen let the furry things, no larger than lizards, scurry out. Some little people—brownies, I figured—bumbled from room to room. I watched them work and listened to their humming. They reminded me of children, until they spoke, their mouths full of shark-like teeth.

I wandered the house. Every room had windows, which wasn't possible, considering the home was built *into* a hillside, but everything here wasn't possible, so what were a few windows in a cave-house?

I found what had clearly been Talen's favorite room. From the wide window, the view of Safira stretched far over hills and into valleys. Warm, scented air breezed in. I touched the wall beside the window, and magic spritzed across my fingers. The walls lit up with familiar silvery circles and faded again in moments.

"My home welcomes you," Talen said. His coat was gone and his waistcoat hung unlaced. Leaves were still snagged in his long hair, and an odd new-to-Talen smirk rested on his lips.

"Your home is perfect."

"It was full of life for a long time..."

Until Oberon had changed the course of Talen's life forever.

"I'm sorry..." A silly thing to say, but I was struggling to find any words that did this place justice.

"It was a long time ago." He breathed in and stopped at the window to admire Safira, as he gathered his thoughts.

"This location is easily defensible. We'll see any force long before they arrive."

Always so practical. "I was thinking more along the lines of how beautiful Safira is."

"It wasn't always like this. Before... before it was full of dark and light fae. It was... different. Oberon tried to destroy it. We battled here, so close to Faerie's heart I was sure we would win, but Oberon already had the polestar. We could not survive its light, and so the dark ones fled..."

"Are there any dark fae left here?"

He fell quiet, studying me. "You sense them." Not a question.

"I feel like what I see isn't everything. Like there's something I'm missing, but it's right in front of me."

It seemed to be the right answer, because he laughed and leaned against the wall. "You are more fae than you realize."

"I'm saru."

"Saru are fae. We are all degrees of fae. Vakaru are fae, and so are humans." He saw my face fall. "That doesn't make you any less saru. Just that... Faerie welcomes you here the same as She welcomes me. It was Oberon who changed our fates, not Faerie."

Faerie loves all Her children.

The Nightshade returns. Now is the time for all Faerie's children to return.

"Ailish knew we'd come here." I needed to speak with the water witch before Eledan could stop me. "Do you think she knows we're here?"

He smiled like I was a child for asking. "Every creature on Faerie knows we're here."

"Even the Hunt?" I whispered.

He bowed his head. "It is possible. Secrets are difficult to keep here."

I gripped the windowsill and gazed over the valley, down into Safira. I'd been raised on Faerie but knew so little about it. "You say I am part of Faerie. Ailish said the same, but I've never felt like I belong."

"Because you are incomplete."

He said it like it was simple. Maybe it was and I just hadn't been ready to hear it before. While the polestar was in pieces, I would never belong. Emotion knotted my throat. "Talen..." I gripped the sill tighter. "I won't survive the polestar, will I?"

"I do not know." He hadn't moved from his spot against the wall, and I didn't want him to. If he came close and swept me into his arms, I'd use him to forget and pretend we'd survive this, and I couldn't afford to. Not anymore.

"If I die, Eledan dies, right?" My voice wobbled.

"That seems likely, given how the polestar is as much a part of him as it is you."

I bit the inside of my cheek and tasted coppery blood. "Good."

I couldn't look at him. Even without the bond, I knew he was hurting. He'd loved and lost before. "My people will be safe, Faerie will stay here and not war with others, and the humans will take Halow back. It will be as it was for a thousand years. There will be peace." I could make that happen. All I had to do was restore the polestar and stop the Hunt, balancing the light and the dark weapons once more. Oberon was gone. Eledan would be gone. Faerie would be settled. The killing would stop. It only required the lives of one saru girl and Faerie's forgotten prince. So small a price for universal peace.

Talen's arms were around me. He scooped me up, turned my back to the window, and propped me on the sill. His hands were on my face, holding me still. I had no choice but to see the bright tears in his eyes. "I cannot watch you do this. I can't lose you. You're the only part of me that feels, Kesh. Without you, I do not know who or what I am. Without you, there is no meaning. I would die in your place if you'd allow it. I have never known a soul as bright as yours. I cannot see it burn out. I won't. There must be another way." His voice caught, and those diamond tears fell, taking pieces of my heart with them. Did this always happen when immortals loved mortals? It seemed so wrong, so unfair. I would do anything to save him, to save them all.

I kissed him and tasted salty tears on his lips. His tears or mine, I wasn't sure and it didn't matter. Outside, rain pattered on leaves, stirring up the garden's sweet scent and Talen's magic. He crushed me close and kissed me like he could save me. If love could save lives, ours would. Just not my life.

"COME OUT, Wraithmaker... I have a surprise for you."

I blinked, stirring in Talen's arms. We lay tangled on his bed. His earlier kisses still tingled my skin, warming me through. "You let me sleep?" Surely I'd been dreaming and the voice had woken me. A voice I knew well but hadn't heard in years. The memory of it faded into the past where it belonged.

"No, I allowed you to drift for a while. You didn't sleep." His strong arm looped around my waist. He reeled me in, against his naked chest. I breathed him in, wishing I could stay in his arms all day, but Sirius was out there looking for Ailish, the Hunt was loose, and Eledan had an entire world at his fingertips. I could not afford to rest.

"I thought I heard... a voice."

"Someone is outside. I planned to ignore them until they went away."

But the voice... I pressed the heel of my hand to my head. I knew who that voice belonged to, and he couldn't be here.

"You're cold?" Talen brushed a hand down my arm, over the goosebumps.

"No—"

"Wraithmaker?" the voice crooned. Male. Rough. "Come entertain us, Wraithmaker."

Talen's eyes narrowed.

The sound of a whip cracking shot through me. I tore from Talen's arms, snatched on my pants and undervest, and grabbed my tek-whip. I headed for the door before Talen could stop me.

"Kesh, wait..."

Kellee approached from one of the side corridors. "Who is this asshole?"

I veered right, keeping Kellee behind me. "I'll deal with it."

Another whip crack jolted through me. Not a metallic sound, like mine. This was the unmistakable *snatch* of leather tails.

Sota was already outside, where he'd likely been standing sentry all along. His guns were open and on display, and there, a few steps down the terrace, stood a fae I'd hoped never to see again. Long salt-and-pepper hair had been pulled back from a severe, narrow face and bound so tightly that it gleamed against his skull. He hadn't aged a day since he'd first sneered through cell bars at me and the other saru children who had survived the harvesting.

"There she is..." His right cheek pulled upward, lifting the corner of his mouth. "You haven't changed, Wraithmaker."

I should speak, but all the words had jammed in my

throat. The last time I'd seen him, he'd whipped me to within an inch of my life. Only by Oberon's grace had I survived.

"Dagnu." His name on my lips tasted foul. Dagnu. *Bad blood.* My jailor. The fae who had thrown me into the arenas as a child so I'd have to fight to survive time and time again.

He laughed and looped the thin whip around his hand and elbow. "My saru gladiator is all grown." It was the same whip he'd always used. I'd know its tails anywhere. He would oil it before visiting the cells every day. I smelled that same sweet oil on him now.

"Leave," Talen hissed, appearing at my right side.

Dagnu sneered at him. "You have no authority here—"

"You know who I am. Leave or suff—"

"The king took your wings, *Nightshade.* I know who you are—a useless ornament dangling from the Wraithmaker's fingers. You and that filthy vakaru and this"—he threw a hand at Sota—"monstrosity of human-made tek, you are all her ornaments. Isn't that right, Wraithmaker?"

Kellee's growl bubbled to my left.

"What do you want?" It was my voice but without the internal screaming trying to drown out my thoughts. I'd known he was alive—Aeon had made it clear that Dagnu had remained in his life—but to see him again after so long reminded me of who I had once been.

"Are you here to entertain us?" he asked, ignoring my question. He spread his arms, and for the first time, I saw the flank of fae behind him. Some sidhe with darkness in their eyes, like the fae at the docks, while others appeared more outwardly vicious, made of claws and teeth. They hooted and snickered, whispering, "*Wraithmaker, Wraithmaker.*" Their combined voices started to eat into my skull and burrow deep.

"The Wraithmaker is dead," I said, making sure they all heard.

Dagnu mock-lunged at me. I recoiled like I had in the past, and even though it didn't happen, I saw the whip come down, saw his leering smile and rough hands.

He chuckled darkly. "Not yet she's not."

"Kesh," Sota said. "Say the word and *he's* dead."

Dagnu's mouth jerked around a grin. He pointed at me. "Oberon stole you from me. You know how this ends. You've always known. Come crawling back to me when you're ready, *saru*." Chuckling, he turned and strode down the steps, away from the terrace. His train of sidhe followed, their gazes hungry for murder.

He was long gone and the pixies had returned to squabble in the bushes, but I still hadn't moved. "Kesh..." Sota dared to approach first. "What did he mean?"

You know how this ends.

"Talen." I looked over him, through him. I saw the whip come down and felt it bite into my back, my arms. I heard my whimpers with each lash. "We don't have time for this. Find out where Sirius has gotten to."

He nodded and started down the steps.

"Don't touch... Dagnu," I called, stumbling over the name. I wiped my mouth, swallowing excess saliva.

Kellee watched me, keeping his expression lawman neutral, though he likely knew my seeing Dagnu had undermined everything I'd worked to forget.

"No more secrets," Kellee said. "Remember? We're together in everything."

I closed my eyes and squeezed the whip, still coiled, unused, in my hand. "He's nothing. Forget it."

How could I tell him everything Dagnu had done? The beatings and relentless healings so I could fight again. Making the Wraithmaker dance at the crack of his whip. Dagnu and the arenas had taught me how to fight, and he'd taught me to despise the fae for the monsters they were.

I swallowed. Kellee wouldn't forget, and he wouldn't stop asking his questions.

"He's nobody, Kellee. Don't ask me again."

"Kesh—"

"Kellee, please, let it go." I retreated inside the house, his gaze on my back. I knew he cared, but he'd also go after Dagnu if he learned even a fraction of what that fae had done to me. Dagnu's life was not Kellee's to take. It was mine.

CHAPTER 13

"Something happened while I was away." Sirius greeted me on the terrace while the others spread out inside Talen's sprawling knoll to make sure nobody else had sneaked inside.

"Nothing important," I denied, keeping my eyes on the wild gardens instead of on the simmering guardian beside me. "Ailish?"

"I've sent out a summons. She will arrive in due course."

He fell quiet, and when I finally arched an eyebrow and stole a look at the guardian, his scowl remained as hard as ever. "What?"

"I do not like to be lied to."

I laughed so suddenly a clutch of wisps shot out of the bushes, spinning and dancing their dazzling light. "Oh really? You weren't lying to yourself all those years you were in denial?"

He turned his head away, showing me his proud profile and nothing of the pained look in his eyes. I shouldn't have said it. I could hardly mock him when I'd fallen into my own lies often enough. "I'm sorry, that was wrong of me." Dagnu had rattled me more than he should have, but that was no excuse to take it out on Sirius.

I considered placing a hand on his arm, but he'd positioned himself just beyond my reach, probably deliberately. Our library kiss seemed like a lifetime ago. Two days ago, I'd found the real Sirius under his hardcore guardian guise and lost him again just as quickly. Maybe things would be easier if I knew what I was doing, but it seemed as though we were all being swept along by the same uncontrollable tide as we tried to grasp at something steady, only for it to slip between our fingers. I didn't know how to stop the Hunt, or how to love a guardian. Compared to his long life, mine was a blink, and if I didn't figure out what to do next, it would soon be over.

"What happened between you and Ailish?"

"It is in the distant past." He continued to glare at the glittering Safira some ways down the valley, doing his utmost to hide his face.

"That doesn't make it any less important."

His shoulders shifted an inch. He reached for the half wall, needing the support, and leaned his thigh against it. In seconds, he'd aged years. The memories were bad ones. "The Autumnlands knoll was my seat of power. Long ago, before the courts became divided, it had thrived. Ailish and I... we were lovers."

I had not expected that answer.

"An immortal life is a long time to love, and we do not always choose wisely." He blinked at the ground, and when he lifted his head again, the rigid and untouchable guardian's prickly exterior melted behind a shy smile. "I did not see her ambitions until it became almost too late to stop her. It was not love she wanted from me, but power. With her true intentions revealed, we fought. She attempted to end my life. I left her with a reminder not to cross me."

Her facial scarring... he had done that to her.

Sirius shooed off a couple of pixies scrabbling over the low wall. "Every time she peers into her healing waters, she sees the fruits of her deceit."

His hands tightened on the wall. The real hand paled from clenching too hard. I was still trying to reconcile the old Sirius—the emotionless fae—with the new Sirius, who felt so deeply he cut himself off to keep anyone from wounding his heart again. That softer, more vulnerable Sirius stood beside me now.

I gently covered his tek-hand with mine. "After I was harvested, I was thrown into the arenas and expected to die. When I survived, I caught the overseer's eye. He took it upon himself to train me."

Sirius looked at our hands and then up at my face. "I always believed Oberon trained you."

"He honed skills *Dagnu* had already instilled in me ... It's a saru name. His real name is Ryande."

"Ryande." His brow knotted. "I know of him. He has a vicious reputation among the sidhe. Oberon expelled him from his forces. I never learned the reason."

And that vicious reputation was only based on what other fae knew of Dagnu. More went on in the gladiator cells than the fae cared to think on. If Oberon had slighted Dagnu and stolen me from him, it would explain why Dagnu had reappeared, after Oberon's death, to reclaim me. I wanted to believe I'd changed and grown enough to face Dagnu, but a mix of fear and hatred left me uncertain.

"It seems he hasn't forgotten me."

"Did you think he would?"

"I'd hoped..."

"And what do you plan to do about him?"

"Right now, nothing."

"That would be unwise," an ethereal, flowing voice said from behind us.

Ailish drifted closer. A dark hooded cloak had replaced her blue gowns. She looked like something that lured humans into the woods to devour them later.

"Fire Lord." The hood dipped, but she kept it up, hiding her face.

Sirius nodded.

"Your colors are much returned. Faerie approves of your choices." The hood swung my way. I glimpsed her beautiful half, her lips turned up in the light, but the hood's shadow hid her eyes. "Your jailor would rather see you dead at his feet than free. Ignore him at your risk. He will hinder your path ahead. There is a way to have your vengeance and win half of Faerie's heart, but it remains to be seen if you are strong enough."

"If I'm not?"

"You'll die."

Of course. "Is there an end to all of this that doesn't see me dead?"

"Those answers will cost you too much, mortal. Ask lesser questions."

She had helped me revive Eledan, which had led to Oberon's death, but that only meant she'd helped me remove Faerie's pretender king. With Sirius's words still fresh, I recognized that Ailish had her own motives, and they involved Eledan, of that I was certain. "Eledan made you a promise. What is it?"

"We bargained, he and I." Her mouth moved seductively, keeping her smile.

"Does it involve me?"

"Your fates are entwined."

Apparently, getting answers from her was as easy as

getting them from Eledan, or any fae. They did so enjoy playing their word games. The problem was, I didn't have an eternity to figure out the rules.

"You helped me before, so help me now. Tell me what I have to do to make everything right. You wanted me to help Faerie, and that's what I'm doing. So help me."

Sirius's tek-hand tightened around mine, offering support without making it obvious. He'd heard the frustration in my voice.

"You are becoming more. Beyond that, I cannot say."

"More what?"

Her hood lifted. The shadow retreated up her face but still cloaked her eyes.

This was useless. "What *can* you tell me?"

"Everything and nothing."

Sirius began, "Ailish—"

"Hush, guardian." She took me by the shoulders and dug her fingers in. Head bent low, she said, "You must survive yourself to unlock your truth. You know this."

What did that even mean? "I don't understand your riddles."

"You will."

"Why can't you just tell me?"

"Because discovery is worthless without the journey." Her slash of a smile cut across her face. "You know how this ends. You've always known."

Those were Dagnu's words. Part of me wondered if she'd brought Dagnu here, but why? She seemed to want to help, but fae were never what they seemed. She wanted me for something—*needed* me even. Or needed what was inside me.

"Witch," Sirius snarled, "if you don't give us something of worth, I'll burn the rest of your face."

I expected the words to hurt, for her to shriek, but she

cackled and stepped back, freeing me from her icy grip. "Oh, Fire Lord, you never change. It is a good thing she is by your side to quench your flames."

"Can you give us anything of worth?" I asked.

More cackling, and I questioned Sirius's past romantic choices. "Of worth? Yes. Priceless, in fact. In the Autumnlands library, there is a book buried beneath the dark. That book is more than it appears. The secrets hidden inside its pages will help you, but you'll open it to find nothing in its pages. Bring it to me and I'll read its words."

"Why can't you get it yourself?"

She lifted her chin. "I am forbidden from entering the Autumnlands knoll."

"If you speak of Eledan's book, my knoll was destroyed, the book along with it," Sirius said.

Oberon had plucked a book from Sirius's library shelves and used it to demonstrate where the Hunt had come from. *The Origin of the Wild Hunt*. Right after, the Hunt had devoured Sirius's knoll and Aeon, and it would have killed us all if Talen and Shinj hadn't saved us.

"Not destroyed, just healing... and sleeping." Ailish turned her attention to me. "Bring me the book and you'll have your answers."

It was a lead, but I didn't trust Ailish. "What do you get out of helping me?"

Her hood shifted, deepening the shadows. "It is time for all of Faerie's children to return and for Faerie to be whole as She was before the sidhe lords demanded order."

"You want the unseelie back?"

She nodded once, a slow bow of the head.

"How is that possible?"

"It has already begun."

"How, when they were banished far from Faerie?"

"All of the dark are drawn to the fountains of light."

Sirius sighed. "The ages have ravaged her mind. Asking her more questions will yield fewer answers. We know Eledan's book survives. That is something. As for the rest, she'll drive you insane with her questions masquerading as answers. Enough, Kesh."

Ailish cackled. "You spoil my fun, guardian."

Fun? Was that all this was to her? Was I worth nothing more than a joke?

"This is my life!" I snapped. "And I don't have much of it left to live, so don't fuck with me, fairy. If you have something to tell me, tell me straight." I hovered my hand over my whip.

Ailish grinned. Sharp, pointed teeth glinted behind her red lips. "I'll tell you this for free, Messenger. You are on the cusp of change, not just for you, but for all of Faerie and Her children. Remember, you will need both the light and the dark to prevail, but do not allow either to seduce you. You must harness the power within you and the power you have gathered around you, or your battle will end in failure."

As her outline ghosted away, I wondered if Eledan would have given me more useful answers.

I slumped against the terrace wall and mumbled, "Go to Safira, they said. It'll be fun, they said."

"That is the opposite of what I said."

I had no choice but to laugh at Sirius's growl. He appeared alarmed that I would dare laugh at him, then his stiffness eased and the tiniest smile cracked his armor. That smile warmed me through.

"All right." I let the laughter fade. "It wasn't a complete loss. We know we need the book. I don't suppose you read the book?"

"Did I read a book written by a nothing prince filled with pages of woe-is-me? No, I did not read his self-indulgent book. I don't understand how the book found its way to my library or why Eledan did not destroy a thing detailing his nightmare."

Because he needed it, should his nightmare ever slip its leash; it would have answers. "We have a lead, and Ailish believes the dark fae are returning. That will go a long way to healing Faerie's rift, if it's true. Peace will return to Faerie once all Her children are returned. She told me that before."

He was closer, his warmth wrapping me tight. I looked up and lost my train of thought deep in his green eyes. His hand brushed up my arm, his gaze tracking its progress as though fascinated that he could touch me without suffering painful repercussions. I recalled seeing him nailed to a cross and the moment he'd sacrificed everything to save Aeon and me before the crystal palace fell. It seemed impossible for this ancient child of Faerie to look at me as though I were the special one. "We just have to figure out how to get a star back into the sky without killing me."

"Faerie hasn't killed you yet, Messenger," he said. Was that a touch of pride in his voice? His words pulled my gaze to his lips. I recalled their scorching touch as he'd unleashed years of desire on me. We stood as close again now, anticipation a flickering fire between us that could turn into a raging inferno at any second.

"Not for lack of trying, *guardian*."

He bowed his head, just enough for desire to sing through my blood. Between one moment and the next, he hesitated, withdrew, let me go, and stepped back, slamming his barriers back into place. "We should prepare to leave Safira. Trouble will find us the longer we stay here."

I nodded. "You're right. Inform the others."

He left the terrace, taking his warmth with him, leaving me chilled. We'd shared a moment, but he'd cut it off before it could become something more. Perhaps that was for the best? If he'd been burned by love before, and that wound still pained him, what could I offer beyond more heartache?

Sota emerged from the same doorway.

I freed my whip and clutched it in my fist. The cool, solid feel of tek grounded me and helped shake off the sense of loss Sirius had left me with. "Are you okay with this?"

"Whatever you want, Kesh, I'm with you. Maybe telling Kellee and Talen would be best. You did say no more secrets..."

"No. Kellee will stop me, and Talen will always defer to Kellee. I have to do this without them. One last thing. They'll understand." I checked that nobody was at the windows to see us leave and vaulted over the low wall, dropping into the gardens below.

Sota landed effortlessly beside me. "Just like old times."

And just like old times, I had some trouble to clean up before leaving Safira.

SAFIRA'S SETTLEMENT center felt like a dream populated by wild wonders. Before I left Faerie as a queenkiller, I'd only been exposed to the sidhe, the regal light fae who inhabited the courts and attended the arena battles. I'd heard tales of weird and wonderful creatures, but without seeing them, they'd been no more real than humans had been. Drifting among Safira's population, I refrained from staring, not because they were strange, but because they were so beautiful in their differences. They observed me, warily stepping out of my way or stopping to watch Sota and me pass. We weren't subtle—me with my tek-hip and Sota, a tek-man, at my side. Most of the folk shied away. Some wore suspicion, curiosity and dislike openly on their faces. At least they were honest, unlike the sidhe lords I'd grown up with.

"Do you think Kellee has a tail?" Sota asked.

"What?"

Sota stared at a furry-faced, pointed-eared fae with a long, sweeping tail. She strode by us, flicking her tufted tail. "He'd rock a tail."

I snorted. "He doesn't have a tail."

"How do you know?"

"I've seen his…" I made a cupping gesturing, realized I had no idea what I was miming, and dropped both hands.

Sota scrutinized my face. "All of him, all at once, every inch?"

I didn't have enough real memories of seeing Kellee completely naked and made a mental note to correct that. Dream memories didn't count. I'd gotten pretty familiar with him in my dreams, but in reality, we'd done little more than fool around. However, there was one thing I knew for certain. "Yes, no tail."

"I guess." Sota sighed. "He wears pants too well to hide a tail."

Did vakaru once have tails? It felt like they should have tails. I'd ask Kellee, when he wasn't so tense.

We meandered down winding pathways between high houses, Sota enthralled like a kid visiting Calicto's Galactic Zoo for the first time.

"Hulia has a tail," I added.

He tripped and caught himself. "Really?"

"I haven't seen it, but she's intimated a few times."

His eyed widened. "I need to see it. Do you think she can open jars with it?"

I laughed.

His expression swiched toward curiosity, then he twisted

to catch sight of his own ass, circling on the spot. "Do you think I could get one?"

"Aren't you content with ten fingers?"

He stopped circling and jogged back into step beside me. "But to have a tail! Don't deny it, you'd totally have one if you could. I've seen you looking. You have tail envy."

"I don't want a tail." I shoved him playfully off his stride.

"You know your whip basically is a mechanical tail, right?"

"Wraithmaker." A huge boulder of a fae blocked our path, bringing an abrupt end to our chat. "Overseer Ryande has requested your presence."

Dagnu. I nodded, swallowed the acid burn on my tongue, and followed the huge fae through darkening alleys into a market slung with fairy lights and sprinkled with glittering wisps. It would have been pretty if not for the fae leaning against the edge of a table. His leather whip, clipped to his hip, caught my eye, and for a few seconds, it was all I could see. That whip had once been my whole world. I'd lived by it. Planned my words around it. Killed and bled so I didn't have to feel its bite again. Old fears tried to clutch at my heart and shrink me into a ball of whimpering saru. After everything I'd been through, every monster I'd faced, I'd thought I'd be prepared to see that long cut of leather again. I wasn't.

Dagnu pushed away from the table, leaving the dozen or so common-fae gathered behind him. "So faithful, saru. You return to me, as you should."

"Kesh, I—" Sota began. Four fae rushed him, captured his arms, and yanked them behind his back. A kick to the back of his knees dropped Sota to his knees. He fought, pulling one of them off balance.

"Wait, stop!" I pushed out a hand toward Dagnu. "Stop! Let him go."

"Kesh, let me hurt them." Sota's glare burned. He could kill them all. All I had to do was say *yes*.

"No." I held Sota's stare. *Don't.* We did not need more enemies. "Just stop," I told Dagnu. "Let him up. He won't hurt anyone."

Dagnu tapped the coiled whip against his thigh. I'd used to pass the minutes by those taps, knowing the pain would begin soon. "I don't think they want to." His deep, rough voice wasn't like the smooth, musical tones of most sidhe. I'd always likened it to stone grinding against stone, and that hadn't changed. What had changed was how much smaller he seemed. I remembered him as a large, dark threat, a nightmare condensed into fae form, but that terrible sense of foreboding had been lost during my time spent with Oberon.

I was the nightmare now. All the fae here knew my history. Queenkiller. Oberon's obsession. The massacre at New Calicto. They knew it had been me and the drone, now shaped as a man, I'd brought along. I was no friend to the fae.

"Dagnu, this is between you and me."

He crossed into the open area at the center of the square, his fae entourage forming a circle around us. Anticipation zinged in the air, lifting the fine hairs on the nape of my neck. We had formed something of a fighting arena, and here I was, facing my old teacher, but not as his student, as his equal.

He wore leather from head to toe, but his wasn't like the scout leathers, or even the sidhe leathers from the courts; his were made of patches of leather sewn together, reds and browns with a few greens thrown in.

"Do you still feint left when your opponent tackles you high?" He laughed and shook his head, his tails of braids lashing down his back. With a flick of his fingers, the whip tails dropped. "I tried to beat that out of you, saru, but your stupid head wouldn't learn."

Sota bucked, trying to pull free. I pushed my hand down, letting him know he didn't have to fight this for me. I had this under control, just the way I liked it. The only hold Dagnu had over me was the one I gave him.

"Would you like to find out?" I asked.

"Come, kneel to me, saru." He reached behind him with his free hand and produced an iron saru collar. My vision blurred, doubling that ring of metal. A loud thudding hammered inside my head. "You should never have been allowed off your leash. Had you stayed with me, the king and the queen would still be alive, and Faerie would not be suffering as She is."

He tossed the collar on the cobblestones between us. It clattered, ringing like a bell far and wide.

I could do this. He was just another fae. I'd fought much worse. I had to do this. I approached him, passing the collar, and stood eye to eye with the only fae I despised more than Eledan.

"Kneel," he sneered.

How similar they were in their demands.

"Let Sota go and I'll kneel."

He held my stare, testing for lies in my gaze, and then jerked his chin to those watching from behind me. A glance back revealed Sota climbing to his feet and shaking out his clothing. He nodded to let me know he was okay. I smiled back at Dagnu.

"Well?" He sniffed. "Kneel."

Blinking slowly, I bowed my head and started to dip to my knee. The tek-whip sizzled in my grip. Down another inch. Power thrummed across my skin. He believed I hadn't changed, believed I was still the Wraithmaker trying to make the fae see me, make them *love* me, as though I needed their adoration like I needed air to live. But the Wraithmaker was dead, and the woman in her place was something far worse.

I tossed my whip back, stretching out its tail in the air behind me. Sparks rained. The whip lashed in a wide arc, looping it over my head, and slung itself around Dagnu's neck. The surprise on his face turned to rabid hatred. He snarled and snapped, making the kind of noises unbefitting a lordly sidhe.

I yanked on the whip, jerking him by the neck. He stumbled and dropped to his knees, our positions reversed.

I stood over him, my whip's coils sizzling into his fae skin. "I am your queen now."

A shimmer of movement at his side. A bone dagger flashed. I danced back too late, and sharp pain flashed up my thigh. He slashed again, wildly, and snatched my whip from around his neck while I stumbled.

He flung the dagger. The blade hit me low in the waist on my right side, tearing through clothing and skin before clattering to the ground behind me. The shock was worse than the pain. He'd gotten through my defenses. He'd made me *bleed*.

Dagnu's burst of laughter tittered through our audience. "Queen?" He staggered backward and wheezed, rubbing his scorched neck. "Because the Mad Prince says so?" The crowd jeered and snickered. "A king with a tek-heart is no king at all."

Eledan would find no love here, not among Dagnu's crowd, and neither would I. I dabbed at my waist, and cool, slick blood greased my fingers. While bonded with Talen, I could have healed the minor wound, but now I wasn't sure.

"And you..." he purred. "What are you, if not a mongrel pet that should have been left in the saru harvester to rot?"

Tek spritzed to life, tingling over my fingers and up my arm, the whip thirsty for more violence.

"Death follows your stench, saru," he sneered. "It is a wonder the Hunt has not caught up with you yet."

Did he know how close he was to the truth? "Or you."

"And what is my crime? Fostering you? Caring for your forgotten friend? The saru gladiator needed extra *care* after the king took you, but he soon fell into line..." He leered, stroking his whip through his fingers.

The rage came out of nowhere, spilling the kind of vengeful fire into my veins that Kellee would have told me to shake loose before it got me killed. The fire had burned all rational thought away, though. I lifted the whip, cracked it overhead, and swung its tails at Dagnu. He lunged right, avoiding my attack, and shot his whip in low, hoping to hook my ankle and yank me onto my back. I skipped to the side, pulled my whip back again, and cracked its tails, snapping sparks in the air above us, giving him no choice but to divide his attention between the whip above and me below.

The lust for the kill sang through my veins. I was made for this. *Created* for this.

He flicked his whip from side to side, like a beast's angry tail, and sidestepped the small space we occupied. I circled him as he circled me. "There's that fire. You were always so passionate a killer, so different from your saru kin, so hungry for their blood, for us to love you."

He needed to stop talking. I'd make him stop talking forever. No more saru should have to suffer under him. I didn't know the details of what he'd done to Aeon, but I knew enough. Dagnu would die here today.

The crowd blurred in the edges of my vision, while Dagnu's figure was diamond sharp.

"You cannot stop me, Wraithmaker."

"I told you..." I tightened my grip, feeling more power spill through me. *"The Wraithmaker is dead!"*

The whip flowed, like it was alive, and struck too fast for him to counter. It tore open a gash in his cheek, raining his blood over the stones. He yelled out his rage and tried to lasso his whip in the air, but his skill was lacking. Power trilled through me—not Talen's, but something older and brighter, a piece of true Faerie. It sang to me, lifted me up, and made me whole, made me more than this little fae could ever be. He dropped his whip hand and stared, eyes wide and mouth open, as I bore down on him. Just like on the balcony with Talen, I had become something else and pulled the shadows into me, wrapping them close. I heard the darkness calling to the light, to me. A million voices, each one a thousand light-years away, but they burned as brightly as any star.

Dagnu dropped his whip. "What are you?"

He fell to his knees, the fight draining out of him.

They all fell like cards, the entire crowd collapsing to their knees with a single name on their lips, the same name I heard chanted in my head, the same name that had haunted me for months. "Nightshade."

Knowing slotted into place. He was right, I wasn't the Faerie queen, that had never been me, but I could be their chosen monster.

Nightshade.

My whip glowed like a beacon of white fire in my hand. *I* glowed. Light encased in shadow. I breathed in, drawing life and power and Faerie into me, and felt power flex outward. It reached with shadowy fingers for all the dark things hiding and forgotten in the nowhere spaces, and the darkness breathed life into them, calling them home. The unseelie. *My* unseelie.

Cold iron touched my neck.

The latch clicked, and from one blink to the next, I was on my knees, drowning and gasping, lost in the sudden, wrenching disconnect. Dagnu's boots, I saw those.

Iron squeezed, bottling the rising power in my chest. Dagnu had picked up the collar in the fight. I should have known, should have expected a trick, but he'd seemed so small... I'd underestimated him, and now he had me.

His fingers sank into my hair. He jerked my head up and leered into my face. "You might be the Nightshade, but you're still mine, little saru, and you'll always be mine."

"Actually, the Messenger is taken," came a lawman's smooth drawl.

I blinked through the haze and saw my vakaru, with my silver fae and my guardian standing on either side of him. Sota... where was Sota?

"And she beat you before you pulled that collar out your ass." Sota's cold voice. "So you'd best let her go before we make it personal."

"You have no claim to her!" Dagnu's fingers dug tighter. The collar tightened. *Can't. Breathe.* "She was mine long be—"

A shot rang out. A single precision blast.

Dagnu fell with a solid thump. I blinked up at Sota's outline. His gun ports smoked. His tek-eye glowed, but his mouth wore a modest smile. "He was about to launch into a villainous monologue and ain't nobody got time for that."

Sota reached behind my neck, and the collar fell away, allowing me to breathe again, in more ways than one. Power trickled back into my veins. Nothing like I'd felt before, but enough to remind me I was becoming something else.

Sota hauled me onto wobbly legs, neatly propping me against him so I could at least appear impressive while surrounded by a few hundred silent fae faces. They knew me now.

Ailish's cackle sailed into the silence. I searched for her hooded presence but couldn't find her.

The crowd parted, opening a path out of the square.

Kellee nodded, but its tightness had nerves fluttering in my gut. Talen's keen eyes scanned the crowd, his presence warning them to back off. Sirius led the way, forcing the locals to skitter out of his path.

"You hurt?" Sota whispered.

My side ached where the knife had cut into me and my neck itched, but I'd live. "No, I'm okay."

His arm tightened around my waist. "Screw having a tail. I want Nightshade wings like yours."

ellee had gone into silent sentinel mode, which was the only clue I needed to know I was in a whole world of trouble.

We were back in Talen's house, in one of the spare rooms, so I could clean up and catch my breath. Dagnu was dead, and though I should care, I didn't. He was just another fae left dead in my wake, and he'd deserved it. No more saru would suffer under his whip.

I'd stripped off my upper leathers and vest, leaving just the chest wrap on, and examined the jagged tear at my waist. It oozed blood, but it could have been worse.

Kellee's glare prickled the hair on the back of my neck. I'd told him I wouldn't leave him. I'd told him we were together. I'd told him no more secrets. And I was a lying bitch. But I'd had good reason. "You would have stopped me."

He simmered silently in the corner across the room.

Sota breezed in through the door and dumped a bowl of fresh green leaves on the bed. "I have no idea," he said, "but Talen said these leaves will seal the wound. He also said don't eat them." He picked up a fat green leaf. "It resembles aloe—"

"*Leave*," Kellee growled, the word barely decipherable.

Sota stiffened and threw a look back at Kellee. "You're a dick."

Kellee stalked forward and snarled, revealing blunt teeth, so we weren't in full vakaru mode. Yet. "Get out, Sparky, before I ask why you didn't stop her from risking her life when you're supposed to be her last line of defense."

"Hey, you don't judge him, okay?" It was not okay to blame Sota. "I asked him to help, and because he's a good friend, he agreed. He's the only one I could trust not to lecture me or try to stop me."

Touches of red swam in Kellee's dark eyes. "Of course he went. He'd do anything for you, and you took advantage of that, just like you did with Aeon, and look where that got him."

"*What!*"

"Wow." Sota dropped the leaf, and folding his arms, he looked at Kellee with enough sass to rival the marshal's barely contained fury.

"Out!" Kellee's teeth snapped together.

Sota rolled his eyes over to me, adding a question in them at the end. As much as I appreciated him being here, he'd rile up Kellee and that was the last thing we needed. I nodded and Sota left, leaving the door ajar. He wouldn't go far.

Kellee snatched a leaf, tore into it with his teeth, and came at me like he was going to smother me with that single leaf. I had the wall at my back and stood my ground. Running from a vakaru was a bad idea.

He scrunched the torn leaf in his hand, squeezing out the sap, and reached for my waist. I batted his hand away. He caught my wrist, held me back, and shoved his goo-covered hand into the wound.

Pain snapped up my spine. "Ah, dammit." I kicked him

hard in the shin. "Don't fucking touch me." He didn't budge. How dare he pick on Sota and say those things about Aeon. He knew how much it hurt. "Asshole."

"It's better it's done and over with fast."

I watched his lips move, observed the blunt teeth behind them, and knew I was safe to pant out the pain. With his face angled downward and his attention on the wound, his hair fell over his eyes, hiding their color from me. He'd been close to the edge of his control since killing Oberon. If he did go vakaru, his eyes would be the first warning, then the claws, then the teeth. After that, I had better be ready to fight.

He looked up, dark eyes flecked with a hint of gold. "Afraid?"

My teeth chattered. "Cold."

"And probably almost in shock after what I saw."

His hand on my side shifted, and the pain started up again. I closed my eyes and stumbled back, needing the wall to hold me up. Kellee let my wrist go, allowing me to steady myself. "What did you see?"

"You, going full Nightshade, like Talen."

He said it like it happened every day. *Oh hey, you sprouted wings and darkness, but it's just another day of the week in the life of the Messenger.*

"Was it bad?" I brushed my hands over my arms to friction warmth into my skin. I was cold, and now that the adrenaline had worn off, my body was telling me all about it.

"Not bad. Just... different." Kellee shifted the leaf again, positioning himself even closer. "Talen says there's no knowing what the Nightshade's power might do to a mortal body."

I swallowed with a click. The Nightshade... me. "Did Talen know this would happen?"

Kellee pulled a slow breath in and sighed, likely to steady

his own racing emotions. I wasn't the only one trembling. "In the beginning? No. A mortal shouldn't be able to adopt the Nightshade's powers, so my guess is he wasn't concerned. After you started changing, though, he suspected. Don't go thinking he meant for this to happen. He's only ever tried to protect you from the worst of him."

When Eledan had severed his wings, I'd reached out to protect him, and taken his burden on board, shattering the bond.

Kellee withdrew his hand and went looking for a towel or cloth to clean the goo from his fingers. "How's that feel?"

I poked at my side and found it numb, the wound sealed shut. "Feels good." I wasn't quite as cold now either.

He returned with my top balled in his grip and held it out at arm's length. The way he kept his distance and his eyes downcast, I couldn't help but wonder if I'd damaged *us*.

I took my clothes from him, and before I could say another word, he headed for the door.

"Kellee, I had to go, and it had to be me alone, not Talen or Sirius... or you. You know why."

"Sota?" he asked, not turning, but at least he'd stopped walking away.

"He's tek. I... I wanted to unsettle them. If I'd taken you and the others, whatever happened, the fae would have pinned the victory on you. It had to be me, just me. Dagnu was my past. I had to be the one to deal with him."

"It's not that." His right hand locked into a fist. "One day, you'll leave, like you did earlier, and you won't return, and I can't live through that again. I won't. So I think it would be better for the both of us," he sighed, "if we don't take this thing between us any further."

"What?"

"You and I end now."

Staring at his back, I mumbled, "I don't understand." What was he saying? That we were over?

He turned, and the regret on his face cut a fresh wound. "You're a hard person to love, Kesh. It's killing me."

I blinked, stunned. He let those words settle and seemed as though he might say more, but instead, he turned his back on me and made it to the door.

"Marshal Kellee, stop right there."

He braced an arm against the doorjamb, his body slouched like someone already defeated.

"You're giving up on us because you're afraid I might die, is that it?"

His shoulder muscles locked.

I wouldn't let him throw us away because of what-ifs. "I don't accept that, and neither do you. Did you turn into a coward while I was gone? Because, sure, I bet loving a mortal sucks in the worst way. We die, it's what we do. You're going to make us suffer because you can't stand the thought of outliving me? I've never heard such karushit in my life and certainly never expected to hear it from you. How dare you walk away from me, from us, out of selfish fear. You're better than that, and we both know it."

He bumped his fist against the wall. "By cyn, you drive me crazy."

"No, you do that to yourself."

He pulled the door shut in front of him and turned. His eyes glowed their multicolored rings, tripping my heart. "You think I'm afraid of us?"

"Why else would you walk away?"

He started back toward me, but the intent in his stride had me looking for an escape. I could make it to the window if I ran. The whip was on the bed, halfway between us. Window or whip? Flee or attack?

He smiled. The tips of his fangs gleamed.

"You're a nightmare to love, Kesh. Half the time, I don't know if I want to protect you, fuck you, or fight you. In one breath, I admire you, in the next, I wonder if I even know you. You play kings and queens like they're your puppets, and here, on Faerie, you're something—someone else again. You asked me if I'm afraid of us?" He stopped at the end of the bed, holding himself back. "I'm fucking terrified of us. And now you're the *Nightshade?* What am I supposed to do with that?"

What was *he* supposed to do with it? What was *I* supposed to do with that! I laughed, not caring that it sounded cruel. "Do you think I've ever had a choice?"

His brow tightened, gaze thinning. "Do you believe you haven't?" His fingers twitched, drawing my eye to the claws stretching free. "Eledan had it right—"

My mouth twisted. "You listened to him?"

"While you slept, he asked me if any of us really knew you. He asked if you'd manufactured everything from the beginning. Tell me you didn't. Tell me you didn't plan everything."

Had he lost his mind? Had Oberon's blood messed with his perception? "Of course I didn't. What do you think I am?"

"The polestar, the Nightshade, the Messenger, and a Faerie queen. That was all a happy accident, was it? C'mon..." His mouth slanted. "I'm done listening to your karushit, Kesh. Tell me the truth."

I crossed the floor and looked my vakaru in the eye. Denials tingled on my lips, but on opening my mouth, the words wouldn't come. The hurt in his eyes turned my thoughts over and revealed the truth. I had wanted the fae to bow to me. I'd wanted it since I'd clawed at the earth, locked inside my saru cage, since Dagnu's whip had come down the first time to snuff out the fire in me. I had manipulated and lied my way through life and thrived. Now here I was, something and someone else to thousands of lives. A Messenger to the saru and Halow humans, the Nightshade to the unseelie, Mylana to the fae, and a queen to Eledan. He was right. The sluagh bastard. I had taken the opportunities where I'd found them. Kellee was looking at me like I was a stranger, but I hadn't chosen those names. I'd chosen to create the nothing Calicto messenger girl, Kesh Lasota. I was still Kesh, but he couldn't see the real me behind all the other mantels thrust upon me.

He smiled a sorry smile that looked wrong on a face, with eyes as dark as the night and teeth as sharp as knives. "It's all right. I wanted the truth. Now I have it."

I lifted my hand toward his face. He turned his head away.

"Only some pieces of it. You're missing a vital part." I caught his clawed hand and spread his fingers over my chest, over my heart. "Inside, I'm just Kesh. Please see me, Kellee, the real me, the girl I wanted to be, the girl you brought back from Eledan's dreams, the girl you tried to save in the sinks. I'm not those other names to you. I never wanted to be. Those other parts of me, they're missing my heart." My voice wobbled around the knot in my throat. "You have my heart, and if you can't see that... well, maybe you should walk away." If he turned his back on me, it would break me. Without him, without Sota and Talen and Sirius, I'd be lost. Without them, I didn't know who I was either. They kept me real.

He went still, something dangerous and sharp in his eyes. If he thought me to be everything he despised, this would be the moment to finish me, to take his claws and slice me open. He could walk away from Faerie, from the war, from the Hunt, and go back to being Marshal Kellee. Maybe if it ended here, I'd have done enough to change Faerie for good, to change my soul for good too.

I let my lashes flutter closed. It would be all right. I trusted him to make the right choice.

His hand clamped the back of my head, claws sinking into my hair. His mouth crashed over mine, capturing me in a kiss that claimed and owned, that stole all breath and reason right out of me. Relief stirred a madness awake, a need to pull him close and never let him go, to own him back and make him mine down to the bone. I broke the kiss with a gasp and threw my head back. His hot mouth fell to my neck, his tongue wet and teeth sharp. I had my fingers knotted in his hair, holding him in check. He was a moving, panting, heated creature in my arms, walking a thin line between monster and man, and I'd never wanted him more and in all the ways as I did then.

"You slay me, Kesh." The words fluttered against my neck. A promise. A surrender.

"Don't leave me." I wasn't sure if I'd spoken aloud, but it didn't matter. Kellee scooped me against him. His hands cupped my ass and hauled me up. I locked my legs around his waist and my arms around his neck, and kissed his mouth like I could crawl inside him.

My back hit a wall and a piece of furniture to my right toppled over. Something crashed to the floor. Kellee smiled against my mouth, and my laughter bubbled free.

I spied the bed over his shoulder, my whip coiled on the covers. "There's a bed right there."

"No bed." He growled into my neck and dove his hot hand down my back, into my pants, clutching me tight against him. Then he was plastered over me, his entire body pinning me against the wall. I gripped his shirt and tore the fastenings open, giving me access to the warmth of his chest so I could soak him into my skin.

We were moving again. He dumped me on a table or dresser. I didn't look. Didn't care. The height put me at the right angle to feel the hard rod of his arousal push against my inner thigh. I tore at his belt, and when it snagged, thwarting my attempt to get him free, I straightened and ran my hand down, over his erection, eliciting a groan that coiled raw need low in my belly. Tightening my grip resulted in my vakaru looking at me with half-closed eyes, the need in them as hungry as the light in his unseelie darkness.

He grabbed at my wrist to hasten me along, but I plucked my hand free and lifted my eyebrows.

"Ah-ah. Did you really think I'd be that easy?" I nodded behind him.

His heated look lingered on me, then, reluctantly, he turned to see what I was gesturing at. My whip. His chuckle was as dark and delicious as rich chocolate. "You think I'm going to let the Nightshade truss me up and fuck me any way she wants?"

"No."

That stalled him, and his grin turned into a question. He glanced again at the whip, thinking he'd missed something. I bolted. He grabbed for me, as I knew he would. I lunged for the whip, twisted, and sent the tails flying. One hundred and eighty pounds of vakaru tackled me in the chest, and with an *oomph,* he'd knocked me onto my back on the bed. He dug a knee between my thighs, but I'd been here before with him. I waited for him to lean left and bring his arm up. Once his weight was off center, I shoved his shoulder and hooked his leg at the same time, dropping him onto his side, only the bed ended too soon and we both fell off. Not part of the plan, but now I had him pinned under me, looking wild, with his clothes askew and pretty hair all mussed up.

I straightened, rocking my hips to keep him thinking with his dick, and admired the pretty marshal from the sinks who'd followed me home. He'd gained some rough whiskers, and there was the obvious fact he had inhuman teeth and eyes, but that cockiness was still there.

"Here's the deal." I fell forward, letting my hair hem us in so his eyes shone in the dark. "I'm going to play the Calicto messenger working below the law, and you're going to play the marshal."

His hand roamed my thigh. I smacked it off, prompting a very un-marshal-like growl.

"Oh really?" he drawled in that smooth voice he liked to unleash on unsuspecting females. His hand was on my thigh again, then on my hip. His fingers skipped down to the front of my pants and flicked at the fastenings as the tip of his tongue wet that smart mouth.

I caught his free hand and looped the whip around his wrist, expecting him to resist. He watched me work, his dark vakaru eyes curious.

"You, vakaru"—I flicked his nose—"are mine."

His eyes flared, his right leg hooked over mine, and in the time it took me to breathe in, I was on my back. The animal growl that rumbled out of him and through me spritzed a tiny dose of fear into the lust. I still had his wrist caught in my whip, still had the whip firmly in my hand, but as Kellee's kisses traveled below my breasts, avoiding the numbed cut, and down to the hollow of my navel, his fingers freeing my pants laces, I bit into my lip to keep from demanding more.

He flicked his eyes up, the beast so close I wasn't sure how much of the man remained. He reared up, dragged my pants over my hips, and jerked me closer. I could have kicked him while he fought with my clothes and sent him sprawling, but I liked where this was going too much to stop it.

His strong hands parted my thighs, the whip rattling at his wrist, and he kissed my inner knee. His teeth lightly grazed. His chest heaved. He'd never willingly hurt me. He had control, even now. Checking my face, he couldn't fail to miss the heat in my cheeks. He trailed his mouth down my inner thigh.

His mouth touched the innermost part of me, warm and soft. His tongue flicked, knotting my body with need. His hands claimed my thighs and pulled me down beneath him, until I was looking the beast in the eye. I pressed my hand to his cheek and thumbed the corner of his mouth, feeling it lift into a smile.

"Will you love me?" I whispered. "Not the names or the myths and legends, just me? Just Kesh?"

His dark lashes shuttered his eyes, and for a terrible second, I thought his fear had a hold of him again. Then he opened his eyes, and the man was there, his beautiful gaze soft once more. "Always."

And he meant it. When I was dust and gone, he'd love me, because he was Marshal Kellee, and my heart would forever be safe with him.

He kissed me, rocking with me, and plunged two fingers inside, brushing the swollen, sensitive bundle of nerves with his thumb, making me writhe. When I arched with a gasp, he nuzzled my neck, whispering, "Who has whom at their mercy, Messenger?"

That was a good point. Wasn't I meant to be holding the marshal's reins? How far would he let the game go?

I reeled the whip in, shortening his leash. "I thought you didn't do submissive?"

"I don't."

The challenge returned to his eyes, daring me to test him. I was game. Pulling him down, I kissed him like he was made of glass and might shatter in my hands. I explored his mouth and nipped at his lips. When he tried to push and take, I hooked my leg around his and locked him tight, anchoring him to me in two places. Shifting my hips tipped his weight sideways, and when he didn't resist, I rolled us over, trapping him beneath me once more. The sharp teeth and his claws had vanished but vakaru colors still shone in his eyes. With his pillow of dark hair, braided in random places, and intense unblinking glare, he looked untamed, like something I could capture and keep forever.

Lowering my head, I tasted the rise of his right pec, felt him shudder, and twirled my tongue around a salty nipple. His free hand tried to investigate my shoulder and slide down my back, but I caught it and pinned it. Now I had both hands pinned above his head. "No touching unless I say so, lawman."

A rumbling, the kind that might scare off petty criminals, sounded inside his chest. His eyes promised wicked delights and all the things he wanted to do with my body. But he was mine now. While I ran my tongue over his abs, I roamed my hand beneath his waistband and found the prize I'd been looking for. He tensed beneath me and slowly arched, giving himself to my hand.

I tightened my grip, making him jerk. "I said, no moving."

"Kesh, you're killing me here."

"I'm just getting started."

His growls rumbled louder. He really didn't do submissive, and this game probably wouldn't last long. There's patience, and then there's a vakaru's patience.

Mouthing down his chest and probing with my tongue, I listened to his breathing tighten and quicken, working him over until he writhed, and panted, and gritted his teeth to hold himself back. By Faerie, he was delicious spread beneath me, poised to come in my hand.

His hand tore free of my grip and plunged into my hair. He yanked me up him and attacked my mouth, driving his tongue in, stealing my breath and my thoughts. His rough hands dropped to my hips, whip trailing behind, and I let him haul me off the floor and spread a hand against my back, pushing me down over the end of the bed. In the next breath, he spread me open and thrust so damn deep I couldn't swallow the cry, then went beyond caring that someone might hear us. He had me locked beneath him, driven like a damn nail into the bed, and I wanted more of him, so much more. We'd dreamed of this. I didn't know if he remembered, but I did. The reality was harder, faster, rougher, like I needed it to be. I fisted the sheets and demanded more. And Kellee gave it to me.

The whip and its grip on him forgotten, I lost myself in the sex. There was nothing else in the worlds, just us, skin to skin, body to body. He shuddered, caught me by the back of the neck, and fell forward. His teeth sinking into my shoulder only added to the riot of feeling, and when his free hand reached around to find the point that would bring me to a cresting ecstasy, all I knew was Kellee. With his teeth in my shoulder, his cock in my body, and his hand at my neck, erotic pleasure tore through me. His touch made me suddenly alive, wrenching another cry out of me. He began thrusting again and withdrew his teeth to rise above me. I looked back, caught the sight of the wild, bloody creature behind me, and pushed my ass against him, changing the angle. The wildness in his eyes blazed red, and Kellee threw his head back, cried out in some ancient and dead language known only to him, and spilled his seed.

I wasn't afraid.

I'd almost lost him by locking him out. It wouldn't happen again. He was as much a part of me as they all were. Sota. Talen. Sirius. And Kellee. The four pieces of my heart. I loved him, loved them all more than any dream of toppling the fae, of being seen, of ending the war or saving the saru. I'd give it all up for them, and that was the truth.

He trembled, his body going slack, and catching me watching him, he tossed me the most wicked of playful smiles and pulled us both down onto the bed. His fingers traced over the warm bite mark in my shoulder, healed from his clever vakaru kiss.

Closing my eyes, I melted against him, sensing his trembling had more emotion behind it than a post-sex comedown. "You're mine now, Marshal, to the end of all the worlds and back again."

He locked me in his arms. I expected some smartmouthed comment to make light of the moment but none came. I twisted to find him watching me, his dark eyes too bright and glassy. For the first time since I'd met him, his expression was open and raw, letting me see everything on his face. Marshal Kellee was afraid. For me.

I LAY WRAPPED in Kellee's arms, trying to slow the seconds, but I didn't have that power, and all too soon, Sota knocked at the door and informed us that the carriage was waiting. There wasn't enough time in all the worlds for all the moments I wanted to live with Kellee. My mortality was as much part of me as my saru blood, but as I lay against his chest, listening to his strong heartbeat, feeling his soft breath flutter against my neck, I wished this could end another way.

He'd loved before and lost that love, just like Talen had. If I could have saved them that heartache, I would have, but we all knew how this ended.

After dressing, and with Kellee wearing a new kind of smile, we left Talen's knoll behind and passed through Safira to where the carriage and its horses waited. Sirius's wild horses chomped on their vine-reins and stamped the ground. They looked ready to bolt, and I couldn't blame them. The thought of journeying to the Autumnlands knoll, knowing the Hunt was likely nearby, was not a comforting one.

All manner of fae beasties lingered nearby, sometimes poking at Sirius's marvelous carriage when they got close enough. It was impressive, as were the males climbing aboard.

By cyn, if anyone could end this war, it was them—us. Together.

I was the last one to the carriage, and before climbing in, I turned to regard the wild folk of Faerie. They weren't unseelie, but they were Faerie's first children. They weren't as wary as they had been. They knew me and knew change was coming. I nodded, acknowledging their respect, and hauled myself into the carriage.

Kellee and Talen sat opposite each other, appearing as ragged and wild as the creatures we were leaving behind. I liked this new rawness. It felt authentic.

Sota took up his spot by the window and stared outside, lusting after all those extra tails.

I pulled the door closed. Kellee thumped on the roof, Sirius cracked the reins, and the horses whinnied, jolting against their tack to yank us into motion.

"Next stop, the Hunt's backyard," Sota mumbled.

He wasn't wrong.

Wetness dripped onto my thigh. I looked down to see a splatter of dark liquid soaking into my trousers. Wetness cooled on my lip. After dabbing at it, my fingers came away glistening red. Blood. I could taste it and feel it lining the back of my throat.

Talen was the first to move in. "Pinch here." His warm fingers touched the bridge of my nose. I copied him. "Tilt your head back," he said, calm but concerned.

Blood swished around my mouth. I swallowed, tasting too much. More blood flowed around my mouth and down my chin and neck, soaking into my collar. It wasn't stopping. Why wasn't it stopping?

The carriage swayed. Air tightened. Cool sweat flushed my face. I reached for Kellee, knowing I wouldn't make it, and saw him grab for my hand. Then I plummeted through the smothering dark and kept right on falling.

CHAPTER 15

"Mother Faerie works in mysterious ways," Eledan said, sounding like his usual irritating self.

He and I stood in front of a never-ending wall of mirrors. Too high to climb over, too long to walk around, and with nothing else around us, I was stuck here.

He was all done up in his purple and silver attire but missing a cloak. Purple ribbons were laced through his braided black hair. Why did he have to be so pretty? Maybe I could smash his face into the mirror, although seeing as this was likely his dream, he'd probably disappear right through it.

"What did you do to me?"

"Me?" He acted hurt, like he couldn't believe I'd dare suggest such a thing, and flirted with a coy smile. "Why, I was surprised to hear you calling out to me, especially after how we left things—"

"I was not *calling* you." Ugh.

"Your subconscious knows your wants."

"The only thing I want from you is that heart out of your chest again."

He tossed me a querying look, part curiosity, part concern. "A mortal Nightshade? Faerie must be desperate. Was queen not enough for you?"

Ignoring him seemed the most favorable idea. I turned away and walked along the mirror, stroking my fingers along its cool surface. If Eledan hadn't summoned me, what had happened in the carriage? I could still taste blood. It had been real. Kellee and Talen would be trying to wake me. This was just temporary. It had to be.

"What do you want from this, Kesh?" Eledan asked. His reflection trailed behind mine like a good little mutt on its leash.

"I'm not talking with you."

"Where do you think you are running to, *my queen*?"

I stopped. His reflection jolted to a stop. "Somewhere far from you."

"Your fear reveals much."

Clearly, I wouldn't get rid of him just by walking away. Turning on my heel, I looked him in those perfectly sculpted dark eyes. Rich blue irises, the color of Faerie's sky in the winterlands. "I'm not afraid of you, Eledan."

"I know." He smiled. Just a simple smile, but on him, it was so much more. His smiles were weapons, like the rest of him.

I grabbed him by his immaculate jacket and flung him against the mirror, pinning him beneath my fists. He didn't fight, barely reacted. "When will I wake up!"

Laughter danced in his eyes. "Well, that depends on what put you here. Assuming, as seems to be the case, it wasn't deliberate."

He was poison. His words were poison. I'd pushed off him, about to walk away, when a huge shadowy creature loomed in the mirror, over Eledan's reflection. A thing of churning darkness with wings of night and a shining beacon for a heart. I blinked and it was gone, leaving my reflection in its place. Just Kesh Lasota, my clothes askew, my hair tumbling free, my saru eyes wide and pupils dark. I blinked and saw the same girl with a crown of bleached ash wood on her head. Blink. A saru with rage in her eyes, her clothes bloody and torn. Blink. A messenger, with her tek-enhanced whip and drone over her shoulder. So many faces. Above them all, the shadow with wings still loomed.

Was that shadowy thing how Kellee had seen me?

Eledan noticed my shock and glanced behind him, like he didn't know what I'd seen. I stalked on, needing to move.

"I assume you and your harem are stirring up the fae to rally them against me?" Eledan said, still following.

Considering how Dagnu had spoken of Eledan, if I had been trying to cause trouble, it wouldn't have taken much persuasion. "You don't feature in my thoughts."

He laughed at the obvious lie and quickened his pace to fall into step beside me. "The sidhe did not appreciate you freeing their workforce."

I'd seen that on their faces when Eledan and I had looked down on them from his knoll balcony. Considering my reputation, it was a miracle none had tried to kill me. Yet.

"They did not take kindly to Mab's killer presiding over them," he added for kicks.

"Why are you telling me this?"

His attention wandered, eyes unfocusing while he stared ahead at the never-ending path. He almost seemed reasonable, and that was what made him so dangerous. "I never wanted any of this," he replied. "I was always the dreamer. It was not my destiny to rule."

Neither was it mine. I stopped and held his gaze,

searching for the karushit behind his words. "Then give up the crown."

His right eyebrow lifted. "To whom? You?" A short laugh. "Faerie must have a ruler, and as you saw fit to kill my brother—"

"You wanted vengeance. You wouldn't have let him live."

"I would have. I told you not to kill him at the crystal palace. You did it anyway."

"Oh, stop trying to paint yourself as the understanding brother. You stopped me because you knew the Hunt was inside him. Had you told me that fact, we might not be in this situation—"

"And when was I supposed to tell you? The moment I awoke, surrounded by my brother's guards, or after my return, when you fled the sight of me?"

I'd only fled because he was bringing the castle down around him and would have brought me down too. "Do you hear yourself? You've had me in your dreams for hours. You could have told me the details of Oberon's curse at any time. *Oberon harbors the Hunt.*" I clicked my fingers inches from his face. "Just like that."

His lips twisted. "You took my heart for him. How could I know you would not do the same again if you learned of his power?"

"What power? He was trapped in that palace. He had no power. You drove him so far he had no choice but to leave the safety of its walls, and by then, he was done with hiding and done with keeping *your* secret." I poked him hard in the chest.

"I have my regrets. Many, in fact. You are one—"

"Oh, please." Throwing up my hands, I marched on. "I'm not falling for your sob story, Eledan. When you wake up, you'll go back to twisting the fae and making them dream so they rally by your side, and you'll take what's left of Oberon's rule, including his pointless war, because you think you have a thousand years of neglect to make up for." I whirled on him. "You don't have to be this person, you know. You can be whoever you want to be. You can choose to be good. Nobody controls you. You're truly free."

A coldness held him still. "Cast aside, I lived *in pain* for centuries. Faerie *forgot* me—"

"Get. Over. It." Rage sharpened his glare. "I would have given anything to have the freedom you enjoyed, and all you did with it was fling it away. Now that you have it back, what do you do? You bitch and moan and throw a fit. Why don't you try doing some good with your immortal life instead of wallowing in self-pity?"

The dream ended as abruptly as it had come. I gazed up at the carriage ceiling. The sudden change stunned my senses into numbness while my words to Eledan rang in my ears.

"She's awake," Sota announced. His face appeared over me. "Kesh?"

My gut flipped and head spun, and I almost reached for the dream. At least there I didn't feel as though I'd been trampled under the carriage, the floor of which I currently lay on. Why did I feel like a ton of rocks had been dumped over me while I'd slept?

We'd stopped moving. Or maybe we had yet to begin?

Sota helped me sit up. Kellee wasn't here, but the carriage door hung open, and his voice drifted in from outside, telling Sirius I was awake.

Talen was looking at me like I might shatter if he touched me. I tried to smile and winced at my throbbing skull. "It's all right. I'm fine."

"Only you could so blatantly lie on Faerie and get away with it." His tone was cold, but his smile was soft.

"Where are we?" Pressing a cool hand to my temple helped.

"The Autumnlands knoll." Outside the carriage's open door, Faerie's twilight licked at the grassheads, making them glisten so the whole field shimmered like a lake. Where Sirius's knoll had been, and where the Hunt had risen, the earth had been scalped, exposing a huge patch of barren soil. Ailish had said the knoll was sleeping, but from my position, it looked dead.

"I've summoned Shinj," Talen said, following my gaze, "but she's reluctant to approach until we need her. She senses the Hunt nearby."

"I'm all right." I gently peeled Sota's grip off my arm. "Let's do this."

"Perhaps we should go into the knoll without you." Talen saw my expression and quickly added, "I'm concerned for your wellbeing."

"When has splitting up ever been a good idea?" Sota asked him.

"You'd be with her."

I got to my feet while they bickered and climbed down from the carriage. "I'm just tired... that's all."

Kellee and Sirius abruptly ended their furtive discussion. I lifted a finger as Kellee opened his mouth to either ask if I was all right or tell me to stay topside. "Don't say anything. I'm fine. Let's get the book."

Nobody dared to mention the blood on my clothes. Much of it had been wiped off my face and neck while I was out, but some still itched around my collar. I'd passed out, that was all. It happened to humans all the time. It wasn't common in saru, but it did occur.

Kellee worked his jaw, like he did when he was pissed, and planted a hand on his hip. "Did you see Eledan while you were out?" Beside him, Sirius gazed toward the scarred patch of earth above the knoll. At the mention of Eledan, the weight of his attention returned to me.

"Yes."

"And?" Kellee pushed.

"Nothing." Mentioning the mirrors and what I'd seen in them wouldn't help anyone, and the argument with Eledan had been one of many.

"Nothing?" Kellee's eyebrow arched.

Always with the questions... "He doesn't know where we are. He mentioned the sidhe being pissed and tried to get me to feel sorry for him. The usual Eledan nonsense." I waved a hand, dismissively. "I think he's floundering as much as we are, which is good. It will keep him distracted."

"He only shows you as much as he wants you to see," Sirius said.

I sighed. "Yes. Thank you. I'm becoming quite adept at deciphering Eledan. So, shall we get into this knoll, get the book, and get out of here before the Hunt notices we're back?"

Kellee poked his tongue into the corner of his mouth and found a nearby shrub fascinating, determined not to look at me.

"What?"

Sirius cleared his throat, green eyes darting. "Talen and I are going inside."

"We are?" Talen asked, climbing from the carriage.

"The rest of you will stay outside," Sirius continued, "and watch for any sign of the Hunt. Sota, stay close to Kesh. Your tek presence will shield her from the Hunt."

"We're splitting up?" Sota asked and rolled his eyes to me. "Splitting up never ends well."

"In this instance, it's better we divide our resources and

potential targets." Sirius stood his ground, expecting an argument. I'd seen that look on him a hundred times. We didn't have the time to talk him around. The longer we stayed out in the open, the more at risk we were. Splitting up made sense, even if the idea ramped up my anxiety.

"You know the book you're looking for?" I asked.

Sirius nodded. "Oberon left it on the table in the library. The knoll, if I can wake it, will help me find it again."

Kellee wasn't arguing with Sirius, likely because he wanted to keep me out of the hole in the ground where Oberon had almost ripped the polestar out of me.

Talen's lips lifted at one corner. Eledan taking his wings had shocked him, but all things considered, he'd never looked better. Like Sirius, Talen had gained a vitality he had been missing before. The glitter in his eyes spoke of his returning strength. He might even be stronger now than at any other time since I'd known him. He was more than capable of retrieving the book with Sirius.

"All right. Kellee, Sota, and I will stand watch."

Sirius nodded, and Talen fell into step beside him. Together, they trekked through the grass toward the patch of scarred land.

Kellee tracked them with his keen vakaru senses until the grassheads obscured them. He jumped when I touched his shoulder and quickly went back to observing Talen and Sirius.

I slid my hand down his arm. His muscles were bunched so tightly his arm felt like stone. "Talen will be all right."

"It's not him I'm concerned about."

Ah, Sirius. I could explain to Kellee how Sirius had been my silent guardian for years, how he'd been forced to endure my torture alongside me, how Oberon had nailed him to a cross for daring to protect me, but words wouldn't be enough to convince Kellee that any fae was worthy. Only actions would do that, and I knew from experience that Kellee was difficult to impress.

I eased my fingers into his.

"Do you trust him?" he asked without looking away from the distant pair of fae.

"With my life."

The ground rumbled just enough to shiver the nearby grass, and in front of Talen, the dirt rose until it was twice his height. Once it had stopped climbing, a hollow opened in its facing edge.

Talen and Sirius disappeared inside the Autumnlands knoll.

"I really don't like splitting up," Sota said, moving to my side.

Neither did I.

The fire-horses tethered to the carriage behind us snickered. A swift, cool breeze lifted dust off the grass and swirled it in the air. Kellee frowned at the darkening sky. "I'll go find a vantage point to better see over this grass. Stay here."

I let his hand slip free and watched him melt into the grass until even glimpses of his dark hair vanished. The wind whipped a chill around me that tried to work its way down to the bone. I folded my arms and hugged myself tight.

Sota's hidden forearm gun ports opened with a soft whirr. He shrugged. "Maybe we won't need them."

I smiled back, neglecting to mention how, on Faerie, hope was an invisible shield that rarely worked against real monsters.

CHAPTER 16

alen

THE KNOLL REARRANGED itself around us, reopening collapsed tunnels and breathing out, blasting us with cinnamon- and sandalwood-scented air. Sirius's outpouring of Autumnlands magic tickled my senses, wanting to take my hand and run with me, while also brushing up against my skin as though it wanted to climb inside it.

"Did it look like this before?" I asked, shrugging off his magic's invasiveness. It had been so long since I'd walked on Faerie and without my wings; it was taking me time to reacclimate to the magic's peculiar touches and whispering wants.

"No."

My own restrained magic flexed and stretched, trying to slip its leash. That, too, was new to me.

"It's showing us enough to get us to the library. It still suffers from... what was done here. Reopening the entire knoll is impossible." He avoided mention of the Hunt, not wanting to prick its ears.

He strode ahead, ringed in warm reds, his spicy, earthy magic tingling on my tongue. As a Wild One, Sirius was rooted to the earth, to Faerie. His magic was Hers, and she permitted him to use it. It must have been quite the revelation for him to learn of how Faerie approved of Kesh. It would have taken a great deal of personal adjustment for a fae as old as him. Although I sensed that initial adjustment had happened long ago. He appeared resigned now. Perhaps, when this was over, he would tell me how his love had come to be, if the pair of us survived.

The library came into sight, the walls aglow enough to light the way. Books lay strewn about the floor among jagged splinters of a table. Sirius crouched and picked up fallen books. After checking their spines, he arranged them in towers beside him.

The Origin of the Wild Hunt. I searched through the titles at my feet for the prince's work. "Is it true he created the original nightmare?"

"The Wild Ones *persuaded* him, but yes, his mind created what we call *the Hunt*," he said, whispering its name.

The fae could be highly persuasive to anyone open and accepting. The Wild Ones had probably used Eledan's fear of being forgotten to promise him power.

"And we're taking this book back to the Wild Ones?" If they had caused this, returning the book to them seemed like a mistake.

"After I've read it and gotten what we need from it, yes."

Sirius was a Wild One and Faerie's guardian long before he became Mab's guardian, and Oberon's thereafter. Older than me. Older than the courts. Older than order itself. Kesh trusted him. Kellee did not. As familiar as I found him, I wasn't yet convinced by his motives.

He rocked back on his heels, his long dark coat bunching on the floor. "Kesh is dying."

My hand froze over a book, a tome with an archaic title that sounded as dull as dirt. I forgot the title, and the book I was meant to be looking for, and looked over at the guardian.

Sirius didn't turn, but he'd stopped organizing the books. "She's mortal. The fragment of polestar hidden in the saru bloodline found its way to her because the time was right for it to resurface, as all of Faerie's hidden things resurface, but it was never meant to be contained inside a mortal body for long." He dropped his head and looked over his shoulder, meeting my gaze. The guardian's green eyes glistened. "She has suffered more than anyone I've known. Every breath, she has fought for. She does not yet know freedom. It is not right for her story to end this way."

"It won't." The words beat like drums in my head. "I won't let it end that way."

The brightness of his eyes dulled. "I am Autumnlands. I know and understand death as though she were a friend, one who visits immortals from time to time but never stays for long. Autumn embraces Kesh... Her time approaches."

"I understand." I dropped the book and stood. "But do you know what I also understand? I spent three centuries buried in tek, fighting death. It wins when you let it win. Kesh will not let it win."

"She knows."

He was right. Kesh knew she was dying. She'd known since she'd learned she had part of Faerie's night sky inside her, made worse by her attempt to protect me, taking too much of the Nightshade into herself.

"She knows, Talen, and she's accepted it." He straightened with a book in his hand. "I... we should respect that."

The book was Eledan's, and now he'd found it, he looked at me with all the sorrow of the worlds on his face. It took me a moment to realize the significance of his words and why he was telling me this now.

He might not have read the book, but he knew what was inside its pages.

And so did I.

The polestar pieces had to be reunited and returned to Faerie's sky. The light would balance the dark. The dark fae would return. The Hunt would once again be Faerie's justice. Faerie would be at peace, and the war would end. All it would cost was the death of an immortal prince and the life of the mortal woman I loved.

"When we were bonded, our shared link healed her—"

"And made her vulnerable to your considerable power as the Nightshade."

That had been a mistake. I had never wanted to hurt her, just keep her safe. That was all I'd tried to do. Her life was so fleeting. I'd been afraid the worlds would take her from me. I should have realized not even I could change Kesh's fate.

"She's strong," I added. I knew the Nightshade's powers. The wings wouldn't have chosen her if she could not bear their weight.

He smiled, as though my words barely covered how strong we knew her to be. "I know she is."

"Together, we'll find a way."

The polestar, the Hunt, the dark fae needing her as their new guiding light. Surviving just one of those things would be difficult for a fae. For a mortal? If it were anyone else but Kesh, they wouldn't have a chance.

A smile lifted my lips. "Have a little faith in our Messenger. She might surprise you."

He took those words on board, tucked the book under his arm, and nodded. "Let's return to the surface."

A ground-shuddering rumble trembled through the knoll's walls. I turned as the tunnel collapsed, cutting off our only way out of the library. Dust settled, revealing a wall of rock where the door had been moments before.

"Sirius?"

He tilted his head, listening to something I couldn't hear. "The knoll is... afraid."

The Hunt.

"Get us out of here. Now."

He closed his eyes. His throat bobbed, and a small knot of concentration appeared on his brow. When his eyes fluttered open, his cheek twitched. "It's not answering. We're not going anywhere until the Hunt has moved on."

"Kesh is out there."

"I know that..."

I checked the buried doorway and ran my hands over the tightly compacted stone.

"It won't let us go until it's safe," Sirius added.

Bookshelves lined the walls. There were no other doors or windows. We were buried inside a sentient hole in the ground. "There must be another way out."

"There is nothing else we can do."

There was. "Command your knoll to open a doorway, or I'll summon Shinj here and blast a hole in your precious home."

Fire licked at the green in his eyes. His hair turned a shade darker, to the color of blood. "That would be... unwise."

"Then you'd better start talking to your hole in the ground, *Wild One*." He looked as though he might unleash his considerable power. "Do you love her or not? If you do, as Eledan revealed, nothing would stop you from getting back up there."

The fire in his eyes stayed, the threat delivered and understood. I might not be the Nightshade, but I was still both seelie and unseelie fae.

He turned his back to me and pressed a hand to the wall. "Be ready. The knoll doesn't react well to commands."

I mentally tugged Shinj. I'd be ready and have Shinj overhead. I hoped it would be enough.

esh

THE BREEZE LASHED Kellee's loose, dark hair against his face. He sniffed the air. "Death," he growled, fangs lengthening.

The Hunt was coming.

The ground shook beneath my boots, and where the knoll had reopened, the earth collapsed, sending up a blast of dust. Talen and Sirius were still inside.

I lunged toward the knoll, but Kellee caught my arm. "There's no time," he warned. Behind him, lightning cracked through a purple sky.

We couldn't fight the Hunt, not even with all of us here.

Sota looked at the sky, his red eye expanding to absorb whatever data he saw beyond my spectrum. "We have six minutes to hide."

Hiding wouldn't help. Thousands upon thousands of fae had tried. Nothing escaped the Hunt.

Kellee returned to the carriage and the restless horses.

With his claws, he sliced through the vine-reins holding them in place and walked one to me. The horse's eyes rolled. Its nostrils flared. The animal was close to bolting.

"You ride, and don't look back," Kellee said. Nodding to Sota, he added, "Go with her. Your presence will shield her."

"What about you?" Sota asked.

Kellee took the reins from the other flame-touched horse, and sinking his hand into its fiery mane, he hauled himself onto the beast's bare back. The fire didn't hurt him. "I'll draw it away." He tightened the reins, bringing the horse under control as much as possible.

Nobody outruns the Hunt.

"Kellee...?" He couldn't stop the Hunt alone.

His horse shied and stamped on the spot, trying to unseat him. He yanked on the reins and leaned closer to its neck. "Do it, Kesh."

"How will we find you?" I placed my hand on my horse's back and one in its mane, expecting heat but finding it cool, and hauled myself onto its warm back. The horse stamped on the spot.

"I'll find you." He dug his heels into his horse's middle and they sprung forward, toward the knoll. "Go!"

Taking Sota's hand, I pulled him onto the horse behind me. His arms clamped around my waist.

"Ready?" I asked.

"As I'll ever be."

The sky boiled. Clouds became rolling mountains, and inside the storm, an enormous figure took shape, its two eyes like two blood moons.

Kellee's horse reared and screamed its fear. The wind tore in, blasting across the land, trying to flatten the grass. Kellee's beastly eyes glowed in the sudden darkness. "Go!"

I kicked my horse. Its flaming hooves dug in, and it drove

into the trees so fast it almost unseated me. I had hold of the reins, but I doubted the animal cared that Sota and I were on its back. Fear had it in its clutches now.

Hunkering down, I clamped my thighs tight against the warm flanks and scanned Faerie's thick undergrowth as it blurred by. Branches snagged and whipped at my face and clothes. Faster, the horse galloped, its heart a drum, its breathing ragged and wild. Sota's grip tightened. *Faster*, until there was nothing but the hammered breathing, blurred bushes, and the blind hope that we'd get away and Kellee wouldn't do something foolish.

alen

THE KNOLL WALLS moved and groaned. Its lights throbbed in a dark, warning red. Hands spread against those walls, Sirius poured power through the touch. His autumnal reds glowed, his outline a crackle of energy. It wasn't enough. The knoll was not letting us go, not while the Hunt was close. And it *was* close. Its oily touch probed at the back of my mind for a way into my fear, where it would root around and turn over my fears, using them against me.

And as Sirius fought the knoll, somewhere above, Kellee, Sota, and Kesh faced the Hunt alone.

I touched two fingers to my temple. <<Shinj... come to me>> The warcruiser's thoughts touched my own, slipping in around those of the Hunt. The ship had no voice, that was what a pilot was for, but her emotions were clear. Sparking, crackling fear. Sharp anxiety. <<I cannot reach Kesh. Find her. Protect her>>

Her answer was acceptance and loyalty. Shinj was coming.

ellee

THE BLOOD of Faerie's dead king sang in my veins, setting ablaze my thirst for battle. Sickle-shaped claws stretched, desperate for purchase. Raw, unseelie strength poured through muscle and bone. The restlessness I'd been feeling since drinking Oberon dry coalesced into power, and as I stared down a nightmare the size of a mountain, I smiled.

Inside the storm—jabbed by lightning—a man-shaped figure reared up, but it was no more man than the sky was. It studied me, its attention everywhere, on my skin and sliding under it, seeking the heart.

My horse stamped and screamed, shaking its head, but the horse was a wild, proud thing too, like me. The beast was mine to control, like the long-dead beasts of Valand. It would not flee.

"The last vakaru..." The voice seemed so loud it might shatter my skull, but the words weren't spoken. They sounded

in my head, insubstantial like dreams. *"One of the brothers created you, the one whose blood you stole. Did his death taste sweet, vakaru? Did it taste like vengeance for the millions of vakaru lives he took? Did it taste like justice?"*

Justice. I knew it well.

The storm rolled closer, pouring across the forest like smoke. It gathered in the meadow and turned the grassland to a lake of darkness. It could reach out and crush me like it had crushed Aeon. But while it was focused on me, Kesh was escaping.

The blackness swirled around, making my horse snort and paw at the earth. Its flaming mane blazed brighter, seeing off the dark as we danced around, following the dark's leading edge.

"Is that what you are? Justice?" I called.

The darkness became a figure again, but only as tall as my horse. It had no features, just an outline of someone vaguely male, and the eyes... if I looked too long in those eyes, I'd hear the screams of all the immortal souls it had taken. Forever trapped, forever punished. That fate could be mine.

"Justice? Yes. You have the taint of a thousand souls on you, lawman. Have you not killed as many as the prince who created you?"

I had, but not by choice. "Do you blame the slave for the actions of its master?"

The Hunt hissed its displeasure, startling my horse. My words had struck close to something it felt. Did it count itself a slave or a master?

"Oberon created the vakaru to kill, and when we fought his design, he killed them all."

"All but one..." The voice poured into my thoughts, coating them in oil, but I was already unseelie and part of Faerie's dark, where this thing had been birthed.

"What do you want from us?"

"Freedom."

"You already have it."

"No. It began with the death of a king, but it has not ended. There is one left who must die for me to be free."

"Eledan?"

"The Wild Prince. He has the key..."

Key...

A memory bounced back. Eledan, his forearms raised and brought together. The warfae marks shifting, realigning, becoming one—becoming the key to stopping the Hunt. He had shown me the truth, and now the Hunt was inside my head, diving into the memory, trying to rip it free. The dark blinded and the howling storm deafened, until all I knew was that memory, turned over and over: Eledan revealing the key etched into his skin. I couldn't hide it. The Hunt flowed, filling me up. The horse screamed, but I no longer felt the beast beneath me. Just the dark.

Was this death?

No, not for me.

I'd fought this long, come this far, I was not giving in now. Doubling down, I pulled on the parts that didn't know how to surrender. Poison for blood, rage and thirst for the kill. Ageless. Ancient. I would not allow the memory of my vakaru to die with me here.

Clutching my head, I pulled on my faith for honor, for justice, for all the things I stood for and had done for centuries. The Hunt withdrew a beat. I remembered the lives I'd saved, the good from my recent past, all the wrongs I'd tried to right. I fought for the good and always had. The Hunt pulled back. It twitched and snarled, lashing out. "I did not come here to be mind-fucked by Faerie's mistakes!"

The dark twitched. The Hunt had *faltered.*

Power burned me up, power and light, and Faerie... I felt

Her then, the weight of the world, listening, watching, guiding. I'd felt it before, on another world in another time when I'd reigned over a people, but I'd known and loved Her then as Valand. Valand had been Faerie. I was part of Faerie too. This world was as much a part of me as my home had been. Her warmth flowed in, and instead of fighting it, I allowed Her to breathe into me. And Kesh, I felt her presence too, so warm, so light. Talen's silvery touch wrapped closer, lending a sharp edge to the light burning through my veins. Sirius's heat flared, and the horse reared, kicking at the dark. Sota's metallic tek sizzled and itched, driving back the darkness.

The Hunt folded in on itself, shrinking around its throbbing, warped center.

It wasn't enough.

Despite the power connecting us, we weren't ready.

A roar cut through the air, coming in low overhead. I ducked in time to see the multicolored undercarriage of a vast warcruiser plunge downward.

The Hunt pulsed and pulled back, retreating in on itself. *Fleeing*.

Fire, born out of the heat of reentry, licked at the ship's enormous bow, setting the sky ablaze. Her heat boiled away the Hunt's darkness.

Shinj would not be pulling up from the dive.

Her bow hit the boiling darkness, and for a few breathless blinding moments, there was nothing, just light and silence. Then the shock wave hit.

alen

"SHINJ, NO! *No!*" I slammed my hands to my head and forced the order home, but it was too late. The dive was critical. She would not survive. *Don't...* A soft warmth reached me, like the last embrace from a friend I would never see again.

"OPEN THE KNOLL NOW!" I grabbed Sirius. Fire flashed across my hand, as sharp and bright as a lightning strike, jolting me back.

Sirius's magic flooded the library, rolling over me in waves of scorching heat. Fire licked up his coat, over his shoulders, down his arms, and lapped at the knoll's wall, where his hands burned into the stone. He strained against the knoll, trying to force the walls open, but either he wasn't strong enough or his connection to the knoll was too weak, giving it the freedom to disobey his commands.

"Sirius," I warned, shaking the burn from my hand. "I don't care how you do it, open the knoll."

His eyes flashed. Through gritted teeth, he said, "You. Are. Not. Helping."

The knoll lurched sideways. Shinj severed my link, cutting the connection so death wouldn't drag me with her. I reeled back, suddenly unburdened. The ground quaked and roared, throwing me against a wall. Faerie screamed. Noise, and heat, and agony. It was too much, and I knew what it meant.

Sirius clutched his head, trying to temper the wail. His magic spluttered and collapsed around him.

The cacophony lasted just moments, but it had felt like years.

A serene quiet fell, and an absence chilled my veins. The absence of a friend.

The knoll's door rumbled open, mocking me.

Panting, Sirius leaned against the knoll wall. He lifted sorry eyes to me, knowing he'd failed.

The Hunt was gone.

And Shinj was dead.

esh

KELLEE'S wild touch burned inside, like Talen's bond had, only Kellee's was a spicy heat that threatened as much as it aroused. Its sudden appearance yanked the breath from my lungs. Power blazed, fire on a touchpaper, and as the sensations stole my mind, I realized it wasn't one touch I felt, but all of them... Kellee, Talen, Sirius, Sota, and even Shinj, the ship. In the sensory onslaught, the horse's reins slipped from my fingers.

Thunder rolled, but instead of ending, the noise rumbled louder and closer, like one of Calicto's enormous earth-eating mining machines that would tunnel below the sinks, rattling our habitat containers.

Not thunder.

I glanced back, past Sota's fierce expression. A mushroom cloud, made of purple fire cut with lightning, swallowed up the sky.

The shock wave hit. The horse dropped beneath me. I tucked myself into a tight ball, hoping I didn't hit something too hard on the way down. Sota's grip clamped closed. Noise. Blood. Pain. Screaming. Not mine. Something *other*. It lasted an eternity, then cut off.

I tested my arms and legs, easing myself open. Trees smoldered. Some had been torn from the ground and lay uprooted, their missing canopy revealing towers of smoke.

"Kesh?" Sota gently pulled at my arm.

"I'm all right."

Our ride, however, was not. A branch had skewered the animal through its chest. Its eyes were open but flat and unseeing.

"We need to get back there." I brushed my clothes down and tugged at my whip, making sure it was still fixed to my belt. Something terrible had happened.

"Kellee said he'd find us. We should wait."

"I don't care what he said. I'm not leaving them."

"But the Hunt?"

"It's gone ..."

He blocked my path, putting his tek-self in the way and puffing himself up. "You don't know it's gone, and Kellee said to wait. Kellee was right, I am your last defense. I should have stopped you from fighting Dagnu. I'll protect you until the end, and if that means protecting you from yourself, then that's what I'll do."

He wasn't budging from my path. He didn't have his guns out, but the steely glare warned me not to push him. It had never occurred to me that he might stand against me like this, but I trusted him. Maybe this time he was right.

"I feel it... It's gone, Sota," I said calmly. "I have to go back."

He held my stare, trying to pin me in place with his daunting laser eye. "I don't like it. We should wait for Kellee."

"What if they need our help?" I straightened up to him. He lifted his chin. He was stubborn enough to argue with me, but then, he'd learned that from Kellee. "I know you want to protect me, but I don't need protecting."

"If you don't need protecting, why am I here? Why do you need me at all? Protecting you is my sole purpose. If you take that from me, what am I then?"

I'd almost forgotten he wasn't human. Just because he'd changed shape didn't mean he'd forgotten his coded objectives. But this was more than code. It wasn't just determination making him stand firm. Behind his code, a living mind needed to feel wanted. "You're here because you're my friend."

"Listen to your friend." Ailish's smooth voice poured into the clearing and over me. She emerged from the tree cover, draped in blue gowns, stepped over the fallen tree trunks, and drifted closer, half her pale face hidden by her hood's shadow.

Sota reflexively engaged his guns and angled his sights on her. She eyed him as if he were a curious toy.

"It is not safe to return to the knoll. Come with me and we'll wait for your vakaru."

"She's made of water and dust," Sota side-whispered.

She chuckled. "And you are a metal man on Faerie. I have never seen anything like you before."

She offered me her slim, light-fingered hand. Her sleeve pulled back, revealing smooth skin so pale it was almost translucent enough to see the beat of blue blood through her veins.

"Come with me, and we'll talk more of the polestar. Those are the answers you seek?"

"Do you trust her?" Sota whispered.

"She can hear you, you know." Did I trust her? No. On Faerie, the only thing I trusted was my crew. I didn't even trust my own eyes or the picture of Ailish they showed me. "What was that explosion back there?"

"The beginning of the war to end all wars."

I'd heard those words before... Kellee had told me how the fae thought the Nightshade would lead the unseelie and end all wars. People assumed the Nightshade had failed. But what if the Nightshade was never meant to be one person? What if it were four people around a central point? Four stars circling another at their center. Before the explosion, I'd felt Talen, Kellee, Sota, and Sirius connect to the part of me just stirring awake. "Are my men alive?"

"Yes, and they will come for you, but your journey is your own." Ailish's good blue eye glinted. A smile lifted her mouth. "You're beginning to see. Come, allow me to show you the rest."

"Kesh, following a fairy into the woods is the worst idea you've ever had. It's right up there with the time you tried to make me waterproof."

Ailish was a Wild One. I knew she had once walked the crystal palace corridors when the palace had been open to all fae, dark and light, unseelie and seelie. I knew she was as old as Faerie, and she likely had many faces, not just this scarred one. I wasn't what I appeared to be either, and I needed answers. I needed to know if there was a way to survive this. A way we could all survive.

I took her hand and grabbed Sota's, adding a reassuring smile. "I have my protector right here."

alen

KELLEE'S CLAW-TIPPED hand shot out of the wreckage. Wrapping my fingers around his, I heaved him from beneath the debris. He coughed, brushed dust and dirt off, and took in our surroundings.

It looked nothing like the land I'd left behind when I'd descended into the knoll. The grass, the meadow, the trees— all gone. Flattened, churned up, and tossed aside, and just beyond the knoll opening lay the mountainous wreckage of Shinj, her back broken, her lights dark.

"Where's Kesh?" I asked.

"Hopefully miles away. I put her on a horse and told her to run." Kellee's eyes shadowed as he absorbed the warcruiser wreckage.

"The Hunt would have killed you," I explained, "and gone on to find Kesh and Sota. Shinj knew that. I told her to find Kesh, but she knew it wouldn't have been enough. One or more of us would have died here. She sacrificed herself to save us."

"She chose this?" he asked, claws receding and the red sparks in his eyes fizzling out, replaced by a subtler green. He wrestled with his thoughts, brows coming together. Perhaps he believed I'd ordered her to her end.

"She chose to save us, yes," I replied. "She was free to make that choice." I missed Shinj's warmth, and with Kesh's absence, I hadn't felt so isolated since the prison. The solid ground with which I'd become accustomed these past few months had turned over beneath me. First, the Nightshade mantle had been cut from me, then Kesh's bond, and now Shinj was gone.

I propped myself against a rock, churned out of the ground by Shinj's impact, and took a few moments to smooth over my rattled thoughts.

"You all right?" Kellee asked.

I nodded, knowing my voice would betray how I was nowhere near as "all right" as I let on.

Sirius approached through the piles of churned earth, Eledan's book clutched in his tek-hand. His guarded expression had gained a few cracks around its edges. Tiredness made his eyes glassy. He did his best to stand tall, but it didn't last.

Anger crackled off Kellee, and he snarled. "Shinj was worth a thousand of you."

"Kellee..." I sighed. "He tried to help." It would be easy to blame him, but knolls were a force of Faerie. There was nothing more he could have done.

Sirius bristled. "I did not foresee this outcome."

"None of us did." I nodded toward the forest. "The Hunt could return. We should meet up with Kesh and keep moving."

Kellee lingered, his breathing increasing. "The Hunt is going after Eledan," he grumbled, scratching his jaw. "We can't allow it to get to him."

"Why?" I asked.

"His warfae marks aren't just marks. They're a key." He waved off any imminent questions. "I know because he showed me." He cleared the growl in his throat. "I didn't remember until the Hunt started rooting around in my mind. He showed me in a dream while torturing me. Eledan's marks form one key to the Hunt's freedom." He jerked his chin at the book under Sirius's arm. "That's what you'll learn in there." He swallowed and ruffled his hair, dislodging dirt. "Also, I think we're all connected in more ways than just Kesh. When the Hunt was inside my head, I..." He paused to collect his thoughts. "Shit, I don't even know how to explain it. You felt it, right? Our connection?" Sirius and I nodded. "We are the answer. All of us. Together."

"Including Eledan?" I asked, needing confirmation.

"Maybe. The way things are going, probably."

"I'll find Kesh and Sota," Sirius volunteered. "You both need to return to Eledan before the Hunt reaches him."

Kellee growled at the idea of *saving* Eledan. It didn't sit well with me either, but for someone who had been forgotten for so long, Eledan clearly had more to do with everything happening than we'd first believed.

Sirius whistled. A fire-touched horse emerged from inside the remaining tree cover, black skin quivering and its mane of flames licking the air. "Take her. She'll get you to Eledan."

The horse plodded toward Kellee and lowered its head for his hand.

"Without Shinj, our options for sanctuary are limited," Sirius told me. "We'll need to regroup somewhere."

"Nowhere on Faerie is safe," Kellee said, scratching the

horse's nose. It snorted its approval and nudged him in the shoulder. The horse was likely part unseelie and recognized the same in him.

Kellee was right. The Hunt would eventually find us. We needed another option. "Meet us back here with Kesh and Sota in twelve hours," I told Sirius. "I'll have a way for us to get clear of Faerie." I neglected to tell him our temporary escape would be a tek shuttle from the *Excalibur*. He had enough on his mind without my adding a trip on a tek-leviathan to it.

Kellee swiftly mounted the horse and offered his hand. I settled behind him on the beast's back.

"Ready, fae?" Kellee asked.

The mountain of Shinj's broken carcass caught my eye. I sent my mental farewells to my friend, wishing things had ended differently.

Sirius lingered and observed the fallen ship. He sighed, and after a few moments, he added, "I can return her body to Faerie, if you believe the vessel would have preferred that?"

Scavengers would come. Eventually, Shinj would return to Mother Faerie, but Sirius was offering to save her that decay. "Thank you."

He approached the nearest section of ship. His warm, spicy magic brushed against mine. Knotting vines laddered up the warcruiser's enormous bulk. Moss and grass spread, smothering her dull gray skin with bright greens. In minutes, the warcruiser had been painted with Faerie's living flora, and beneath, the earth—Faerie—would welcome her home.

Thousands of warcruisers had fallen in the first war. I'd hidden among their floating carcasses in the debris zone, where Kellee had found me searching for a spark of life to resurrect. Those ancient remains would never be returned to

Faerie, but Shinj would, as it should be. She had earned her peace.

Sirius glanced over. I nodded my approval, afraid the lump in my throat would choke off any words.

"All right, hold on," Kellee grumbled. I looped my arms around his waist. He kicked the horse into a canter and then a gallop, following old tracks through the undergrowth, startling wisps and pixies into the air.

Were Sirius's intentions truly aligned with ours? Save Kesh or save Faerie? It was becoming increasingly clear we might achieve one but at the expense of the other. Like us, Sirius would need to choose his loyalty and soon.

esh

As we walked, the spaces between towering oaks darkened, becoming thick and warm. Wisps darted and buzzed, creating dancing light and layered shadows.

"Where are we going?"

Ailish ghosted ahead, moving eerily quiet through the brush. "Somewhere I think you'll like."

"Why can't we talk right here?"

"You're a woman of many questions."

"Because nobody will give me a straight answer."

Sota's gun ports had dropped open some time ago. He trailed behind me, watching our six for Kellee and any *problems.*

I planted my boots in the mossy earth. "This is far enough."

Ailish halted and turned, showing me the beautiful half of

her face. Her smile was deliberate but only skin deep. "Your males are approaching. There is nothing to fear."

"Then we can wait for them right here." In a dark forest, in the depths of Faerie, where there were creatures who would happily hunt us all. "You have a surplus of time?"

"I do, but you don't, *mortal* Nightshade. Tell me one thing..." She picked her way over the leaf mulch and stopped close enough to touch. Her blue clothes sparked beneath the darting wisp-light. Yips, clicks, and pixie songs filled the quiet. "Would you trade everything for a chance at immortality?"

"What?"

"Everything..." She gestured down the length of me. "The Nightshade mantle, the polestar driving light through your fragile veins. These things are killing you. With every breath, you die. Every second slays you. Your males are immortal. Even the tek-man will long outlive you. You are their weakest link. You were not made to live, but what if I could change that? What if I could take the threat of death and decay away? What if I could soothe that aching, mortal body and make it last forever?"

My heartbeat became so heavy, I tasted it in my throat. "You can do that?"

"You saw my home. One of many. My waters heal and can do more."

It seemed wrong to want something I shouldn't have, but while bonded with Talen, I'd had the strength and power that went beyond a saru lifespan. I'd healed quicker. I'd been stronger. Faster. If I accepted her offer, I would get to live. I wouldn't have to leave Kellee alone. I'd always be there for Talen. Sirius wouldn't have to watch me die one last time. And Sota... Sota would always be my friend.

"Your males... their love is fierce. They fear your death,"

Ailish whispered. "They seek ways to help you survive, but you, a mortal saru, cannot survive the polestar. Give it to me and the Wild Ones will return it to Faerie's sky."

"You would do that? You *know* how to do that?"

"We will."

"Then you don't know how to return it, not yet. Why not?"

"The person who has the information keeps it from us."

"Who?"

"The Wild Prince."

Eledan. Again, fate walked me back to him. The Wild Ones wanted the knowledge, and he kept it from them, likely because he trusted them as much as he trusted me. Or could there be another reason? Eledan was always one step ahead of us, playing his games, seeding ideas into our dreams so we never knew for certain whether our thoughts were our own. He'd been inside each of us. He'd wandered the minds of the palace saru and no doubt visited sidhe dreams too. Separated, there was no knowing what he was planning, but whatever it was, the Wild Ones, like Ailish, had run out of patience with him.

"You have freed all the saru," she went on. "What other battle must you fight, Kesh? You have done enough. Agree to surrender the polestar and the Nightshade mantle and I'll give you immortality. You no longer need to fight. *Kesh* is all you'll be." Her sing-song voice made the offer sound reasonable. It was just a matter of saying yes, and all the hurt, the pain, would go away.

"Don't bargain with them..." Sota urged, standing close behind me, like always. My conscience. My friend.

He didn't know what it was like to feel death stalking him like it stalked me now. I *was* dying. I could feel it, like a thread unraveling. The end was approaching. The polestar must be returned to the sky and the light and dark put to rest.

"You never wanted any of this," Ailish whispered, moving in closer.

"No, I didn't..."

"You've wanted freedom before you knew what freedom was. You've fought so long you don't know any other way. I understand..." She reached out a hand to stroke my cheek. "You don't need to fight any longer."

I swatted her hand away. "I thought I was supposed to fight for Faerie? Isn't that what you said? Faerie loves all Her children. I was to embrace the light and the dark, not give it up to you..."

Her clear eye flared. She curled her hand toward her chest.

"Something has changed." I stepped closer. "Is it the Hunt?"

Her nostrils flared, as though I'd insulted her. If it wasn't the Hunt, then what?

She stiffened. "He told us he would give us the Nightshade."

Eledan again. I recalled the snippets of conversation I'd overheard here and there. In the crystal palace, moments after he'd woken, Ailish had asked him to remember their deal: *"You have not forgotten your oath to the Wild Ones."* He'd bargained my life to the Wild Ones in exchange for their support once he woke up, knowing none of the sidhe courts would welcome him back with his tek-heart. Now that he was awake and the Hunt was back, the Wild Ones wanted him to pay up. They wanted my power as the Nightshade, but Eledan hadn't yet given me up.

The Water Witch was not my friend, and she looked at

me as though I were her dinner. I dropped my hand to my whip and flicked its tails loose.

"Then what are you waiting for? You want the Nightshade, so take me..."

Sota's guns whined, charging up.

Movement among the shadows drew my eye, and all around, figures took form, coalescing out of the air or revealing themselves among the bushes. Horned creatures, tails lashing, all Wild Ones, but they didn't attack. They waited, their eyes aglow and full of want.

The unseelie chose their Nightshade. The title was earned and held. I'd only recently earned the wings, but if they could have taken them from me, they would have already. On Faerie, magic couldn't be taken; it had to be given. That was why Ailish had offered me immortality and freedom... For the polestar. Really, it was a surprise it had taken any fae this long to bargain for the greatest weapon ever known.

Power snickered down the whip, crackling it back and forth like a loose live wire. The Wild Ones hissed and recoiled from the alien tek.

"Say the word and I'll cut them down," Sota offered, voice chillingly calm.

"I don't want to hurt any of you." Raising my voice, I sent the words far into their number and on into the dark woods.

"Just accept the offer!" Ailish snapped. Her blue gown glowed and rippled, as though she *were* water. "Surrender your names to me!"

I'd never surrendered to Faerie or anyone. I wasn't about to start now. "No."

"Stubborn fool!" Her glow brightened, lifting her off her feet. Her gowns flowed, bleeding into the air, expanding her outline. As her hood blurred, light fell on the skeletal side of her face, revealing her true visage.

Two could play that game.

I breathed in and mentally jabbed the new, emerging part of me, summoning the same inky power I'd had on Eledan's balcony and while fighting Dagnu. It filled my veins, pouring into my thoughts, making me *more*.

Ailish laughed. "The more you use it, the more it kills you. So fragile a thing it is to be mortal!"

"Stop this!" A column of fire moved toward us out of the trees like an apparition. It took me a moment to recognize Sirius inside those flames. His hair had become long tongues of flame, his body and clothes a pillar of fire.

Ailish's waters throbbed and lapped outward, flowing and then receding. Her beauty wilted. Lines cut into her smooth skin, her body curling in on itself. "Fire Lord... this is not right!" Her musical voice cracked. "She was promised to us, the Wild Ones! Her names are ours!"

"Promised by whom?"

"The Wild Prince, in his dreams."

Sirius stood among them, wearing a disapproving scowl, like he'd come across a group of misbehaving children. "An oath already stands. You cannot make another."

"But the prince delays!"

"Enough!" Sirius's flaming visage flickered out of existence and reappeared between me and Ailish, so hot I stumbled back against Sota. "If you were foolish enough to bargain with the prince and not specify your terms, you must live with the consequences, else the Hunt will find you."

"He controls the Hunt!"

Sirius's growl sounded more like fire devouring a building than anything male-made. "Silence, Water Witch, or I'll take the side of your face I spared before."

She cowered, her water sizzling to steam and her youthful appearance burning away to reveal the crone behind the lie.

Sirius stared her down until she bowed her head and shuffled backward.

"Eledan no more controls his creation than you or I do." He cast that scornful gaze at the crowd. "Go, all of you, and know this: to invite The Nightshade's ire is to invite death."

The Wild Ones dissolved into the shadows, the forest holding them close. All that remained was the occasional wisp dancing on a soft breeze.

My power had also faded, withdrawing into that new, unknown part of me.

Sirius's flames spluttered and dripped off him, vanishing as soon as they left his body. Beneath it all, his skin had paled and his eyes had dulled to a washed-out green. He swayed on his feet. I rushed in and caught him by the tek-arm before he could stubbornly shove me away.

"I'm fine..." he grumbled.

"It's a wonder Faerie doesn't strike you down for that blatant lie. Hold on to me." His arm folded around my waist and locked tight enough to tell me he was suffering. He wouldn't lean on me if he weren't. "What happened?"

"The ship, Shinj, struck at the Hunt. Shinj did not survive."

Oh, Shinj, no. And Talen. He was so close to the ship. "Is Talen all right?"

"He is angry and hurt but hides it well."

"Kellee?"

He winced. "The vakaru is always angry."

"Not always. He's had a hard time. We all have." We hobbled to a fallen tree. "I should have been there."

"No. Had you stayed, you would have died."

Sirius dropped onto the fallen log and leaned forward, sinking his hands into his hair. His shoulders shuddered.

Sota raised an eyebrow at the guardian's obvious exhaustion. More had happened to weaken him, but demanding answers would only shut him down. I knelt in front of him and placed a hand on his warm knee. When he lifted his head, pain had changed his face from its hard, stoic mask to a play of sadness and regret. His mouth, always so quick to sneer, pulled down, and his eyes held great wells of sadness.

"Sirius...?"

His tek-arm looped around my shoulders and clamped me so close I got a face full of autumn-scented hair.

"What did she offer you?" he whispered, his voice as wrecked as the rest of him.

"Immortality."

He locked his hand in my hair and pushed me back, his stare severe. "You said no?"

I nodded.

His fingers tightened too much, but not from anger. I couldn't read him, not confidently, but he seemed afraid. He slipped his fingers free, and slumped forward, the fight draining out of him like his colors had.

"Eledan bargained with your life as though you were his to give away," he said. "I'll not let that rest."

Sota, behind me, still had his guns out and watched Sirius with the same distrust he'd had since the guardian had entered our lives.

"It's all right. I can handle Eledan," I told Sirius, moving across to sit beside him on the log. "Did you get the book?"

Sirius reached inside his coat and withdrew Eledan's tome.

I snatched it and immediately opened it. The page was blank. That couldn't be right. I flicked to another page. Blank. I flicked through them all. Every single page was a wash of faded white. "I don't understand."

"Nor do I, but I'm not sure it matters." Sirius lifted his head. "The vakaru—Kellee faced the Hunt, and when it tried to get inside his mind, it unearthed Eledan's secret. The marks on Eledan's body are connected to the Hunt. It's likely yours are as well, cut into your skin to match Oberon's. The Hunt knows it. With Oberon dead and Sota shielding you, Kellee believes it's going after Eledan."

I thumped the book closed and lowered it to my side, resisting the urge to ask Sirius to burn it. "Why didn't Kellee tell me about the marks before?"

"The memory was hidden from him, only to be revealed when Eledan triggered it. The Hunt unearthed it too soon."

This was a lot to take in, and though I'd love nothing more than to allow the Hunt to take Eledan, the last thing we needed was for it to get stronger. So Eledan knew of a key. Was it another failsafe? A magical one should he ever lose control of his nightmare, or something else? "Doesn't Eledan control the Hunt?"

"No. He created it when the Wild Ones took a young, naïve prince and played his ego. He does not control it. Only Faerie's will can control it, once the polestar, and balance, is restored."

"If the Hunt kills Eledan and his marks are lost, what will happen?"

Sirius's auburn lashes fluttered. "Without its creator, the Hunt will spread farther than Faerie and become unstoppable. Sol will likely be its next target."

With their fairytales and stories, and the first war a distant memory, they couldn't fathom battling a nightmare like the Hunt. "We must stop the Hunt from growing more powerful—"

"Kellee and Talen are already on their way to Eledan. They will find and secure him."

Finding Eledan was one thing. Securing him was quite another. If anyone could, it was Talen and Kellee. At least with Eledan closer, I could pin him down about his deal with the Wild Ones. I straightened and nodded at Sota to relax his weapons. Reluctantly, he shuttered them away beneath his skin.

"All right," I said. "So, we should find a secure location and hole up."

"Talen has a plan for that also." Sirius rubbed his temple.

"Then, what do we do?"

"We learn that there is a time for action and a time for waiting." He slipped his tek-hand into mine and drew me down beside him. "And we hope the Wild Ones do not return too soon."

ellee

ELEDAN'S FAIRY knoll looked like a rolling set of hills, with the occasional balcony chiseled into its green, vine-covered edges. Its resemblance to Arcon—moss-covered and overgrown—was no mistake. As it happened, vines made an excellent alternative route up walls and over balustrades, leading me right into the heart of his chambers.

He wasn't inside, which meant I was free to roam while Talen walked in through the front door, causing enough of a stir to draw Eledan out from whatever hole he was hiding in.

The trailing drapes and puffed cushions demanded to be shredded. My fingers twitched, claws itching to be free.

On the ride over, I'd had plenty of time to recall the dream the Hunt had been so fascinated by. Eledan had made sure he would live. *"These marks, given to me and my brother, are the key to the weapon's demise and the demise of both the darkness and the light."*

"I'm telling you this so that, when the time comes, you'll remember and do the right thing."

He'd known this would happen, and here I was, about to drag him out of the fire when I'd prefer to see him burn.

"C'mon, Talen... spook him already," I muttered, drifting from room to room. The place smelled like his poisonous magic, like he was already here, watching. I freed the claws, reliving their itch, and craned my head, popping a muscle in my neck. The ghost of the scar he'd given me across my neck —long healed—itched too. I hadn't yet paid him back for that.

The main chamber door peeled open, and in strode the prince, painted in purples and silver, his oak crown sitting neatly on a head of raven black hair. "... and where am I..." He spotted me, and his long-legged stride halted.

Talen entered behind him, silver and grays to Eledan's bruised purples. The door closed, sealing the three of us inside. That didn't mean we were alone. I'd learned there was always someone, or something, listening here, either from the outside or inside our thoughts.

"Eledan." I smiled, displaying a hint of sharp teeth. "We're leaving."

"As I just told him," he stiffly replied, "there's nowhere to go." He could straighten his back and lift his chin all he liked. Fear wrapped around him, smelling like old, wet metal.

A rumbling started overhead, growing louder.

Talen casually folded his arms. "And had you let me explain, I would have told you there most definitely is."

Eledan veered straight for the balcony, tossing the drapes aside like he wanted to rip them off. I already had a good idea what we'd find.

The small shuttle gleamed in all its angular, human-made tek glory. The Sol Alliance's crest, concentric circles around a central star, sparkled on the hull. Through the narrow observation window, Hulia sat at the controls.

The downdraft whipped dust, magic, and pollen into the air, upsetting Eledan's immaculate appearance. He saw Hulia and snarled. She had stabbed him in the back once, and now here she was, saving his ass. That had to burn.

She saluted me. I mirrored the gesture. Then, wiping off her smile, she gave Eledan the middle finger.

"You fools are no match for the Hunt," he snapped. "Bringing tek into Faerie's sky is an insult—"

I struck him square in the jaw. I'd tucked the claws away, else I might have taken his head off. The weight behind the blow was enough to topple him. His head struck the banister on the way down, knocking him out cold. Now we had ourselves cargo that didn't argue.

"That was unnecessary," Talen remarked.

"Probably," I cracked my knuckles. "But it felt real good."

I scooped up the prince's limp body and slung him over a shoulder. We waited as Hulia brought the shuttle in close enough to lower the docking ramp and open the shuttle door.

"Sugars, y'all didn't tell me we were taking out the trash," Hulia said once we'd secured Eledan on one of the shuttle's fold-out bunks and pulled up, away from the knoll.

Talen took up the co-pilot's chair beside her. "I wasn't sure you'd agree if you knew."

She snorted and ramped up the engines. The shuttle growled, and outside, the purple sky shifted as the shuttle nose dropped, its blasters launching us forward. "Where next?"

"To get Kesh, Sirius, and Sota," Talen said as he effortlessly navigated the shuttle controls. "But we stay cloaked. Once the sidhe courts realize Eledan is missing, they'll come searching."

She winked. "Yeah, but they won't be expecting human tek."

I settled into a pull-down side seat and watched the unconscious prince for any sign he was waking. Hopefully, he'd stay out cold until we were all back on the *Excalibur*. What would happen when he woke and found himself there was anyone's guess.

Just above his jacket collar, the tip of a warfae tattoo peeked out. They likely snaked all the way down his body, if they were anything like Kesh's.

The hate I harbored for him hadn't waned. He'd cut my throat, trapped Kesh in dreams for months, almost ruining her mind, and facilitated the return of the fae to Halow, killing billions. But he wasn't his brother. Oberon's vicious crusade to wipe out anything he disapproved of had been worse than anything Eledan had done. As much as I despised this Mad Prince, I couldn't blame him for what he was, and that only made me want to hate him more.

"When we get to the *Excalibur*, we need to restrain him."

Talen glanced back. "Physical restraints won't stop him. It would be better not to restrain him. If we threaten him, he'll respond in kind."

"What am I supposed to do, treat him like he's one of us?" I rubbed my bruised knuckles.

"No." Talen's tone warned me to back off. But how could I? This bastard didn't deserve to be saved. How was he even still breathing when so many had died?

"Kellee..." Talen swiveled the co-pilot's chair to face me. The fae had too much understanding on his face. "We need him alive."

"He's safe..." I grumbled. "Unless he hurts Kesh, then all bets are off."

"He won't." Talen turned the chair to face the front again,

hiding his expression, but he couldn't hide the regret in his tone. He almost sounded as though he were sorry Eledan wouldn't hurt Kesh.

It revealed the same fears I had. Eledan wouldn't hurt her because the fool loved her and had done since this started. I'd seen as much when he thought he was twisting my thoughts to his whims. Maybe it had happened when he'd had her trapped beneath Arcon, or maybe he'd fallen for her when he'd been trapped in his own dreams. Love had a way of creeping up on us. I'd loved Kesh since I'd seen her fight to come back from the Dreamweaver's grasp. Without Eledan's scheming as the head of Arcon, I might never have crossed Kesh's path.

Now there was an unsettling thought.

Leaning back against the shuttle's bulkhead, I dug my golden marshal's star out of my pocket and rubbed its battered surface clean. These next few days would be difficult. Whatever happened, I'd be there until the end, no matter the cost.

I pinned the star back onto my coat.

esh

THE *EXCALIBUR* HUNG cloaked in the sky above Faerie, the only tek-ship to ever spend time close to the planet without being shot down. While we were technically hidden, I knew we'd be safe as long as we were trying to right all the wrongs of the past. If we veered off course, Faerie would reveal us.

Tek gleamed and rang every time my boots hit the catwalk gallery over the enormous weapons bays below. Every surface shone. Walls ended in sharp corners, unlike inside the smooth, undulating Faerie knolls or Shinj's interior.

Thinking of the ship's demise further darkened my already shadowed mood. Eledan was on board, and I wasn't sure what to do with that knowledge or him. I'd tried so hard to escape him, but he kept coming back into my life, likely because it wasn't my life at all. His life wasn't his either, since Hapters' people had spliced tek and a fragment of polestar into his chest to make him a heart. We were two parts of a star. We finally had all the polestar pieces we needed.

Before I dealt with all of that and what it meant, I entered the med-bay and found Hulia fussing over Sirius. The guardian was seated on the edge of a high med-bed. She stood beside him with a datapad, trying to log his readings, while he grumbled and groused about being *fine* as he latched the hook-and-eye fastenings on his shirt. His tek-hand and arm appeared to be working perfectly. The rest of him was a mess of ragged hair, dirt smudges, and exhaustion.

He saw me in the doorway. "Will you tell your friend if she continues to hover around me, I'll not be held responsible for her wellbeing when I finally lose my patience."

I smiled at his gruffness and approached Hulia.

Her lips twisted. She handed over the datapad. "He's as stubborn as a Calicto drunk. He won't let me scan him for injuries and insists he's fine." Barking a laugh, she threw a hand his way, making him flinch. "Look at him. He's a mess."

His scowl cut so deep it must have hurt. "Technically, if he says he's fine, then he is fine," I said. "We've all been through a lot."

She rolled her eyes and flounced toward the door. "If he gives himself an aneurysm, don't blame me. Oh, and honey... you don't pay me enough to go within a mile of Eledan. He can rot in his room."

If Eledan was awake, he likely wouldn't be in his room. Kellee had argued to restrain him, but there wasn't enough rope or chain in the worlds to hold Eledan for long, and tying him up would only piss him off.

"I don't pay you," I reminded her with a smile.

"That is also something I'll be bringing up at the next meeting, along with the fact Talen's zombie mind-slaves are freaking me the fuck out."

"Duly noted." Zombie mind-slaves were better than conscious Earthens who couldn't handle the fact they were orbiting Faerie. He wasn't hurting them, just easing their minds. Given how Captain Pierce had attacked Kellee to get her hands on the polestar, and how she'd executed a number of Sirius's fae crew from Hapters, the Earthens were lucky to be alive.

Hulia was gone with a flick of her dreadlocks. The door whooshed shut behind her.

"She is a feisty namu," Sirius remarked, wincing and rolling his shoulder, shifting his tek-arm.

I set the datapad down on the end of the bed. "*Are* you all right?"

"I would prefer to be on Faerie, where I can replenish my strength." He flexed his tek-hand and rippled his fingers.

"Is the arm causing you discomfort?"

"Some," he admitted. "I almost forgot it on Faerie, but here, surrounded by all this, it aches."

Before I could talk myself out of it, I planted a very Talen-like kiss on his forehead and ran a hand down the side of his face, marveling that I could get so close to him without him threatening to murder me.

He froze, gulped, and looked up. The honesty in his eyes stripped us both raw. Like this, he was just Sirius, my silent guardian. I was only beginning to understand what that meant and knew we might never be able to explore where these feelings could take us. If he still had those feelings. He seemed to, but even now, he was restrained.

"Rest," I said. His face was so warm, his skin fae-smooth. "We're safe here."

"The book. Eledan—"

I pressed a finger to his soft kissable lips, which tried to move around my touch. "I will handle Eledan, and the book can wait."

Switching my thumb with my fingers, I checked his gaze to make sure he wasn't about to fly into a fit of rage over a saru violating him, and brushed my mouth over his, trading soft breaths. His arms folded around my lower back and pulled me snug between his knees. The kiss deepened, turning slow and surprisingly gentle for my guardian. But he was already wrung out, and I had others waiting on me. Breaking away, I eased from his grip.

His hand snagged my wrist, pulling me up short. "Stay with me." It sounded like an order, but the softer request reflected in his eyes.

For someone who didn't know how to convey his emotions, he was doing a damn fine job of it. There was no way I could walk away from that low-lashed pleading look, not when it came from the honest heart few had seen.

His chest expanded, and his glare shifted away. "What we started in my library, I know the memories were not good ones for you, but I would not change that kiss—"

"Is that what you think? That I don't want to remember it?" I laid my arms gently over his shoulders, smiling down at my vulnerable guardian. Beneath all that armor, he was a complicated soul. When I kissed him, it turned into a heated, hungry thing, as though our time were running out and this might be our last moment together. I knew that feeling. I felt it with them all, like each conversation could be our last. How could I leave them? Why did it have to be me?

A cool tek-hand claimed my back while his other sought my face, his fingers smearing the tears he found there. Then my fingers were working at the shirt fasteners he'd done up, opening them so I could feel him beneath my hands and soak up every precious quiver and tremble I ignited.

"I wanted you to say yes to Ailish..." The words brushed my ear. His fingers sank into my hair, holding me close as though afraid to let go. "I still do. Is that wrong?"

"I wanted it too, but I've come too far to surrender now. I have to see it to the end. *We* have to see it to the end."

"You are brave... braver than I am."

Wrapping him in my arms, I held him close and listened to the beat of his immortal fae-heart, to the rhythm of his breathing, committing his soft hardness to memory. Maybe he'd listen to my heart, and hear my breathing, and he'd remember me. Perhaps, in his memories, I could live forever.

CHAPTER 26

Arriving late at the meeting in the *Excalibur's* observation room revealed tensions had already flared. Kellee had moved to the back of the room to keep himself from sinking his claws into Captain Pierce, who stood on the other side of the long meeting table. The bank of screens behind her flickered and blinked, the tek fighting off Faerie's influence and failing.

Talen, always the mediator, had planted himself midway between Kellee and Pierce, and Sota stood off to my right, quietly observing and analyzing.

"Where's the guardian?" Kellee asked.

"Resting."

Talen and Kellee shared a glance that indicated they were content to leave Sirius out of this.

"How long will this go on for?" Pierce demanded. She wore her dark blue Sol uniform like it was armor that could protect her in Faerie-space, and Kellee had found his marshal's star. Maybe their symbols helped them when they were so far from home. Pierce's appearance had frayed at the edges in the short time I'd known her. Kellee had told me she was a woman made of iron and would do anything to protect her people. I knew that compulsion well, but she'd also attacked and tortured Kellee, which made her my enemy. The only reason her ship and her crew were here was to keep *Excalibur* useful. Now, with Shinj's death, this tek-leviathan was all we had. Keeping Pierce and her crew compliant required the finesse of Talen's touch, something we had no time for.

"Pierce..." I approached the table. "We have an opportunity—"

"My, my..." Eledan strode into the room, demanding all eyes turn to him. "I must have missed the invitation to attend this prestigious meeting?" He'd ditched his royal robes for a snug-fitting plain shirt and black pants. Earthen clothes. He had braided his long hair into multiple tails, bunched at three places down his back. No crown. He resembled his alter ego Larson, with that same easygoing human demeanor to charm his way through life. The ear tips and ridiculously good looks marked him as fae, but all his stiffness and formality had vanished. The sudden dissonance lost me my train of thought.

Kellee growled.

Eledan sauntered around the table to Pierce's side and perched himself on the edge beside her. He studied the captain—like he did everyone, dissecting her with his glare— then glanced at the rest of us.

"Do I know you?" Pierce asked him.

"You dreamed of me." His mouth tilted, dialing up the charm a notch. "Many times. Do you not recall? Never mind. Do you know who you negotiate with?"

She blinked, her thoughts tumbling over his appearance and his words. It must have been unsettling for her to see someone she thought a dream come to life. "Who are you?" she whispered.

He waved her off. "That one..." He pointed at Talen. "He can empty out your human mind with a single touch. You might not even feel it. Just the smallest brush of his fingers and he can whisper in your ear to slit your throat, and you'd do it, after killing your entire crew, of course."

"Eledan," I warned.

"That one..." He pointed at Kellee. "Well, you know all about that one, having dreamed of him every night since you met him. He's somewhat twitchy, partly because he gorged himself on my brother's blood, and partly because he's an animal most of the time, anyway." Eledan hesitated, making sure Pierce was riveted. "The drone behind me, recently upgraded into a man-suit, could kill you before you opened your mouth to beg. You once had him strapped down and probed in all the wrong ways. You can bet he harbors a grudge for that. And Kesh? Kesh is something of an anomaly. You've only just met her, right?"

Pierce's throat bobbed. Her eyes darted round the room. Eledan's words were exposing her fears.

"All those monsters and more, Kesh controls them. So ask yourself what kind of monster she must be for the others to fall in line behind her?"

"Eledan," I sighed. "You're not helping."

"Not helping *you*." He gave me a pointed look. "This Earthen should know the creatures she liaises with. It's only fair."

"And what about you?" she asked in a small voice. "What kind of monster are you?"

His devastating smile was all the more disarming now that he was wrapped in human clothing. "The one you never see coming."

"Kesh, get him out of here before I do the Hunt a favor," Kellee warned.

I checked Talen for his agreement, saw his soft nod, and mentally counted out my frustration. "Eledan, come with me."

He didn't have to obey, but as he left the room alongside me, I wondered if he hadn't made a nuisance of himself to separate me from the others.

He ran his hands along the smooth, metal walls. The tek behind the panels must have burned him, but he showed no sign of discomfort. "A marvelous piece of human engineering. Humans—Oberon's creations—really are ingenious." His voice carried far into the empty ship, drifting into hollow spaces and farther, into the quiet darkness.

He just had to mention his brother, didn't he? "Are you going to idolize him now he's dead?"

"I can hate him and admire his accomplishments. Don't you feel the same way about me?"

"I'm supposed to admire you now? For what?"

"Making you what you are."

I planted my boots on the grated metal catwalk. The whip at my hip buzzed, itching for me to pull it free. "Do you want me to hurt you? Because that's where this conversation is going."

"It's true. I made you who you are." His blue eyes sparkled. "And you know it."

He was trying to get a rise out of me, but it wouldn't work. "Your bargain with the Wild Ones, tell me about that."

"Ah, they approached you?" He shrugged and leaned back against the wall, appearing so casually human that I wanted to wrap my fingers around his neck and rattle the truth out of him. "One promise cannot supersede another. They were fascinated by you as soon as Sirius introduced you that day in

Ailish's cave." He saw my alarm. "You did not think me idle while I dreamed?"

"You bargained my life away to them?" Just hearing it reignited that itch to wrap my whip around his throat and squeeze the immortal life out of him.

"I suppose it looks like that from your perspective. The truth is, I made a deal that protected you. They cannot take you by force. They can't move against you while my deal stands."

"You think you're *protecting* me? Really? Is that how you see this?" I circled my hand between us. "I don't belong to you, Eledan. My life is not yours to bargain with."

"Yet." He bristled. "You're being overly sensitive. A *'thank you, Eledan, for saving my life'* would be appreciated."

Faerie help me, I was going to kill him with my bare hands. If I did kill him, I wouldn't be able to stop the Hunt and the worlds would fall into darkness and chaos, but by cyn, killing Eledan might be worth it. "And why are you protecting me?"

"Because I need you." He straightened away from the wall and prodded me in the chest. "I need that polestar fragment in your saru blood." His gaze roamed over me, pupils widening, darkening. "I need you, as the Nightshade, to bring the dark fae back to Faerie. Haven't we been through this already?" Closer, he stepped, so close I could taste him. "I need you and your harem of monsters. I need this tek-ship, and I need to go back to Calicto. So, let's get on that, shall we?"

Calicto? "What?"

"Do you have a better plan?" He lifted a hand to touch my shoulder or arm, but reading the fury on my face, he dropped it again and eased back a step. "If you do, tell me so we can proceed."

"What plan? You haven't told me any plan. You've just listed your demands, and frankly, you're in no position to demand anything. The Hunt wants you and your warfae marks. You're the key—"

He waved a hand and started down the corridor, apparently needing to be somewhere else.

"We saved you." I followed him, quickening my pace to keep up.

"Don't be so naïve. I'm here because I want to be."

That would mean he'd anticipated our arrival, as though he'd known we'd bring a shuttle to retrieve him. That was impossible. "You can't claim to have planned this."

"Can't I?"

"Hey." I grabbed his arm and yanked him around to face me. "You don't get to claim to have masterminded all this when we both know, deep down, you're just a frightened, homesick fae who dreamwalks because it's the only place you're not alone."

He blinked, long and slow, waiting for my words to settle. The humorous sparkle in his eyes sharpened. His brows cut in, and his easy smile thinned. "Those people who invited you for a meal on Hapters, do you remember them? The nice farming couple who took a liking to you and Hulia? How do you think they knew who you were?" He gripped my wrist but instead of pushing me off, he held firm. "Do you truly believe Lord Devere happened to arrive on the correct warcruiser, out of hundreds, and stumbled upon you? The lord who dreamed of fucking a saru?" His fingers tightened, and my treacherous heart raced. "Kellee didn't escape the Earthens. Pierce let him go because I was in her head. The only reason Kellee and Talen are here is because I soothed your silver fae's rampant dark fae side, stopping him from unleashing his power on the entire *Excalibur* crew. And Kellee... Marshal

Kellee was the first mind I seeded with ideas of the Messenger. He wasn't too keen on the strange girl from the sinks who carried illegal weapons, but after I planted some ideas, he couldn't stop thinking about you, couldn't stop *dreaming* about the Kesh Lasota who might *save* Halow if he could just wake her from the Dreamweaver's spell."

Oh, no, no, no... He didn't get to do this again. He didn't get to rip the rug out from under me. What was he saying? That he'd manipulated Kellee into... helping me? That he'd started this? That was impossible. It couldn't be. But I had met Kellee after meeting Eledan. This all began with Eledan killing the mineworker and framing me for the murder. What if there was more to it? What if Eledan had been in our heads since I'd run into Kellee in the sinks?

What if Eledan had given Kellee the mental shove he'd needed to be in my apartment right as I returned from Arcon? I'd called it a coincidence, but what if luck had nothing to do with it?

I tried to yank my arm free before his words hooked in deeper and deeper, but it was too late. The words were already eating away at what I thought I knew. Was anything between Kellee and me real?

"Let go..." I pulled.

He yanked harder and threw a steel-like arm around my back, trapping me so close his magic crawled across my skin and spilled over my tongue. "And your precious Sota?" Eledan's blue eyes flashed, their depths suddenly infinite. "He's not *your* Sota. He's my eyes and ears in the real world and has been since I dismantled him in Arcon and rebuilt his processes according to my design. You believe Hulia chose to upgrade him? I've been in Hulia's mind since you stole my heart the first time. I gave her the idea to put him in an Arcon-made tek-body. Sota is mine. Hulia is mine. Kellee is mine. Talen is mine. And you, my queen, were always mine. I let you believe the illusion of being in control because it's easier for me if your monsters believe in their cause—if they believe *in you*." He stroked his finger down my face. "So, my dear queen, your life *is* mine to bargain with. If you stopped fighting the truth and saw it for what it was, we could rule the worlds together."

He couldn't lie.

All those terrible things he'd said, they were all true.

But I'd gotten us this far, hadn't I? Sjora's arena battle, the dark fae on Hapters, freeing the saru, reawakening Kellee's vakaru wraiths, his love for me, Hulia's friendship, Talen's devotion—that couldn't be Eledan. If it was, then nothing was real. Nothing at all.

The game of lies had been Eledan's game, not mine, and it had started with a Nothing Girl and her nothing life when she'd bumped into a marshal.

His steel grip released, and he backed away, smiling with every step. "I wouldn't tell your monsters, lest you lose control of them. Then where would we be?"

If Kellee learned of this, he'd kill Eledan. Key or not, he'd gut him. And Talen... Talen would know he'd never truly loved me, that it had been Eledan's design. And if Sota learned it was all a lie, it would break his heart.

Oh, by cyn, we were all held together by that unraveling thread, and Eledan held its end.

The corners of his mouth tightened with threatening laughter. "We're going back to Calicto. You'd best find a way to tell them, and make the lie believable, Kesh. Lying is, after all, what you're good at."

His laughter trailed off as he walked out of sight. I should have acted, should have wrapped my whip around his neck...

but it wouldn't change anything. Worst of all, *Eledan had gotten us this far.*

I fell against the wall, thoughts untethered. He'd contaminated every memory. Every word, every touch, I couldn't trust any of it. *Nothing* between then and now had been of my own making. Kellee, Talen, Sota, Hulia, they were all his puppets, and so was I.

All, but one.

SIRIUS LAY ASLEEP, shirtless, and bedraggled on the sheets, exactly where I'd left him in one of the ship's many cabins. His face was a beautiful wonder of auburn lashes and pale freckles. I lingered in the doorway, wondering at what point Faerie had allowed this masterpiece of Her making to become mine and why. Each of my men was unique and precious, just like the star in my veins. I loved them all so much it hurt to think that none of them might freely love me in return.

Only Sirius had been there before Eledan infected my life, and he was the only one I could trust.

Placing a hand on Sirius's chest, I whispered his name, bringing him around.

He blinked heavy-lidded eyes, sharpening their emerald shine. "Kesh, what is wrong?"

"Has the Dreamweaver ever been inside your head?" I settled on the edge of the bed and locked my hands together in my lap to hide their trembling.

His scowl was back, chasing off the dregs of sleep and hardening his face. "Not to my knowledge."

"Why not?"

He sat up and ran his tek-hand through his loose hair,

gathering it back. "I'm older than he is. I suspect it would take too much power to twist my dreams to his whims, though he is capable when at full strength. Why? What has happened?"

I told him everything Eledan had said, reliving the same numbness and loss of control. Eledan had been playing us since the beginning. "We can't tell the others."

He didn't deny Eledan could have manipulated everything, confirming what I already knew: Eledan wasn't lying.

Sirius left the bed, picked up his shirt, slung over a chair, and latched it up. "Keeping this from them could be as damaging as them knowing Eledan played them."

I didn't *want* to keep anything from them, but what choice did I have? "I realize that, but Kellee is on edge. If he learns of this, he will kill Eledan, and as much as I want Eledan dead, we need his marks."

What's the point? The small voice of doubt asked. If none of my choices had been my own, why was I fighting? Why not accept Eledan as my master as I'd once accepted Oberon? How could I stop someone who was inside all our minds, pulling our strings and making us dance?

Sirius rested his hands on my shoulders, and I ran my gaze up the solid wall of chest to his face. A thousand years old or more and he was looking to me for answers. Sometimes, it felt like all the worlds were looking at me for answers. "I'm not sure I can do this."

He tucked a lock of hair behind my ear. "You survived and excelled long before Eledan entered your life. Don't let him take that from you."

"I thought I knew him, I thought I had him under control, but he just let me believe it."

"Kesh, his power lies in suggestion. Don't allow him to undermine everything you've done." He squeezed my shoulder. "We must focus on moving forward. Consider this. Why would he tell you the truth?"

"I told him he was nothing. He couldn't handle it. He wanted me to *see* him and everything he's done. I think he wants to be noticed. It's all he's ever wanted."

"He cares what you think of him, and this led him to make a mistake. Now that we know his level of control, we can manage it. Kellee and the others will understand our need for secrecy, when the time comes to tell them."

Lying to them was the last thing I wanted to do. Somehow, I was supposed to convince Talen to have Pierce move this ship to Calicto. How could I look Talen in the eye and lie?

I rubbed my forehead. "Why Calicto? It must have something to do with Arcon. I know he's stronger there. It's more his home than Faerie is."

"Go to Eledan. Listen to everything he says and doesn't say. He *wants* to tell you, so allow him that and learn the truth."

An aching knot tightened my chest. I rubbed it away. "What if him going back there with all the polestar fragments is a bad thing?"

"We'll deal with it." Sirius threaded his fingers into my hair and tilted my head back. His warmth and crackle of spicy magic wrapped me in its embrace. "There has never been a force stronger than you and the others in all of Faerie. Trust in yourself, Mylana." He sealed the words with a gentle kiss, but his touch, his assurance, did little to ease the hollow pain of doubt in my chest.

aerie churned and throbbed, suspended in the purplish starscape outside the panoramic window of *Excalibur*'s command deck. With only a skeleton crew manning the ship, I had the deck to myself. I'd told Sirius to gather the others in the obs room, where I'd tell them about our new plan to head to Calicto, for reasons I hadn't yet figured out. Instead of following him, however, I'd veered off and found my way here, observing the living planet below us. Sentient. All-seeing. Like a goddess. I'd heard how Faerie loved all Her children, of how She had been torn asunder when the dark fae had been driven from Her surface. And those stars twinkling all round? I'd heard of how Faerie had given Her polestar up to return balance against the use of the Hunt—Eledan's creation, crafted from his nightmares at the behest of the Wild Ones. One saru had been seeded and harvested, reared under the whip to kill her own, and shaped by a king as his key to securing the polestar. It seemed impossible that this person was me. If we were all Faerie's children, why had I never felt like I belonged?

I pressed my hand to the thick glass, almost covering Faerie behind my palm.

"Beautiful, isn't She?" Eledan asked.

Pulling my hand back, I turned away from the stars to watch him weave between the control consoles and ascend the steps onto the deck. I'd assumed he'd find me. There was nowhere I could go, no world far enough away, to escape him. The sight of him reawakened the strange push-and-pull feeling that told me to kill him, but also lured me toward him.

I expected his smug smile and horrible laugh, but he stopped beside me and gazed out at Faerie, his expression thoughtful.

Here we were, two parts of the polestar, once again in the sky above Faerie. Would Eledan and I simply cease to exist once all the pieces were back together?

"The polestar will kill me," I said. I already knew the answer, but I wanted to hear it from him.

"Yes."

"And you?"

"My death is... likely. Although, as I'm immortal, I have a higher chance of survival than you." Faerie's churning colors reflected in his ice-blue eyes.

"Did you know that when you had the Hapters people fix your heart with a fragment?"

"It was a risk I was willing to take." His cheek pulsed. He kept his glare locked on Faerie and away from me. "I do not want to die."

"Maybe if you hadn't been such a dick your entire life, Faerie would have looked more favorably on you."

He blinked, slowly turned his head, and softly laughed. "I could say the same about you."

"Everything I've done I did to survive."

"You killed thousands of fae at the Game of Lies."

That aching knot tightened again. I shifted on my feet. "They were there to watch me die."

His smile was on the move. "And so mass murder was a justifiable punishment?"

"Murder? Your brother wiped out the vakaru because they became too powerful. He would have wiped out the humans too. *You* let him back into Halow, so you don't get to lecture me on murder."

"Yes, my brother committed genocide," he calmly replied. "Not me."

So, Eledan was good now? "As Oberon's general, you killed thousands of humans in the first war."

"Yes, I did. That was war. I also spent much of my time teaching humans how to better their tek, and in some cases, like Hapters, I taught them how to combine tek with the magic sleeping on their planet, considerably enriching their lives."

How could he stand there and justify himself to me? "Oh, please. You did that for yourself. Everything you do is for yourself. You admitted as much, so don't try to convince me you're something you're not."

He smirked like he'd won an argument I didn't know we were having. "You still don't see it."

"See what?"

"We are so alike."

Now I laughed. "We are nothing alike."

He faced Faerie again. Humor glittered in his eyes and in the twitch of his lips. "We both do what we must to survive."

"You're fae. All you have to do to survive is show up."

The ache in my chest thumped in time with my heart, growing hotter and heavier. I rubbed it again. "Why do you want to go to Calicto now? Is it the well below Arcon?"

"I have made mistakes—"

My laugh cut him off. Eledan admitting he'd made mistakes? What was next, Faerie freezing over? He arched an eyebrow at my outburst of hilarity. He truly was a piece of work.

Heat throbbed across my chest and cinched around my lungs. Laughter forgotten, I gasped, or tried to, but my lungs locked and my throat closed. My knees hit the floor. Pain jolted up my thighs. My thoughts raced to catch up and think around what was happening, but everything was too slow. A wall of blinding white hit, stealing my sight and feeling. The only thing left to cling on to was Eledan calling my name.

ellee

RESTLESSNESS ITCHED IN MY VEINS. Talen had sent Captain Pierce off to ready the ship for travel, as Sirius had suggested, though we didn't know our destination. Now I rattled around the obs room, waiting for Kesh to show up. Talen and Sota watched the screens observing the silent *Excalibur* decks and external docking points on the ship. Sirius waited by the door like guardian-shaped furniture, and I paced, because if I didn't move, I'd need to kill someone.

Sirius had implied Kesh had a plan, and we were sorely in need of one.

The door hissed open. Eledan carried Kesh, convulsing in his arms.

Talen and Sota moved in. Eledan barked an order, Talen replied, but I heard nothing. The unexpected shock rewired old instincts.

Eledan set Kesh down on the table and held her there,

fighting her jolting arms. Talen pressed a hand to her forehead, instantly stilling her.

"What did you do!" Talen demanded of Eledan.

He might have replied, but in the next breath, I had him against the wall, my right-hand claws lodged firmly in his middle while I clamped his neck in my left hand. Nothing had felt so damn right as feeling his poisonous blood running down the back of my hand. His throat was next. I'd tear it out like I had Oberon's.

Sota fired. The blast hit my hip and scorched, shooting pain deep into the killing thoughts and shattering them enough for reality to soak back in.

I wasn't meant to be killing Eledan.

By cyn, outside of Oberon, I'd never wanted someone to die so badly.

Eledan smiled. "Release me or the drone will fire again, and it will be to kill."

Sota's presence buzzed against my senses. I couldn't see him while locked on Eledan, but I felt him close. "Sota?"

"Do as he says."

Hate paled everything else. I leaned so close to Eledan that his magic flared, sickly sweet. Warm fae blood soaked my clothes and dripped onto my boot with a steady *tap-tap*. "What did you do to her?"

"Nothing—"

"Kellee, leave him." Talen's voice was cutting.

If I killed Eledan, wouldn't it end? What if the Hunt was tied to his life as its creator? Wouldn't killing him stop it? It seemed like a reasonable risk to take, and by cyn, I wanted him gone. Heat beat through my jaw, teeth extending. I'd killed Oberon, still had him in my veins. Killing Eledan felt more right than anything had since we'd arrived on Faerie.

A cool hand touched my shoulder.

"Kellee…" Talen's voice pulled my thoughts away. His violet eyes demanded I look, and see, and hear.

"Let. Him. Go," Talen said, and every word thudded at the door to my soul, demanding I let Talen in.

My grip on Eledan's neck loosened. My heart slowed. The lust for the kill fell away, and a strange peace soaked into my body.

He's controlling me.

"Kellee…" His tone had changed, turned querying to match the new concern in his eyes, and so it should.

I yanked my claws from Eledan's middle, ignoring his gasp, and bared my teeth at Talen. His hand sat innocently on my shoulder. His reach inside my mind was a thousand cold veins of silver, prodding the parts that made me who I was and turning them to his control. Hundreds of years we'd been together, and the one time he tried to control me was to save Eledan?

I brushed his hand off, and the sickening eel-like sensation of his invasive touch snapped and fell away. "Don't *ever* get inside my head again."

Talen's eyes flashed silver. If he came at me, I'd do more than sink my claws into him.

"She's stable but unconscious," Sota said. He'd moved to Kesh's side at the table. Kesh's eyes moved behind her closed eyelids. She dreamed, but not with Eledan, it seemed.

Eledan stumbled against the table, clutching at the bloody patch growing on his shirt "We were talking and she collapsed. There's nowhere safe left on Faerie to take her. You have to turn this ship toward Calicto."

"Why Calicto?" Sirius asked. He'd stayed by the table, by Kesh, where I should have been.

I backed away from them. The wound in my side pounded, and flesh itched as it tried to heal around shredded fragments of clothing. Sota had shot me to save Eledan. Talen had entered my mind to save Eledan. Eledan leaned over Kesh, the anguish on his face almost as real as Talen's.

"The well below Arcon," Eledan told them, wincing and breathing like it pained him. "I can heal her there. Perhaps buy her more time before the polestar... before it's over for us."

"What's wrong with her?" Sota asked.

Eledan glanced at Talen, as though expecting him to answer, then to Sirius.

The guardian answered, "She's mortal."

"We'll take her to Calicto now," Talen said.

This was what Eledan wanted.

He'd maneuvered them into a corner, and none of them could see it.

"Do you have something to say, vakaru?" Eledan asked, sensing my glare riding his back.

Talen rested his hand on Kesh's forehead. Sota watched Kesh's sleeping face. Only Sirius watched Eledan and saw the smile the Mad Prince cast my way.

"Nothing to you."

KESH WAS stable but unconscious in the *Excalibur's* med-bay and under Sirius's constant guard. From the chair beside her bed, he acknowledged my arrival with a shift of an eyebrow and discreetly slipped his tek-hand from hers. Whether he didn't want to be seen showing her affection or didn't want the drama, I couldn't be sure. From the pieces of information I'd picked up, Sirius had loved Kesh—or Mylana, as he knew her—for a long time, but he had been trapped behind Oberon's rule, just like the rest of us.

"You did well not to kill him," he said, leaning back in the chair to give me the full weight of his ancient gaze. It wasn't often I looked into the eyes of another and felt the weight of eons look back at me.

I rippled my fingers, clean of blood and claws retracted.

"The vakaru were always difficult to control," he added. "Your volatility made you unbeatable in battle, but unstable outside it. A trait Oberon never did breed out of you."

Was he complimenting or insulting me? His face was as blank as always.

"I mean no offense." He sighed, his gaze finding its way back to Kesh. "Oberon often spoke of his vakaru and human experiments. He was proud of you. Without the vakaru, the fae would not have won the first war."

"Do you mourn him?" I hadn't thought to ask, hadn't thought about much since sinking my teeth into the king's neck.

"In the same way I mourn all fae killed too soon, yes."

I stopped at the foot of Kesh's bed. Her chest rose and fell, and her lashes fluttered, but like before, there was no sign of her waking. A slim med-pad on a stand beside the bed blipped her vitals. It sounded like seconds ticking down.

The polestar was eating her up inside. Without Eledan's promise to heal her on Calicto, she might never wake again. "Do you think he'll heal her?"

He took a moment to think on the answer. "I do."

"But he just needs what's inside her. So why wake her at all?"

"It's more than that." He tucked her hand in his shining tek-fingers. Her hand seemed small resting in his. The vakaru in me wanted to knock him aside and claim her as mine, but I had a hold on those instincts, for now.

"There is a magic to her that is not part of the polestar,"

he said. "She is more unique than a thousand Faerie stars, and Eledan knows it." His gaze fell to the star on my shirt. "You wear that as a symbol of hope?"

"Among other reasons."

"We will need it. Eledan has all four pieces of the polestar within his reach. He returns to his stronghold of a thousand years. That is no accident."

"Do you have any idea what he's planning?" If anyone would know, it'd be an ancient Faerie guardian.

"No."

Then we would need all the hope we could find. Cradling my fist in my other hand, I rubbed the itch away. "I should have killed him."

"That would have been unwise. He is all that tethers the Hunt. Without him, there may be no way to stop it."

I knew that, which was why the bastard was still breathing, but he clearly couldn't control it. "What of the book?"

"It cannot be read. The pages are empty."

Typical. We needed something as powerful as Eledan to stop him and his Hunt. Shinj had barely tripped the Hunt up. We needed something bigger. Something equally unstoppable. Something nobody had tamed in a long, long time. Something unseelie...

"The vakaru wraiths on Valand..." I thought aloud. "Is there any way to resurrect them?"

"Bring them back to life? No. But they are not gone and won't be until their spirits are returned to Faerie. We could utilize them in other ways..." His russet eyebrows pinched together.

"How?"

"By the Nightshade."

"Talen tried that on Hapters and failed."

"Talen alone was not the Nightshade."

He caught my gaze, and he knew, just as I'd suspected since the Hunt had tried to kill me: *we* were the Nightshade. We were all connected. Sota, me, Sirius, and Talen, with Kesh at our center. All our pieces had been scattered, until now, until Kesh had brought us together.

Moving to Kesh's bedside, I watched her sleep. This impossible woman had somehow found us. I'd lived a long time on the fringes of nowhere, looking for something I didn't know I was looking for, looking for her. "Do you believe in fate, guardian?"

"I believe in Faerie. And Faerie believes in Mylana."

I held his gaze. No fae could speak lightly of such things. He was as much part of Faerie as Kesh was part of the polestar. He believed in her, like we all did. "How do we rally the dark fae to us? How do we stop the Hunt, for good?"

"We will find those answers on Calicto."

alen

CALICTO LOOKED nothing like the tek-riddled planet Kellee and I had rescued Kesh from over a Sol year ago. From orbit, its surface churned green and blue like Faerie's. As Pierce maneuvered the *Excalibur* over Arcon, some fifty miles below us, Faerie's touch became apparent. Calicto hadn't started out alive like Faerie, but it was now.

Hulia set the shuttle down in the open plain in front of Arcon's pyramid-shaped building and lowered the ramp. Pollen and magic puffed into the small cabin on the exchange of air. Kellee sneezed and swore, then helped maneuver Kesh's hovering stretcher down the ramp behind me. Kesh remained unconscious.

As soon as my boots settled into the mossy ground, a new, invisible touch wound around my legs, exploring, tasting. New Calicto was an extension of Faerie now, and as alive and aware as we were.

"Holy shitballs." Sota scanned our surroundings, made up of strange, little trees with weeping branches and sparkling brooks burbling across what had once been an all-tek plaza. Arcon loomed like a mountain of greenery.

"Life signs are too abundant to track," Sota announced. "I don't recognize any of the species here."

To prove his point, a six-legged critter scurried out of the bushes and scuttled to the nearest pool. Tek tickled my senses, and as I watched the creature lower its antennae-bristling head to drink, the tek-scales along its back flared to absorb the heat.

The creature was tek *and* magic. I scanned the nearby bushes, listening for pixie chirps, and found them among the branches. Their little bodies were the same as any pixie on Faerie, but these had an extra set of wings made from metal and mesh.

Tek fused with magic, just like the trinkets on Hapters.

Just like Kesh had made Sota.

And just like the heart that kept Eledan alive.

It shouldn't have been possible.

"I thought magic hated tek?" Sota asked, echoing my thoughts.

Eledan descended the ramp. "It's evolved," he said, like the answer was obvious. He stopped at the edge of a stream and lifted his head, admiring Arcon towering out of the undergrowth. *His* Arcon. His teasing smile suggested he'd known this would happen. "Faerie always finds a way."

He touched Kesh's med-stretcher and had it drift behind him.

Kellee started after him. I blocked him and Sota, earning frowns from both. "You need to stay here."

Gold rimmed Kellee's dark pupils. "To hell with that. I'm

not letting him take Kesh in there to do whatever the cyn he wants with her like last time—"

"I'm going," I interrupted.

Sota had fallen into the stillness that happened whenever he forgot about pretending to be human. His instincts demanded he protect Kesh, but whatever Eledan was about to do would trigger those instincts.

"Kellee, you know you're not in the best frame of mind, and Sota, what happens in there may trigger your protocols to protect. Kesh needs you both out here, waiting for her when she wakes."

"You promise he won't hurt her?" Sota asked.

I couldn't answer that, as well he knew. "I will do everything in my power to keep her safe."

"If anything happens to her..." Kellee trailed off, his eye color bleeding red.

He knew me well enough to know I'd never put Kesh's life at risk, but my controlling his emotions to prevent him from killing Eledan had driven a wedge between us, which might never be dislodged. I'd known the risk then as I knew them now. This had to be done.

"Guard the shuttle. There's no knowing what monsters Faerie has created here."

Sota backed off, his eyes cast downward, but Kellee's stayed the entire way across the plain. Eledan had stopped at the foot of Arcon's vine-blanketed steps. He rested a boot on the bottom step and looked up at his old home. Glittering motes drifted in the air, catching Calicto's light, filtered through its new atmosphere. Faerie had always terraformed worlds, but I'd never seen the process firsthand before. New Calicto was beautiful, even with its hybrid tek-and-magic base.

Eledan arched an eyebrow and raised his gaze to me. "Afraid the vakaru might lose control?"

"Yes."

He chuckled. "He's tried to kill me several times, and here I am."

"Because he wasn't really trying."

His smile died. "This is as far as the stretcher will go. We'll have to carry Kesh deeper into Arcon."

There was no *we*. Easing my hands under Kesh's light body, I cradled her in my arms and climbed the steps. Vines and fauna slithered out of the way, revealing a dark cavernous mouth. It took a great deal to unnerve me, but passing into Arcon and feeling a thousand eyes observing me from behind hidden walls sent a shiver down my spine. I'd stepped into the mouth of something alive, and I wasn't sure what that meant.

Walls moved, and the floor opened, leading us spiraling downward. Dallying wisps lit the way. The well had turned Arcon into a knoll, but this knoll was like none on Faerie. Creatures made of tek parts scuttled around my boots and up walls.

"Is this your doing?" I asked Eledan, who strolled ahead. I expected my words to echo, but the trailing greenery devoured the sound, adding to the claustrophobia. One wrong step and the knoll could seal us inside. Knolls were well-known for their temperamental nature. Was this knoll friend or foe?

"It's merely what happens when a well is left to claim a world without intervention."

"But tek and magic fused together?"

"My brother feared such a union. He considered it blasphemy."

"Do you consider this blasphemy?"

"I would have, before Faerie neglected me. Now, having

lived among humans, I consider this inevitable. I assume you've seen my heart, and you've certainly seen what Kesh did with Mab's gift in Sota. This is, after all, Queen Mab's life magic at work."

"*Your* magic."

He dipped his head in acknowledgment.

The same magic that had run through Shinj, and Oberon's warcruisers, could create life from nothing, and here it was, as Calicto's beating heart. It felt significant. "Where are we taking Kesh?"

"She's dying. I intend to change that."

"Why help her? Isn't it the polestar you want?"

He walked on. The air cooled, and tek-wisps settled on roots poking out from the tunnel walls.

"You are as old as I am, perhaps older. You once fought a war, and like the vakaru, you lost. The years go on, and nothing changes. The same cycles begin again and again. As fae, we are not immune to these traps, but I saw another side. I stood outside Faerie and looked in. You know what that view looks like."

I did. I knew the loneliness, the isolation, the confinement behind a glass prison, both real and imagined. The chill tried to gnaw through my skin. I pulled Kesh closer, keeping her close and warm as much for her as for me.

"Faerie is shortsighted," he added. "Calicto is the future."

Then he wanted Faerie to spread far and wide, to Sol and farther. And he'd be its ruler. Everyone would finally notice the ignored prince.

"What does any of that have to do with Kesh?" I asked again, and all I received in answer was a cutting glance in warning. Did he even know the answer?

The deeper we traveled, the more magic hung in the air, its silken trails tasting like spun sugar. Deeper still we walked, into the old mining tunnels a mineworker had used to stumble across an ancient Faerie well. A discovery that had gotten the worker killed and Kesh framed for murder. The presence of burgeoning magic pushed in from all sides, like water pressure. It searched for a weakness or sought to drown me in magic. My defenses flared, my unseelie side stirring awake and pushing back. Kesh's breathing became labored, her mortality fighting against Faerie's touch.

"How much farther?" I'd barely finished asking before the tunnel opened into an enormous chamber, with a large, glowing green bubble at its center. The bubble pulsed and rippled, magic churning, throwing off enough light to stretch long, dancing shadows behind us.

Eledan approached the well, his aura taking on a similar green glow. The well was three times as high as he was tall, and it beat with magic, the same as Shinj's twin hearts had once thudded life through the ship—only this heart fed an entire planet.

Eledan gestured for me to hand over Kesh.

"What will this do to her?" Life magic rarely killed, but it wasn't meant for mortals either. This much of it... it *could* kill, the same as my bond with Kesh could have killed her in the past.

He offered his hand. "This is not your magic. It's mine. Hand her over or she'll die in your arms. Is that what you want?"

"Why are you helping her? At least tell me that."

He let his smile go, and a fresh honesty shone through all the layers of madness and neglect shimmering behind his eyes. "There is no time for explanations."

Moving closer, I felt more magic throb over me. Kesh trembled, her breaths racing with her heart. She felt small and fragile, like something so close to breaking. I wanted to turn back and leave this place, leave them and take her with me, but she'd never forgive me if I stole her life and her choices from her.

"Why, Eledan?"

Green light pulsed over him and through him. Beneath his shirt, his tek-heart glowed with the same intense light as in his eyes. His guarded expression broke open, becoming raw and desperate.

"Because I've lived a thousand years as a ghost, and she finally saw me. I will not allow her to die."

I searched his face for the trick, for the crack in his words that would reveal the deception, but I found only pain and confusion. He meant every word. Eledan took her from my arms, and in the next step, the green well of energy swallowed them both.

ellee

"Kellee, I'm picking up a ton of blips on this screen, and I don't think they're friendly." Hulia poked her head outside the shuttle ramp door. "Did yah wanna take a look?"

I nodded but watched the opening into Arcon, expecting to see movement inside. Talen and Eledan had been gone for half an hour. I'd felt every excruciating minute pass like each one cut. I trusted Talen, but I also knew Eledan.

"Kellee?" Sota asked, bristling to my right like a pillar of nervous energy and plucking on my already frayed nerves. He hadn't left my side once.

"See to it," I told him, keeping my gaze on Arcon.

He lingered, like he wanted to say more, then retreated up the ramp.

"You'll wanna see this," Sota said moments later. "They're in orbit. Looks like a whole lot of Sol ships just arrived."

Earthens. Given my recent and past history with them,

any discussions between us wouldn't go well. If they were here, that meant they hadn't yet switched on their shiny new defense net.

"Contact Sirius." I ducked into the shuttle and joined Hulia at the flight console.

"Hailing…" She tapped the controls. "He's not picking up."

"Maybe he doesn't know how," Sota suggested, leaning over my shoulder and peering at the raised semitransparent screens.

"He's fae, not an idiot."

"You don't need to get salty, *Marshal*."

"Hulia." Sirius's rumbling voice filled the cabin. "Pierce says we have company. She's asking to hail her people."

"No, don't let her near any comms. We can't trust her."

We needed Talen back. Sirius alone would be enough to stop Pierce, but not if the fleet wanted to board the *Excalibur*. The displays showed the ships converging above our location. They'd soon try to make contact, and after that, Calicto would be crawling with Earthens. If they found Eledan or Talen, we'd have a fight on our hands.

Blinking lights lit up the screen. Outside, I'd bet the ships were darkening the sky. I left the shuttle. "That's got to be almost forty ships."

I could hail them to buy us some time, but my reputation would not win us any favors. Recognizing the tek-warship as their missing *Excalibur*, they'd be looking for a fight. Without Talen, we had no way of controlling the crew or fighting back.

"This is bad, isn't it?" Sota asked, staring intently at my face, reading his answer there.

"It doesn't have to be, if we can all just get along."

"Your suggestion?" Sirius asked over the comms.

As far as I knew, since Oberon's demise, the fae had withdrawn from Halow back to Faerie, leaving the system ripe for the Earthens to return. Only now, they'd find it changed, less human and more Faerie. They were as likely to destroy this planet as the fae had. If Calicto was anything like Faerie, though, it would have grown its own defenses.

Pressing the comms button, I told Sirius, "Bring the ship in over Arcon, as low as it will idle."

"The human is protesting."

"She's one unarmed Earthen, Sirius. Use your considerable fae talents to make her *not* protest."

"Kesh would not approve of my using glamor."

Hulia gave me a look of "is he for real?" Admittedly, it felt good to hear how Kesh had him under her thumb too.

"You know as well as I do that Kesh will go to any lengths to protect her own. Just do it."

Sota leaned forward to get a look at Arcon outside the shuttle's window. "If we bring the *Excalibur* in that low, Arcon's magic output will interfere with the ship's systems."

"That's the plan."

The mass of leviathan warship drifted across the screen, planting itself above our location. Afraid of what the magic would do to their ships, the smaller Sol Alliance fleet hung back, forming a halo around the *Excalibur*. It wouldn't last, but it would buy us some time.

"Now what?" Hulia asked.

"Now we go inside Arcon, find out what's going on down there, and get Kesh back and the fae who can control humans." Leaving the co-pilot's chair, I headed for the door. "Sota, with me. Hulia, if those ships start to descend, contact Sota. Hopefully, the magic won't block the signal once we're inside Arcon."

Sota descended the ramp behind me. "I'm er... I'm sorry for shooting you earlier. Again."

"Forget it. I'm getting used to it." I looked up, and sure enough, Sol ships dotted the sky. That high up, they looked like hovering bugs. Each of those bugs could kill us.

"Technically, I can't ever forget it." Sota followed my gaze and then jogged after me. "You were going to kill him. The others couldn't see it like I could, and Kesh said we need him. I am sorry, Kellee."

"I know you are, Sparky."

"We're still friends?"

I paused at Arcon's steps. He looked at me with all the apologies in his eyes. "Never doubt it."

Magic slammed into my back, but instead of knocking me down, it caught hold and squeezed. Its taste poured down my throat and swam into my eyes, blinding and choking me. Just as I realized I couldn't move or breathe, it let go, dropping me to the ground.

"Did you feel that!" Sota gripped my arm. "Look!"

Claws sprung from my fingers, teeth plunged from my gums, and the vakaru in me tore free, unleashed by the powerful rush. Sota dragged me to my feet, but among the sensory overload, I almost didn't claw my way back to being in control.

"Look," he repeated.

A liquid green torrent of light shot skyward, like a reverse waterfall, and at its center, the *Excalibur* throbbed and warped. Vine-like Faerie tendrils exploded from Arcon's tip and thrust into the *Excalibur's* hull, wrapping the vessel in vegetation and turning it into a pulsing mesh of roots. The ship groaned in protest and descended, pulled toward Arcon.

esh

I'D NEVER FELT MORE alive.

The world was awash in power. I breathed it, drank it, drowned in it, and never wanted it to end. Forever stretched in a moment. Faerie embraced me, like Talen's bond once had, only this was *more*. This was everything. I wasn't saru, and I wasn't a body with a heart and a mind. I was stardust. Everywhere and nowhere. Everything and nothing. I was finite and timeless. A hundred thousand souls called and were silenced. A mother cried.

Then I was me again, in a body that felt too small. I remembered everything had hurt, but it didn't now, and inside, at my center, a star pulsed awake and wanting, *needing* its pieces.

I'd been with Eledan on the *Excalibur* when the pain had struck, but this place was far from the *Excalibur*.

Talen was here, hands reaching toward me. Behind him,

where nobody watched, Eledan stumbled, his hand clutched to his chest. His polestar heart hungered too. Its presence reached to me, needing to be one, and the power in my veins ached in answer.

He was hurting, I realized, thoughts slowly returning. In my muddled mind, one thing was clear: he'd done something, changed something, and I was... different. Powerful. Calm. Controlled. Life throbbed below me, above me, and all around. Life magic. It ran through my veins again, lighting me up.

I laughed and heard it echo through the world. So much power... I could reach out and...

"Stop," Eledan panted. "Stop, Kesh. Not yet." He was on a knee, his face ghostly pale, long hair spilling over one shoulder and trailing on the ground. He looked panicked and afraid, the opposite of everything I felt.

Talen was in front of me, blocking my view. He glowed silver, but only because I was seeing the real him, through new eyes. I looked at my hands and moved my fingers, stroking magic in the air. These hands didn't seem like mine. Something fundamental had shifted inside.

"Kesh?" Talen's hands hovered over either side of my arms, wanting to touch but afraid to. Why was he afraid?

The magic pulsed like long, luscious waves rolling up through the floor, through me, and climbed higher and higher, converging on the pyramid's point. I couldn't see it, but I knew its path. Then it pulsed again and again, a beacon sending out a signal.

At the edge, where my thoughts couldn't reach, something familiar answered. Many familiar things with dark thoughts and dark intent.

The unseelie.

We were on Calicto. The information came to me from a

sense of belonging. If this was Calicto, then the well behind me meant we were below a living, breathing, Arcon.

Everything seemed impossible yet so perfect.

"Kesh, say something."

I blinked at Talen and saw that same fear Eledan wore mirrored in his eyes. Whatever had changed, I didn't want him to fear me. Never that. I threw my arms around him and pulled him so close his heart thumped against mine. His arms clutched me against him. His chin brushed my cheek, the gentle caress warm and smooth. He smelled of lilies and honeysuckle and home, and I never wanted to let him go.

"What happened?" I whispered.

"You collapsed. Eledan brought you to Calicto to heal you."

Eledan had healed me? That wasn't all he'd done. I watched him, behind Talen. He staggered to his feet. His gaze snagged mine and held it, even as his body trembled. "The Earthens are here," he said, his voice raw.

Talen pulled me toward the only way out of the underground chamber and away from its enormous beating well of life magic. As we left the ebb and flow of magic, another sound sought me. Voices called out as one, hissing a name.

"Do you hear the voices?" I asked Talen.

"Yes." His pace quickened, guiding me through an overgrown tunnel. Wisps took flight around us—their tiny half-tek-bodies sharp and shining, each one a marvelous union of human and fae.

Nightshade, the voices in my head crooned, growing louder like they had on Hapters, but they weren't asking for Talen. They were asking for me, and it felt right. Everything felt right. Like I was supposed to be here, in this moment. Like I finally belonged.

"The queen of names,

a star unchained,

Faerie's worlds forever changed."

I glanced over my shoulder, unsure the words were in my head with all the others or if Eledan had spoken aloud. He didn't smile like I'd thought he would be. If anything, there was a sorrow in his eyes that matched the longing in his tek-and-magic heart.

He had done this. He had known what would happen when he took me below Arcon, and he knew what was happening now. Still, he was afraid. If he feared our next steps, so should everyone.

"What did you do?" Pulling from Talen's grip, I stopped in the tunnel, blocking Eledan.

He straightened and peered down his nose. He had no intention of answering.

A wisp darted up the tunnel, taking its light with it, leaving just one hanging from a metallic root overhead. We were close to Calicto's surface, and the rumbling from a ship's engines sounded like distant never-ending thunder. The humans were here, on Calicto.

"You did something that frightens you. Tell me."

Talen caught my hand and gently pulled. "There's no time for this—"

"I freed you," Eledan said. It sounded so simple, but as any saru knew, freedom was not simple.

"What does that mean?"

He sniffed and attempted to snarl back, like he always had, but its edge had blunted. "It means as it sounds, and now we should listen to your silver fae. We do not want to be in these tunnels when the dark fae arrive."

The dark fae. The voices in my head. "They're... coming here?"

"You know they are, *Nightshade*." Now his smile was real. "You feel their imminent arrival in your bones."

I felt it in the same place I felt the star throb and churn, and the same place I loved the saru. "How is that possible?"

"Each Faerie well, placed throughout the systems, acts as a stepping stone, and Calicto's is the last before Faerie. They were waiting for their Nightshade to awake and call them home."

"*All* of them?"

"Every last one my brother chased from Faerie." He shoved by me. "They have little else but vengeance on their minds, so we had better be ready."

The last wisp took flight and buzzed up the tunnel, plunging us into darkness. In that darkness, I saw why they looked at me with fear. My hands and wrists shone with a milky glow, the remaining warfae marks like great scars carved into the light, and that was only what showed outside my clothes.

"Fate is in motion..." Talen murmured, his gaze heavy with concern. "We must regroup and ready ourselves for the return of the dark fae and our return to Faerie."

"Kesh?" Sota's voice ricocheted out of the darkness.

"Down here."

The outlines of Sota, Kellee, and Hulia appeared in the tunnel's gloom.

"The humans are here," Sota announced, his red eye glowing in the dim light. "Fifty ships and counting."

"Sirius?"

"Still on the *Excalibur*." Kellee prowled closer, his vakaru eyes reflecting the wisp-light. "We *all* need to get somewhere defensible."

Before his words ended, Arcon had trembled, and the

vine- and root-knotted tek-walls had cracked and warped, *shifting* around us. Arcon was breathing out. *Everything* felt alive. Calicto hummed beneath my boots, a constant presence like that on Faerie. I had the impression of being inside a huge beast that was aware of us, just like Shinj had been aware.

Eledan's careful smile said it all and not enough. The bastard knew what was happening here.

"Follow," he barked, turning on his heel and striding into a tunnel that had just opened up.

Kellee glanced at me in question. I nodded. Arcon was Eledan's knoll. We had no choice but to follow, lest the knoll swallow us.

The floor lifted into a steep spiraling climb. Talen walked ahead of me, keeping Eledan in front of him, while the others trailed behind. Occasionally, the floor trembled and throbbed, and the higher we climbed, the lighter the tunnel became, until the veins in the walls glowed, lighting our path. I touched a branching vein. The greenish light rippled brighter beneath my hand, as though I'd thrown a pebble into a pond, and Arcon beat back against my hand. Whatever was happening wasn't normal. I wasn't even sure whether this was Faerie's touch or something else. Something *Eledan*.

Talen cried out and dropped. His hands shot to his head, clasping over his ears as though he were fighting to keep out something we couldn't hear. Someone growled, likely Kellee, and Hulia snapped an insult at Eledan.

"Quiet! All of you!" I ordered, dropping in front of Talen and touching his knee. He'd squeezed his eyes closed and hissed through gritted teeth, caught in an agony. With the loss of our bond, I couldn't help him.

His hissing breaths slowed. "It's... all right."

Kellee loomed behind him, his face mirroring my thoughts: *this is not all right.*

From behind me, Eledan said, "It's the leviathan ship."

I glanced behind me. Eledan had a hand against Arcon's wall, his head lifted.

"It's alive," Talen breathed. He opened his violet eyes and lifted his head. "Calicto is defending itself with the *Excalibur* by birthing new life inside the tek-ship." He settled his hand on mine. "It's calling for a pilot."

Panic fluttered in my heart—the first time I'd felt it since waking. I gripped Talen's arm and helped him to his feet. "Talen, I don't understand."

"This sentient planet is bracing itself for war against Earthens and grasping at anything in its arsenal—including the ship and me."

"We have to stop it."

"Then you'd better stop the Sol Alliance from firing," Eledan's sardonic drawl answered, humor glinting in his eyes. He was loving every second of this.

"Take us to the seat of power here," I barked at him. "Somewhere we can regroup and assess what's happening."

We followed Eledan through the snaking tunnel. Talen winced and missed his steps, Excalibur still calling out to him. I couldn't lose him to a ship. I'd seen pilots. I'd killed one when it had begged me to free it. I could not let that happen to Talen, but I had a hundred other things to stop first. Namely, stopping the humans from firing on this planet and getting us all killed.

The tunnel mouth widened, and a waterfall of ivy parted, depositing us in a grand, root-infested chamber. My soul knew this room, even if my eyes didn't immediately recognize it. One wall was solid glass. Outside, Calicto throbbed like living neon lights. The sky dripped with Sol Alliance ships.

"Oh, by Faerie..." I drifted toward the glass, drawn by the magnificent sight.

"I know this room," Kellee growled.

"So do I," Sota agreed flatly.

I caught sight of the broken oak table Eledan had once punched me through, and where he'd made Hulia dance and scream. She seethed near the tunnel mouth, her hands locked into fists. I'd rebuilt Sota here, with phantom-Eledan's help. I'd once jumped from these very windows rather than fight a fae unprepared. I touched the glass and watched metallic veins pulse against the outline of my hand.

The history in this room was a living thing inside all our minds.

While we absorbed the room's new Faerie-infested look in stunned silence, Eledan had predictably taken up residence on the oak throne. In his human clothing, he looked like a cross between Larsen and the Mad Prince, which seemed eerily appropriate, considering how magic was merging with tek here.

Eledan rested his hands on the throne's wide arms and spread his fingers. He looked down, his expression locked in concentration.

"Now then..." He sighed. "Time to birth a new reign."

His body jerked, back arching. He threw his head back, or whatever was happening to him wrenched his head back, exposing his neck and the squirming tattoos coming to life beneath his collar.

"Stop him!" Kellee growled.

I thrust out an arm and jolted Kellee back. "No, wait. We don't know what he's doing."

"Whatever it is, it's bad."

Maybe. "Just wait..."

Roots sprang from the throne, knotted, and lashed in the air, then they wound around Eledan's trapped form, tying him tight to the throne. He stared at the ceiling, lashes fluttering, but whatever he saw wasn't in this room. Roots crept up his chest, peeling apart the shirt to reveal the throbbing scar tissue and tek-veins of the heart keeping him alive, then those roots traveled on, lacing through his hair.

Talen twitched beside me. He again clutched at his head and swore. "He's readying the *Excalibur* to fire."

"Can you stop it?" I asked carefully.

"Not from here. I'd need to be... on the ship."

The way he'd added that last sentence, I assumed he meant being *on* that ship wouldn't be enough. He needed to fuse with it, and that wasn't happening. I shook my head, but he flinched away again, teeth gritted. He *was* a pilot. More than that, he'd been exposed to tek for hundreds of years. Fate had *made him* for something like the *Excalibur*. No other fae could pilot a tek-and-magic made ship. I didn't care. I would never let him suffer like the other pilots had.

I squeezed his hand. Destiny couldn't have him. He was mine.

"Kesh, what are we waiting for?" Sota asked. "Whatever he's doing, it's gotta be bad."

I scanned the worried faces surrounding me. Kellee, Hulia, Sota and Talen. They didn't know Eledan had led them by the hand to this very moment. We were each here for a reason. The dark fae were close. Calicto was alive, and together, with each of them, I was the Nightshade. The Earthens were about to pick a fight with the strongest weapons outside the Hunt: us.

Slipping my hand from Talen's, I approached Eledan and focused on that wretched pumping organ exposed in his chest.

He and I were two parts of the polestar, and together, we had summoned Faerie's dark legion. But not all weapons had to be used. Sometimes, it was enough for them to exist.

His heart beat like a drum, louder in my ears than in anyone else's. I stopped in front of him and hovered my fingers over the tek-heart trapped in its cage. All he had ever wanted was to be noticed, to be loved, to be remembered. He had created the Hunt because the Wild Ones had promised him power, but the Hunt was too wild, even for him. He'd fought for Oberon, and his brother had betrayed him, having him slain in battle. But Eledan hadn't died as his kind had assumed. He'd survived, like I'd survived. He'd fought and lived and made mistakes. We all had. And now he was fighting again, but it did not have to be this way. The polestar was a weapon of light, a signal of hope taken from Faerie's sky, and it was by no mistake that it rested in us. He had tried to tell me, and I hadn't listened. He had tried to reach out to me as only a fae knew how, and I'd shut the door on him at every turn.

It was time to try another way.

I spread my hand on his chest, over his heart, and absorbed the strange, pulsating warmth, sliding my touch against scar tissue and tek. The rhythm stuttered, his fear spiking, but before he could pull away, I closed my eyes and reached inside myself, to where that new source of power beat like a second heart. Instead of turning it against him, instead of fighting him like my instincts demanded, I surrendered my power to him, like I'd done many times with Talen. I gave him a true and honest gift, one unencumbered, and whispered, "I see you."

Eledan opened his eyes.

CHAPTER 32

"The *Excalibur*'s standing down," Talen said.

I stared into Eledan's crystal blue eyes, seeing the damaged soul inside. His heart beat against my palm, so vulnerable, even as he commanded a newly sentient planet. Weren't we all Faerie's children? Good and bad, light and dark, unseelie and seelie, wild and sidhe. I had to embrace the dark and the light to prevail.

"Don't fight the humans," I told Eledan. "Don't start the cycle again."

His throat moved as he swallowed. His chest rose and fell. His heart thudded its racing beat.

"You are not your brother. That's a good thing."

His brow pinched into deep-set lines, and then his hand broke away from the oak roots, and clamped on mine over his heart, perhaps to pull me off him or to hold me closer, his face too muddled with emotion to know.

"They'll kill us all," he whispered.

"No. You were right. We are so alike, and I refused to see it. We will end this war. Together. But not like this." It was the only way. I had to stop fighting my past and stop fighting him.

His hand squeezed mine, and slowly, the roots binding him to the throne unraveled. After they'd withdrawn, he stayed seated, his gaze roaming my face, looking for the lies that didn't exist. The time for lies was over.

I lifted my hand from his chest, but he snatched my wrist and held firm, his gaze spearing into mine. Whatever he wanted to say, he didn't voice it.

I didn't need the words. I knew. He had only ever wanted to be seen and heard, and have something real in his life instead of living from one illusion to the next. Everyone in this room, we saw him. Some might not look on him with kindness, but they saw him all the same, and that was all he'd ever wanted.

I pulled my arm free and backed away. "The dark fae are here," I announced feeling the weight of a thousand minds filling Arcon below our feet.

Turning, with Eledan at my back, I admired my friends, each one worth more than life to me.

Marshal Kellee—his marshal's star glinting—looked at me with a strange sense of awe on his face. With his claws exposed and eyes aglow, he was more vakaru than man, and that was how I needed him, because Hapters' dark fae weren't the only souls who had arrived among Arcon's foundation. The minds of countless long-dead vakaru skirted the fringes of my thoughts.

"The legion is here." The words carried deep into Arcon, down into the shadows. "We are the Messenger and our time has come."

I loved these people. I'd do anything for them. "Together, we are light and dark, just as it was always meant to be. There is only one battle left to fight, and it is not with the humans of Sol. We must stop the Hunt and return the polestar to Faerie. That is the only way to end this."

The grief on Kellee's face betrayed him. We all knew how this ended. We'd known all along, but it was right. That star on his chest stood for everything right. He would not stop me from doing the right thing.

Talen stood tall, proud, my untouchable silver fae, but I didn't need a bond to know how his mask hid the pain inside. I would die to save them, and they wouldn't stop me.

"We will return to Faerie with the Dark Legion. That is where this ends."

Magic tingled and stroked around my legs and up my back. Not the blinding, overwhelming blast of the polestar, but its smoother, gentler touch, as though I was now ready to control it. The tek-whip, hooked at my belt, hissed and fizzled to life. Nightshade wings blurred into existence. Like smoke and glitter, they billowed over my shoulders and drifted toward the ceiling. I barely felt their weight, their burden light. I'd come a long way from the saru who'd fought her way out of the delivery crate and into a world that would sooner see her dead than breathing. I was so many things to so many people, and this war needed me to be those things to end it. *You must survive yourself to unlock your truth.*

I was ready.

Talen knelt and bowed his head. Kellee followed. Sota and Hulia did the same, and then, from behind me, I heard a rustle of movement and turned to see Eledan on a single knee, his right hand fisted over his crackling heart and his head bowed.

We were all ready.

"That was the most badass thing I have ever seen," Sota beamed, striding along the *Excalibur*'s new corridors beside me. The ship had taken on a green aura, and just like Calicto, its tek was changing before our eyes—or *his* tek, as Talen had confirmed the *Excalibur* was male. My wings and aura had vanished. My reflection in the *Excalibur*'s glass told the world I looked the same as I always had. Unassuming clothes, and whip mostly-concealed at my hip, beneath my coat. On the outside, I was Kesh Lasota, illegal Calicto messenger, but on the inside, I was something else entirely, but still Kesh. Still me. I'd never give that truth up.

Sota's enthusiasm had shored up my own since we'd returned to the *Excalibur,* shortly after I'd stopped Eledan from killing thousands of people. Eledan had retreated somewhere inside the living ship, while Kellee and the others descended on the command deck, familiarizing themselves with the newborn spacefaring vessel under Talen's guidance.

"What did you do to Eledan?" he asked.

We approached the obs room. "I stopped fighting him."

Sota mulled that over. As a wardrone, the idea of not fighting was alien to him, but he also had personal AI protocols, which meant he was more than capable of thinking instead of shooting.

"Isn't that dangerous?" he finally asked.

The obs room door opened ahead.

"Yes, but I got nowhere as his enemy." I let Sota enter the room first. "Doesn't mean I trust him, though."

Sirius observed Sol's fleet drifting in Calicto's airspace on the screens, his hands clasped behind his back. The smallest smile touched his lips as he saw me and turned away from the screens. Eledan's book lay innocuously on the table, seemingly nothing more than an old tome.

Pierce sat across the table, looking grim and wrung out.

Earthens didn't cope well under Faerie's influence for long. After the *Excalibur*'s transformation, she likely wondered if she was losing her mind. She watched me pick up the book and tuck it neatly under my arm.

"We don't want this war," I told her. "The least you can do is speak with your people and ask them to back off. We haven't fired on them and we won't, as long as they keep their fingers off the triggers too. Do you understand?"

She nodded. "Now that I've lost my ship, can my crew return to the Sol fleet?"

"After you've hailed your counterpart in that fleet and told them how we mean them no harm."

"They won't believe me."

"Then it's your job to convince them."

She sighed. "My crew and I have been off-grid for weeks. They won't accept a message from me, from this ship, when it's clearly infected with Faerie. I'll need to speak with them in person."

"We can change that."

"You'll need to be with me."

Sirius stiffened. He and the others would not react well to my visiting the human fleet.

"Look..." Pierce rubbed her temple. "If I tell them the Messenger is real, if I tell them any of this, they'll think my mind has been compromised and they'll attack. If you come with me and speak with them, we could come to an amicable working solution. Despite our captivity and your fae's... invasive touch, you have not hurt us, and I appreciate that. The Sol Alliance does not want war either. We saw what Faerie did to Halow, but we will fight if we must. You can bridge our differences, Kesh, and stop this from getting worse."

They knew my myth. I had to go. "All right."

"Kesh...?" Sota queried.

"You'll both be by my side."

Sirius nodded, happier guarding me than leaving me to walk among Earthens without him. Kellee would hate it, but knowing his and Talen's past, I couldn't take either of them to an Earthen ship without risking the humans capturing them.

All I had to do was convince the Sol fleet that a sentient planet and ship and a legion of fae monsters didn't intend to hurt them. It wouldn't be easy, and I wasn't entirely sure it was true, but if I succeeded, we'd be one step closer to peace.

I nodded. "I'll have Hulia help your crew get ready to depart. Sirius, hail the fleet and tell them I will personally escort the *Excalibur* crew back to them. Let's make this happen as peacefully as possible. Nobody has to die today."

Leaving Sota and Sirius with Pierce, I headed straight for the command deck to debrief Kellee and Talen, Eledan's book still tucked under my arm. The route had changed, corridors twisting and branching off where they hadn't before, but on arriving, I found them standing at the great curved window, ignoring all the bleeping tek flashing warnings and watching the Earthen fleet shimmer in Calicto's low atmosphere.

Before I left, I had to tell Kellee I'd sensed the vakaru and ask Talen not to bond with the ship. Two conversations I dreaded. My next words could cost me them. So, instead of speaking, I climbed the steps onto the deck and planted myself between Kellee's simmering presence and Talen's icy stillness. We watched the fleet and the stars behind, and I wished I had more time with them, just to stand and watch and be in the moment.

"Do you believe in destiny?" I asked, echoing the same question I'd asked Sirius.

Kellee shifted and cocked his head toward me, keeping his gaze on the fleet. "Before I met you, I didn't."

Talen lifted a single shoulder, agreeing with Kellee. Having them so close reminded me of all the things I'd done, and some things I shouldn't have, and how they'd been beside me through it all. It had been worth it. I wouldn't change a damn thing.

"Kellee..."

Hearing the tension in my tone, he turned to me, his mouth set in a firm line. "If this is about Eledan, I don't care how you did it, just that you could control him—"

"The vakaru wraiths are here."

He flinched and took a moment to digest those words. "What?"

"They're all there. I don't know how... I think Eledan had a hand in it. His heart is Valand's piece of the polestar. It's likely the wraiths recognized it."

Kellee's lips tightened, a snarl threatening to bubble through. "Then it's a trick," he dismissed, unfolding his arms to make way for sprouting claws.

Selfishly, I wished it were a trick. "Not this time. They're here and..." I swallowed, because the next words might lose me my vakaru, but the words meant he'd have a future *after* me. "It's possible the lifewell below Arcon can bring them back."

His face crumpled. He blinked too quickly, and a color I'd never seen before bloomed in his eyes, a blue so pale it was almost white. "Don't say these things unless they are true."

"I wouldn't lie about this, and I don't lie to you, not anymore."

"Did Eledan tell you this?" He didn't wait for my answer and instead glared at the swarm of ships outside the window. "Anything from him is a lie."

"I thought so too, for the longest time, but he lived in his brother's shadow for millennia. He never wanted to rule. He never wanted any of this. He took what he had and made it work for him. He survived. I think he wants Oberon's shadow gone from him. He'll return your vakaru to right his brother's wrongs, if you talk with him."

"You don't know this. He's never done anything for anyone but himself. The cost will be too high."

I had looked into Eledan's eyes, and instead of searching for all the bad in him, I'd looked for the good. Although it was buried so far down it was almost undetectable, I had found it. "He built Arcon for this moment, and he led us here. I know this, Kellee, because we share the polestar, and when I put my hand on his heart, I knew he was sorry for everything he could not stop. A thousand years with humans changed him, even if he believes otherwise. I felt the hollow regret in him. He knows he screwed up. He created the Hunt, and he's trying to make it right as only he knows. We just didn't want to see."

Kellee lowered his head. He looked at his hands, at the claws growing from his nails.

"You need to go to him and listen. I know it will be hard, but isn't it worth it for the chance to bring the vakaru back?"

Kellee jerked his head up. "Come with me."

"I can't," I said. Talen's hands settled around my upper arms, sensing I needed him close. "I have to take Pierce back to the Earthens, and you need to do this alone."

Kellee's gaze flicked to Talen behind me, and the hope on his face made losing him seem all right. He would be okay. He'd be right where he was supposed to be, with his people.

I handed him the book. "Take this to Eledan and tell him to wait for me. He'll know what it means."

Kellee cupped my face, careful to keep his claws angled away. His mouth slanted over mine. His tongue swept in, and the simple saru part of me sang. He meant everything to me, but I knew he'd give me up for his vakaru.

The kiss slowed and pulled apart. He rested his forehead against mine. "Kesh... if this happens..."

"Go."

He swallowed and brushed his lips against mine so I could taste his want and desire and need to stay, but he had somewhere else to be, and his destiny, one I wasn't part of, called to him. He turned away, and with every step, my heart stuttered. I wanted to call him back. When he paused, I grasped at the idea that he wouldn't leave, as wrong as it was. He turned, tarnished gold star in hand. He looked at that star, emotion passing over his face, and then he stepped up and pinned it to my coat. Meeting my gaze, he nodded once, assured he'd done the right thing, and then he left.

Talen's hands tightened on my arms. He pulled me back against his chest. The sound of Talen's heart and soft, measured breathing surrounded me. His arms folded around me. He bowed his head. The side of his chin brushed my temple.

I almost couldn't speak, and when I did, the words were just a whisper. "It felt like goodbye."

 ellee

ELEDAN HAD ONCE TOLD me we were on the same side. He'd told me many things, all of it twisted and manipulative. I'd prefer to kill him than talk with him, but it had never once occurred to me that he might actually be *helping* me. Helping us. And I wasn't entirely sure how to feel about that. But Kesh was sure, and I trusted her judgment. She knew him better than any of us. If he could do the impossible, then I'd listen. I owed Kesh and my people that.

The ship's growing corridors led me right to him in a room I'd never seen before. Wires and tek climbed the walls, making pathways for whatever information flowed along them. It looked like liquid light, like silver veins, and Eledan sat in the middle of the floor, with one knee drawn up to his chest. He didn't look up, and even as I approached, he stayed staring at the same spot on the floor. I'd seen the bastard smile, heard him laugh, seen him mad and vicious, but I hadn't seen him like this. Light rippled over him, catching in his pale skin and highlighting long strands of black hair.

Coming around to stand in front of him, I had to stop myself from dumping his book on the floor near his boots. I could be civilized, mostly, as long as he didn't rub my fur the wrong way. Crouching to his eye level, I gently set the book down and tapped its thick cover. "Kesh said to wait for her and that you'd know what that meant."

He shifted his gaze to take a long look at the book. Was this the first time he'd seen it in centuries?

"I skimmed the pages on the way over. It's empty," I told him.

"Hmm," he mused. "It didn't used to be."

He lifted his eyes, and their usual hardness had softened, as though he were weary. I'd tried not to look too long at him before, not caring for his typical fae appearance, but now I did look, and I saw more to him. More lines around his mouth, more of a slouch to his shoulders, and more of the warfae marks as they snaked beneath his collar. Maybe I hadn't cared to notice him until now, and maybe I'd tried to forget he was also a victim, but it was hard to sympathize with a victim who victimized others. For what he'd done to Kesh, I'd never forgive him, even if she had.

"She also said the vakaru are here. Do you know anything about that?"

The tiredness scrubbed out of his eyes, and their lethal sharpness returned. "She did, did she? And what do you want from me?"

He knew, but he would make me beg. Damn him. "You and I will never see things the same. We are not alike, and we are not friends, never will be, but Kesh believes you want change and that you've been helping it happen in your own way. Is that true?"

He skipped his gaze away and scanned the pulsing veins crawling up the walls. "Creating life is such a special gift, one often forgotten on Faerie, where life is immortal, but not here and not on Arcon. You know what it means to be immortal and forget how precious life is."

I was sure his rambling had a purpose, so I humored him. "I do."

"Your vakaru believed themselves immortal. My brother took that from them, from you."

I gritted my teeth and rode out his abrasive tone. "Can you bring them back or not?"

He winced, breathed in, and held that breath. Why this should be so hard a decision for him I'd never know, but if he agreed, it wouldn't matter.

He sighed out that heavy breath. "For you? No. But for the Queen of Hearts?" He bowed his head, and I was reminded of how I'd seen him in my dreams, and how I knew he loved her.

He huffed a soft, dry laugh. "She said she sees me, but with her, I cannot tell the truth from the lies."

"She sees you. If she didn't, she would have ripped out your heart a second time on that throne."

He flinched, reliving the memory of Kesh doing exactly that, and maybe, just maybe, I felt a pang of regret along with him.

"She will never think of me as she thinks of you."

He was probably right, but *never* was a word so often thrown around it had lost its weight. "Never is a lie."

"For immortals, but not for mortals." He picked up his book, and climbed to his feet, realigning his clothes and running his long fingers through his hair.

His words rang in my ears, reminding me of the ticking clock and how the time Kesh had left was fast running out.

"Come, then, vakaru. Let's see what Arcon and Calicto can do and if they will grant the return of your people."

esh

THE SHUTTLE RAMP lowered and three rows of armed Sol Alliance guards greeted us, glistening tek-pistols drawn and mean looks on their human faces. Tek glinted in their eyes and the lining of their uniforms. Even after waking on Calicto and now residing in an organic tek-ship, seeing humans bristling with so much tek was jarring.

Sota and Sirius flanked me. I waved them down to stop them from shooting into aggressive-defensive mode and getting us killed in a hail of bullets before anyone had drawn breath to say hello.

Lifting my hands, I showed them I was unarmed, for all the good it'd do if things got tense. Sota and Sirius mirrored me. These humans expected submission, despite us being lethal without any obvious weapons.

"Pierce, you wanna come out and show these nice people how we're all friends here?" I called.

Captain Pierce, dressed in her neatly pressed Sol Alliance uniform, emerged from behind my line. "Don't shoot," she told her people. "We have three shuttles waiting to dock. The *Excalibur* crew are all present and in good health." She stepped in front of me, and for the first time, I noticed how much shorter than me she was. Despite her size, she had no problem putting herself in front of three-dozen nervous trigger fingers.

Had Talen or Kellee been here, this would have already turned into a bloodbath.

"We're sorry we borrowed your ship," I said, wondering if *sorry* cut it, but it was all I had. "But the situation required it."

No official had stepped forward, and as nobody replied, we waited. A drone hovered at the back of the line, feeding the footage to whoever was running this show.

"What you see happening to the *Excalibur* now was... unexpected, but we can explain, and I'm willing to explain, if you'll allow me."

The door behind the barrier of humans opened. The lines parted, and a tall, thin male approached, gleaming in his tek-lined Sol Alliance dark blues. I'd spent so long in the company of males with hair longer than mine that this man's grade 1 cut lent him a savage appearance. The shrewd look continued in his cold eyes. This was the man I'd be negotiating with. He looked as though he'd been chipped from stone.

"Lower your weapons," he commanded his troops. Guns rattled as each was relaxed. "Captain Pierce, are you being coerced in any way?"

"None, Admiral."

The admiral's lips twisted. "Your reputation precedes you, Kesh Lasota. The Messenger?" His eyes dropped to the whip at my hip and then examined Sota beside me, reading the clues and confirmation. Before Faerie, I'd been a symbol of hope to Halow's remaining people. I had no idea if that was still the case, or if they knew I was also *technically* Faerie's queen. I probably wouldn't mention that recent development, or the fact I happened to be the Nightshade too. This was complicated enough.

I lowered my hands. "May we talk like civilized people?"

The admiral's penetrating glare landed on Sirius and found its match. The man's eyes narrowed, and Sirius dead-eyed him right back, his spicy magic tickling my nose. He was getting annoyed, and as I'd learned, an annoyed Sirius was about as easy to tame as an angry, wet pixie.

"Okay, all right..." I said, tacking on a smile to ease the tension. "We're talking, see? Your people are waiting to dock. Let's start with letting them go free and continue from there, shall we?"

The admiral nodded and extended his hand. "I'm Admiral Briggs, and on behalf of the Sol Alliance and Earthen people, I welcome you and your escorts aboard the *Chesterain.*"

I took his warm, firm hand in mine and shook. Perhaps this would be easier than I'd imagined?

"Stark, take our guests to their quarters," Briggs ordered.

The soldier sprang into motion. "Sir."

Briggs returned his gaze to me. "Allow me to receive the *Excalibur* crew with Captain Pierce, and we'll meet at fifteen hundred hours."

Being on Faerie time, I had no idea when fifteen hundred hours was, but I hoped it wasn't long. There was a lot more happening than this little meet and greet, and every moment away from Faerie was another moment the Hunt gained strength.

I nodded and followed Stark into the depths of a smaller

tek-ship than the *Excalibur*. Our quarters were small, neat, and functional, exactly as Earthens liked it. I missed Shinj's organic chaos.

Sota appeared at my door moments after Stark had left. "They didn't lock us in, so I guess we're not prisoners?"

"Will wonders never cease?" I mumbled dryly. I poked at the bed, finding it board-hard. I had no plans to stay long enough to sleep in it. I didn't spot any cameras in the room. "Listening devices?" I asked.

"None," Sota confirmed.

Sirius's scowling presence filled the doorway. "These humans and their tek are making my arm itch."

"Your arm can't itch," I told him. "It doesn't have surface receptors."

"Tell that to my arm."

His lips quirked, and Sota double-blinked, then thumbed at the guardian beside him. "Was that a joke?"

"More of a humorous observation," Sirius deadpanned.

Sota swung his wide eyes to me. "He has a sense of humor? When did this happen?"

"On Faerie." I smiled, enjoying the ease of the moment. By Faerie, we didn't get many. "He hides it way down under all the grousing. You have to look for it."

As they hadn't confined us to our quarters, we roamed the *Chesterain*, taking stock of the efficient Sol Alliance crew and their careful glances. Sirius deliberately kept his tek-arm outside his coat, as though it somehow made him closer to them, and many Earthens openly stared at the guardian. Among them, he looked alien. Too tall, his ear tips prominent through his mass of braided red hair, his eyes too green, and his russet red and brown clothes like nothing an Earthen would wear. He soaked up the attention without comment.

Our self-guided tour was interrupted by a guard who

escorted us to a comfortable room, complete with a seating area, desk, and bank of monitoring screens. Briggs waited for us inside. His personal drone loitered at the fringes of the room.

Sota gave it a good once-over and muttered, "Pinnacle Attack Drone."

Which meant that innocuous little ball of tek could microwave our insides before I could free my whip. So Briggs didn't trust us. I couldn't blame him. A Faerie guardian, an upgraded AI wardrone, and the Messenger were a formidable force to meet with.

"Captain Pierce had quite the story to tell," the admiral mused, standing with his back to the narrow strip of windows. Outside, Calicto's curving surface shimmered like a marble in the black. "It will take some time for the Sol Council to work through it all."

Time.

Something I didn't have.

"Sir, there are forces at work on Faerie that could have consequences far worse than Oberon's stalled war."

"The Hunt. Yes, we are aware of its occurrence. Tell me more about this Hunt."

I glanced at Sirius. Faerie's law was his forte, not mine. He nodded and began to relay all we knew of the Hunt, how it was formed, where it had hid, and how it had come to be free. I wouldn't blame the Earthens if they decided to retreat behind their new defense net and stay there, shutting the gate on the rest of the worlds. Kellee had believed they'd do exactly that, but the thunder darkening Briggs's face as Sirius spoke told me a different story. Kellee had once admired Earthens enough to consider allying his vakaru with them. Today, we could right the past.

As I listened to Sirius's deep voice describe the last few

months of my life, everything I'd been through solidified in my mind. I'd blamed Eledan for manipulating us, but reliving events from the outside reminded me of everything he couldn't have controlled. He'd had his touch in everything, but suggestion was just that. The implementation belonged to me, Kellee, Talen, Sota, Sirius, and Aeon.

"You have a plan to subdue the Hunt?" Briggs asked.

"We have its creator, and while he can be unpredictable, I believe he wants this to end, like we all do."

"And he knows how to stop it?" Briggs asked.

I thought of Eledan's warfae marks, the original marks given to him and Oberon, and considered how the Wild Ones had persuaded Eledan to bring his nightmares to life. The book with its blank pages was part of that; otherwise, Ailish wouldn't want it. Eledan, the marks, the book, and me. "Yes, he does."

"If the Hunt is contained or stopped," Briggs considered, "what will happen to Faerie then?"

"Faerie never wanted this war," Sirius said. "She has no interest in Sol or its inhabitants."

"Then how do you explain that?" Briggs gestured at the window and the obvious green and blue ball that was a living Calicto, once a tek-only human world.

Sirius glanced at me, hoping I had the answer.

"That is..." I swallowed. "I'm not sure what that is. There are lifewells all over."

"On Earth?"

"I don't know for certain."

"Do you know?" Briggs asked Sirius.

"It is likely there was a lifewell on Earth. It would have been the source of all life on your planet. I don't know if it's still active. Oberon rarely spoke of Earth or Sol. He saw it as a... failed experiment."

Briggs breathed deeply. I imagined being told you owed everything you knew and everything you were to an alien planet took some getting used to.

"I would like to help you, but it's not my decision. I will need to liaise with the Sol Alliance council. I can do nothing more at this time."

It was enough to know they had no intention of firing on us like they had on Hapters.

The admiral's gaze fell to Kellee's star and recognition sparked. Perhaps he knew it as a symbol of justice? "This is a delicate situation," he continued. "Whatever is happening on Calicto is of great concern, not least because I personally observed a planet *steal* a Sol-made ship out of the sky and turn it into a living creature. We will be monitoring the planet closely, and if we observe any signs of a threat, the Sol Alliance will defend itself."

We'd do the same.

He offered me his hand again. "These are interesting times, Messenger. I believe we are on the cusp of peace, but the Hunt concerns me. If you can subdue it, you'll have my support and the support of my fleet, but beyond that, I cannot make any further promises. Don't fuck it up, Messenger."

I tightened my hand around his and returned his smile. "We'll do our best, Admiral."

CHAPTER 35

ellee

THE BOWELS of Arcon groaned louder the deeper we descended. Wisps tossed their light around, casting crawling shadows along the walls. My vakaru senses itched. Those shadows could be alive. Just because I had unseelie in me didn't mean I was immune to them. Hapters had proven that. Now, all those Hapters monsters were here. I'd have preferred Talen next to me than Eledan.

The *king* walked ahead, dark hair swishing without a care in the world, and here I was, following him into the darkness. This was not how I'd imagined events would go.

The deeper we went, the cooler the air became. It licked at my face and neck, and had my skin bristling. Even the air was alive down here, and I had no choice but to breathe its poison in. Fucking Faerie.

Winged dark fae clung to the ceiling and watched us pass beneath them. They looked like hairless bats, if bats were man-sized. I'd seen the monsters of Hapters. What we found down here wouldn't get any prettier.

"Nightshade..." Hissing voices echoed at our passing. Not for me, but for Kesh. They sensed we were all connected, which was why none had decided to impale itself on my claws. Yet.

The green orb chamber had the same throbbing energy as Shinj's two hearts. Life magic leaked outward, washing over my face, sticking to everything, and trying to smother me in Faerie. I wrinkled my nose, fighting off a sneeze. Shadow after shadow writhed over the dome walls. I'd seen them on Valand, when Talen had tried to subdue them. Those wraiths were my vakaru or their essence. The injustice had my teeth aching.

"Control yourself, *Kellee*." Eledan smirked.

"I am," I growled back, "or you'd have more holes in you."

"Are you sure you can wrangle a vakaru army? It would be a terrible mistake to bring them back only to make the situation worse."

The bastard's smile was hanging out on his lips again. I knew how to wipe that smile off his face. "What's with you and this key you told me about in a dream?"

Sure enough, he straightened and the smile vanished. Turning his back on me, he approached the huge green orb. Light flowed over and around him, not consuming him, just lapping at his edges.

"To do this," he began, raising his voice against the skitter and scurry of claws marking the walls, "there will be a sacrifice."

I wasn't getting my answer about the key, then. "What kind of sacrifice?" I inched closer, absorbing the beat of magic.

"A death for a life." He stared into the green.

"What?"

"Did you think their resurrection would be free?" He slid his attention to me, looking every part the bewitching fae well versed in luring innocents to their deaths. "The lifewell can rejuvenate, but to bring the dead back to life, new life must come from somewhere."

"That's not how it worked when you healed me here before."

"You weren't dead when I brought you here, just close to it."

A death for a life? I couldn't tell if he was full of karushit. He knew I wanted this and would do anything for it. "What life do you suggest?" The thought alone knotted my insides.

Eledan considered the question before looking back the way we'd come. "There are hundreds of dark fae here and more arriving. They seem like a reasonable trade to have your battle-hardened vakaru back, don't you think?"

Kill the dark fae to bring the vakaru back?

I couldn't do it.

I could not take a life in exchange for the lives of others. That was not my way.

"Hmm..." he mused. "So close to having your world back, yet so far."

"You're a real piece of work, Eledan. There's no mystery why Mab didn't care for you like she did Ober—"

I had the wall at my back and Eledan's cool fingers around my throat before I could finish speaking his brother's name. Unfortunately for him, I also had my claws lodged beneath his ribs, ready to thrust in and zip open his insides. His fingers squeezed, and the Mad Prince snarled in my face, his true fae colors showing.

"Go on." I bared my teeth. "Push me. I'd like nothing more than to gut you right here."

The words wormed their way through his rage. He blinked, caught himself, and withdrew, looking down at the tears in his shirt where my claws had dug in. I hadn't cut him, but we both knew I could have.

"If you aren't willing to make the sacrifice"—he tugged his shirt straight—"I will."

"No, you won't. If you want to redeem your brother's fuckups, you won't touch the dark fae. Leave them be. They've been through enough."

"The vakaru are better fighters. We will need them against the Hunt and against those on Faerie who do not want to end this war."

"It doesn't matter." I backed away. This was over. "I'm not condemning the dark fae just because they're convenient for you."

"Don't your vakaru deserve the same?" Green light poured over his face, hollowing his cheeks.

"My vakaru are gone." I had the wraiths, and with the dark fae, it would have to be enough. "If you make a move to sacrifice the dark fae, I'll do everything in my power to stop you, key or not."

He glimpsed my claws. "Then you had better hope Kesh can control the dark fae where Talen could not, because we will not get a second chance to stop the Hunt."

"She will, and if you knew her like you think you do, you'd know it too."

He took one long look at the lifewell. "I suppose I do."

KESH ARRIVED at the command deck with Sirius and Sota in tow. She saw me at the window and tripped over her feet and her words. Whatever she'd been saying to Sota, it was forgotten as she came across the room in a flurry of her dark coat and hair. The slightest flicker of vulnerability about her had me wanting to meet her halfway. I stood firm, watched her climb the steps, and braced for whatever words she flung my way. Instead of attacking, she threw herself in my arms, the press of her soft and warm and achingly familiar. I breathed in her leather and metal smell, wishing we were alone.

"What happened?" she asked.

"There were complications. As with all things Eledan, the cost was too high."

She lifted her head, and the fear in her eyes caught my breath.

She'd thought she'd lose me. I'd been so consumed by the thought of resurrecting the vakaru that I hadn't seen her concern.

She fumbled with the star, trying to unclip it.

"Keep it." She looked up with those fine, emotive eyes, equal parts fierce and vulnerable, and I couldn't stand to see her pain a second longer. I crushed her close, folding her into my arms, not caring about our audience. "You're never getting rid of me."

Never is a lie.

Not for mortals.

By cyn, I wanted to take her away from here and run so far time couldn't catch us, but she wouldn't come.

"The wraiths are here," I added, pushing aside selfish thoughts, "as are the dark fae. Eledan believes the last lifewell is on Faerie. He said the dark fae will travel there next."

"When?" She pulled out of my arms, her barriers slamming down.

"When you say so."

She nodded and absently looked toward Sirius and Sota.

"We had some success. The Earthens won't fire on us, as long as we don't do anything to alarm them."

I snorted. My being alive routinely alarmed them. "I never doubted you."

"Then we should ready the ship to return to Faerie," she said, firm in her conviction. "I need to see Eledan..."

Just like that, she was back in motion, her focus on the task ahead. I rarely felt the passage of time so keenly as when I was with her. Everything in me ached to pull her back, to capture her light and savor it before she burned out.

"Find Talen," she said, already halfway to the door. "Ask him if the *Excalibur* will help us without him having to bond with the ship." The next words she muttered almost too softly to hear. "I can't lose him as well."

After she'd left, Sirius and Sota lingered with me in the quiet, their thoughts likely along the same lines as mine. There wasn't enough time left to love her how we wanted.

esh

"WE'RE RETURNING TO FAERIE," I said, entering the long, narrow hall that had once been a cafeteria but was now more of an atrium filled with sprouting leaves and tangled roots. Had I not been accustomed to Shinj's strange organic living, I would have struggled to adjust to this.

Eledan sat at a table, his book spread before him, fingers flicking over the empty pages.

I pulled out a chair, detaching it from its nest of metal roots, and sat across from him. "It's time you told me about this book."

He continued to tickle the pages, running his fingers over them as though he could see something on its plain age-mottled pages.

"How do you live knowing you die a little more every day?" he asked in that mad, poetic way of his.

I slammed my hand down on the open book. His head

snapped up, a snarl bubbling on his lips. He could growl all he liked. I was done with his karushit. "What is wrong with you? We are going back to stop the Hunt and correct your monumental fuckup. Get your head out of your dreams and in the game."

Dark lashes shuttered over too-blue eyes, my words chipping off some of his attitude.

"Why does Ailish want this book? Why was it in Sirius's knoll, and why is it empty? What's so special about these blank pages?"

He tugged the book out from under my hand, glowered hard, and slammed it closed to spite me. Glittery dust wafted into the air.

"Eledan, there isn't time for your drama—"

He tapped the spine and drawled, "*The* Origin *of the Wild Hunt.*"

"I know what it's called."

After working his jaw, he tried again. "Titles are never just words. *Messenger*, *Wraithmaker*, do you think those titles are just words?"

"No."

"*No?*" He laughed.

My palm itched to slap him. I needed the sane Eledan, not the tek-exposed insane version, although at least the insane version was honest. "So tell me what I'm missing." Folding my arms to keep the urge to lash out under control, I leaned back. "Tell me what my saru mind can't comprehend of your fabulous masterpiece full of blank pages."

He rolled his eyes and sighed. "This book *is* the origin of the Wild Hunt."

"Were you this annoying before getting stuck on Halow?"

Muttering something fae and foul, he flipped open the hardcover, lunged across the table, grabbed my hand, and shoved my palm against the page. Nothing happened. The pages were still blank.

"I don't know what I'm looking at."

"Don't look. *Feel*."

He pushed my hand harder into the paper, and just as I was about to yank free, a cool, slippery void opened beneath my touch. I couldn't see the hole—the page was just a page—but I could feel it. It felt like the nowhere hole Oberon had kept Eledan in. Like it went on forever with no end and no beginning. Like it might swallow me and keep me in its pages forever.

I yanked my hand out from under his and cradled it to my chest, rubbing off the oily feel. "What is that?"

"*That* is an empty book. That is the origin, where it all began, where the Hunt was first conceived. The Wild Ones wanted a horror story, so I gave them one. Those pages are the prison we must return the Hunt to."

The title wasn't just a title; it was a description. The book *was* the origin of the Wild Hunt. That monstrous thing had come from its pages, and it had to go back in there.

"Now she understands." He fell back into his chair with a huff. "So clever and so stupid all at once. I suppose that explains your infatuation with the vakaru..." He rubbed the bridge of his nose.

"How by Faerie do we get the Hunt back into a book?" The Hunt was enormous, and the more it consumed, the bigger it got. I couldn't even wrap my head around wrangling the thing into a book.

"With the light of the polestar," Eledan replied flatly.

I shoved the book away, not wanting its cold, hungry hollowness to leak out. The thing felt like death, like the Hunt itself, and that was why it had been in Sirius's library, I realized. Autumn *was* death.

Light attracted dark. The polestar and the Hunt. Then Eledan and I, as the last two pieces, were bait.

"Do you have a plan?" I asked.

His eyebrows lifted. "One we both survive?"

I took that to mean no. "Okay, so... we need to get the Hunt near the book, right?" He gave me a droll look. He'd been thinking on this for a long time, maybe centuries, and here I was trying to bring something new to the table. "Let's work with that. We lure it in and corral it like Talen did with the dark fae on Hapters?"

"The polestar must be complete for its light to sufficiently tempt the Hunt anywhere near this book."

A complete polestar meant Eledan and I wouldn't be around to see it. "Must it be the polestar's light? Can't it be some other bright light? Can't we... I don't know... ask Faerie for another star?" He gave me that look again, that one that told me I'd been born yesterday and couldn't comprehend how superior he was. "You've had hundreds of years to think up a solution... At least I'm trying." The anger in my voice disguised the tremor of fear. "You're just going to sit there and sulk?"

"Well, yes, I think I might. I have that right."

"Where is the general who commanded Oberon's armies? Where is the prince who fought the dark legions long before they were cast out of Faerie? You weren't always a useless waste of space."

"That prince died a long time ago."

"Why? Because you got trapped with humans? You're capable of more than this. I know you are. You built Arcon. You practically made New Calicto what it is, and you brought us all back here for a reason. So... get off your ass and help."

His expression ticked, something unlocking and turning over. The change was subtle, and instead of mulling over what he couldn't do, an intense new spark brightened his eyes. "Arcon...?" he mumbled, gazing off into the jungle-like room. "Hmm... you're right. There may be another way." When he returned his attention to me, his smile had returned. "How far is Kesh Lasota willing to go?"

"To stop the war and save the people I love? To the end and beyond."

"Good." He stood and scooped up his wretched book. "Then we had best get to work."

ELEDAN'S VERSION OF "WE" apparently meant just him. Moments after I'd rallied him into action, he slipped off my radar and disappeared somewhere inside the *Excalibur*'s evolving corridors. Getting rid of him was never easy, so the fact he'd vanished likely meant he was scheming. As long as he was scheming a way to get the Hunt back in his book, I'd take the fallout when it happened.

I found Talen by asking Sota to scan the ship and went to him inside a strange dome-shaped chamber. Silver veins throbbed up the walls. Glittering dust hung in the air, each speck glowing in time with the silvery throb. I'd seen a similar room on Shinj. Navigation. But this chamber was still growing into its purpose.

Talen stood at its center with his head tilted back and eyes closed. He looked every piece the surreal vision of untouchable fae. His long white hair hung unbound down his back. In the strange pulsating light, each strand gleamed like silver. He'd never looked so alien or so beautiful.

This was where he was supposed to be.

Did the *Excalibur* call to him now?

I considered turning away, but his head lowered and a smile tugged at his mouth. "Stay."

He knew me so well.

"Eledan's book is how we stop the Hunt," I said. "He's gone off somewhere to make that happen, but I don't trust him not to sacrifice us to get what he wants."

He watched me approach, and when I was close enough, he pulled me close, tucking me under his arm so he could plant a soft kiss on my forehead. By cyn, how could he be so gentle in one breath and so devastating in another? I melted against him and sighed, letting the wiry tension fade.

"Eledan manipulated us here..." I whispered, wanting the secret out before it festered. I couldn't keep anything from him, from any of them, anymore. "He played us like we're his toys."

"I know."

"You do?"

"It's his nature. He cannot change who he is. Dreams are his life. Asking him to stop would be like asking him to die."

I'd never thought of it like that. The Dreamweaver was who he was, just like we all were who we were. "The Hunt escaped his book," I muttered, looping an arm round Talen's waist and molding myself to his side. "He says only the polestar can lure it back inside."

"Hmm... light attracts dark. It has always been this way."

His rumbling voice traveled through me, sinking into my bones. I used to wake tucked into his side like this, feeling as though there were no safer place than in his arms. I wanted more of those times. "Do you think Kellee knows Eledan manipulated him?"

Talen smiled. "Kellee knows there's an art to dealing with the fae."

I rested my head against his chest and listened to his

heart. He had talked of dreams being Eledan's nature, but what of Talen's nature? He was a pilot without a ship.

"What does the ship say to you?"

"He is young and afraid."

I looked up to see Talen's distant gaze, his thoughts turning inward.

"The human fleet frightens him," he continued, smile falling away. "Calicto frightens him. We frighten him... I'm attempting to soothe him, but doing so while not connected is not easy."

"Is the *Excalibur* stable enough to take us back to Faerie?"

He paused and listened to something I had no hope of hearing. "Possibly, given enough time to acclimate."

"How much time?"

"A few weeks."

I did not have weeks. "Can you persuade him to go sooner?"

"Kesh..." Talen eased from my arms. "The ship is a newborn. I'm preventing him from ejecting us all into the atmosphere. Asking him to do anything more would be tantamount to asking a child to go to war. There has never been a tek-and-magic hybrid ship. I'm doing the best I can, but I do not have the power to tame him in a few short hours."

"The dark fae will soon return to Faerie. We need to be there, Talen. I don't have weeks. You know that..."

His cheek fluttered. He looked down and, just as quickly, turned that silvery gaze on me again. "I can only control this ship as its pilot."

Memories flashed of the pilot I'd shot to save back on Hapters. I'd known him just minutes, but having seen that pilot and listened to him beg me to kill him... "No."

"It is the only way. The *Excalibur* could be a hundred times more powerful than Shinj. Magic continues to warp the ship's tek, creating vastly superior weapons. Left alone, the *Excalibur* could become dangerous to any and all, but with a pilot—"

"No, Talen." I couldn't lose him like that.

He dipped his chin. "I understand your apprehension."

No, he didn't. He couldn't. Not fully. Or he wouldn't be suggesting this.

"A union will not hurt me."

"Maybe not to begin with, but I saw what a union did to the fae pilot."

"You saw the results of hundreds of years of abuse beneath Oberon's hands."

Irrational anger had the next words falling out of me too quickly to pull them back. "I know what it feels like to be subjected to years of Oberon's abuse, and I don't care. I cannot lose you to this ship. I won't."

He reached for me. "I'd still be here."

"I'm not discussing this." I stepped back, out of his grasp. "I will not see you trapped again. You must persuade the ship to take us to Faerie without bonding with it. Please, Talen. This must happen."

Something dangerous flashed in his eyes, reminding me he was no pushover. "Yours is not the only destiny playing out in front of us, Kesh."

He'd do it without my consent. He'd do it because it was the only way. Eledan had asked me how far I'd go, and I knew if I asked Kellee, Sirius, Sota, or Talen the same, they'd reply with the same answer I had: they'd go to the end and beyond. "Aeon died because of me," I said quietly. "I can't lose you too."

Compassion softened his face, but he would not give in. "It is not the same."

"Just... try? Can't you command it or something? It's new, and you're a powerful fae in your own right..."

He bowed his head again and turned his face toward the ceiling. Glittery dust settled on his cheeks and snagged in his soft lashes. Time seemed to slow. The bright specks rained from the ceiling and froze in mid-air, forming the position of each known star. He was meant to be among them, which was likely why my half-star soul had always called to him, but I was not brave enough to let him go.

The ship groaned like an enormous beached beast and the metal creaked beneath layers of organic material. I couldn't tell if the ship was protesting or just replying. Talen's brows pinched. With his eyes closed, he spread his hands beside him, steadying himself against the shifting floor.

The groaning and creaking reached a crescendo, the ship threatening to rattle apart. If the *Excalibur* exhibited too much unusual behavior, would the humans fire?

"Talen?"

He staggered. His top lip peeled back. He snarled around gritted teeth, and then the noise and movement ceased. Talen gasped and blinked himself back into the room. He saw me and winced. "Don't ever ask me to command him unpiloted again."

"I..."

"You have your wish. The *Excalibur* is returning to Faerie."

He left me alone in the navigation chamber, stirring an icy chill in his wake.

CHAPTER 37

Faerie was not how I remembered.

I observed the planet from the *Excalibur*'s command deck. What had once been a glowing orb of light and color now throbbed all shades of red.

"Shit went down while we were away, huh?" Sota remarked, drawing Kellee's side-eye.

Lightning split the churning clouds. Numerous storms swelled and sloshed like waves, and as we watched, heaving masses of what I assumed was the Hunt's magic heaved off the planet's surface, disturbing Faerie's atmosphere. Shit had definitely gone down. My guess was the Hunt hadn't been too pleased to learn its primary targets had abandoned it. Had we been gone any longer, it likely would have breached Faeries atmosphere altogether.

"And the dark fae are down there?"

"They will be," Eledan replied to my left. "The arena your ill-fated harem met me at to hand you over is also a dormant lifewell. They'll come through there."

That was the place Eledan had made me believe the earth had tried to swallow me whole. Bastard.

"When?"

"When you go there and call them to you."

Great. I had to get down there, amid a maelstrom and be the Nightshade, right under the Hunt's nose. "Sota, I'll need you by my side to hide me from the Hunt as long as possible."

"I got your back."

Kellee glared down at Faerie like he could screw it up in his fist and toss it away. "I should be there. The wraiths may recognize me."

I nodded and asked Eledan, "What do we do once we have our army on Faerie?"

"Channel the polestar," he replied grimly. "The presence of the dark fae will distract the Hunt enough to give me time to prepare the book."

Sirius had left to retrieve the thimble from Talen moments ago. He returned now, with it in his pocket, its presence like a beacon in my mind. Eledan plucked the acorn from his pocket and handed it to Sirius—the only fae we all trusted to have both pieces in his possession. I sensed each piece like they were living, breathing beacons demanding I steal them and crush them. Eledan shot me a raised eyebrow, feeling the same ominous push and pull.

"The Wild Ones and the sidhe will be waiting for our return," Sirius said, keeping his distance as I'd instructed. I didn't trust Eledan not to grab the polestar power for himself while we were wrangling countless fae.

"Of course they will," I grumbled.

Talen wasn't here. I could have ordered him to come, but there was nothing here he didn't already know, and after forcing him to command the *Excalibur*, I didn't feel like ordering any of them to do anything they didn't want to.

"Can you get a message to Sonya?" I asked Sirius. He nodded. The last I'd seen of my saru friend, she'd been in

Sirius's sanctuary with other saru Sirius had been trying to wean off their innate desire to serve. My gut told me she and the saru would help if they could. "Tell her to be ready."

"And the plan?" Kellee's sardonic, liquid drawl rolled over us.

"We get the Hunt as close to the book as we can..." I deferred to Eledan, who continued to gaze at Faerie, blue eyes pinched and mouth set in a hard, slanted line.

"We will have an army of dark fae and vakaru wraiths—wraiths you can control, Marshal, now that you're brimming with my brother's blood. We will have all willing saru at our potential command, the Messenger-Nightshade, an evolved wardrone, a guardian, and myself. The sidhe lords are few and have never liked the taste of battle. They will buckle first. As for the Wild Ones... it's time I dealt with them."

"How?" Kellee pushed, too familiar with Eledan to let him slither out of answering.

"With empty promises," he replied without missing a beat.

"What promises?"

"They want Kesh's power..." Eledan circled a hand in the air. "It's not a concern."

Kellee's eyes narrowed. "The hell it's not—"

"Kellee," I tried to appease.

He glanced my way, pupils rimmed in red. "The last time we went into battle, Aeon and Sirius took you, just as Eledan took you from me in the past. I won't stand here and let you tell me to trust him when we all know he's a manipulative shit. Eledan, you will explain how this ends right now, or this ship isn't moving."

Eledan calmly regarded Kellee like the live wire he was. "You do not control this ship, vakaru."

"And do you think Talen will take my word or yours, *Dreamweaver*?"

Eledan's grin morphed into the type he knew baited Kellee. I shoved him, resisting the urge to turn that shove into a punch. "Stop. There's no time for this."

He looked at where I'd touched his arm and then back up to me, his expression teetering on the edge of rage.

I dropped a hand to my whip. "You can tear strips off each other when this is over." *If any of us survive.* To Kellee, I said, "Eledan made a deal with the Wild Ones for my life."

"He did *what*?"

"The deal stopped them from harming me."

"Is that what he told you?"

"At this stage, it really doesn't matter—"

"Why, because you think you'll die down there?" He came at me with raw vakaru burning in his eyes. "It matters. *You* matter. You're surviving this. We're all surviving this—"

"Unlikely." Eledan snorted.

Kellee lunged. I blocked him, locking my stare on the vakaru desperately struggling against Kellee's control. The beast in him glared through me, until Kellee blinked and eased back beside Sota and far from Eledan, composing himself.

"Kellee..." I spoke softly. "I need you under control."

"Oh, I am... You'd know if I wasn't." He flicked his hands out, banishing his claws before they could fully appear. "You'd all best know this: I don't give a shit about Faerie. I will do whatever it takes to keep Kesh safe, and if that means the whole damn system collapses, so be it." His stare found Eledan and burned. "If you betray us, I'll turn the wraiths on you, and don't think I won't."

"Understood, vakaru," Eledan replied, startlingly reasonable for once.

A few moments passed and the tension dissipated.

"We're really doing this?" Sota asked.

Events had led us right here, either by fate or by Eledan. Halow's fall, Arcon's rise, the Game of Lies, Hapters's dark fae, and Valand's dead... Whatever the source, there was no escaping what would come next.

I took Sota's hand and gave it a firm squeeze. A smile warmed his eyes. "We're doing this," I told him. "Together."

Talen entered the command deck. His gray and silver scout leathers reminded me of the same outfit he'd worn when we'd first met. Their severe cut made his outline lean and sharp. His hair, braided close to his scalp, rested in tight plaits over one shoulder.

"Are we ready?" he asked, formal and distant.

I nodded. "Take the *Excalibur* down to the surface."

IT SEEMED the entire sky was stormy, but where I'd expected devastating thunderclaps, a thick silence and stillness hung over the arena. Faerie was holding Her breath.

If there was ever a time to help me, Faerie, that time is now.

Eledan walked ahead to the center of the old, abandoned arena. Ancient organic arches reached over our heads but had broken and crumbled before meeting in the middle. Nothing seemed special about the space, but if Eledan said there was a lifewell here, I trusted him with that information, if little else.

He climbed a curved set of moss-covered stairs to an overgrown platform and gestured beside him. "Stand here." When Sota tried to follow me, Eledan added, "Not you. Just Kesh."

He reluctantly hung back. Kellee stood nearby, claws out

and senses alert. Sirius lingered behind, flames licking at his hair and clothes like sprites. Talen had stayed with the ship, soothing it and keeping it under control should we need a quick getaway. I missed his guiding hand. He would know whether Eledan was full of karushit.

"Trust me, Kesh, or don't, but make a decision. Time is not on our side."

I stepped onto the spot he'd indicated, expecting something to happen.

"Now what?"

He stepped back and spread his hands, looking at the ground. "Now to add a little of Mab's *gift*."

I waited and huffed. Here we were, standing beneath the Hunt's churning darkness with little to no plan, waiting on the Dreamweaver to get his act together. What if this was all for nothing? But he'd gotten us this far, even if I did despise his means.

The surrounding vines slithered apart, revealing the polished black stone beneath and the shining fae letters, like those I'd seen on Hapters, etched into the surface.

Time, our prison.

Dark, our sentence.

Light, our freedom.

The depth of that meaning clicked inside, shifting a core part of me and awakening the alien power near my heart that I attributed to the polestar. Eledan glowed with intertwining rope-like green light, feeding his magic—Mab's magic—into the platform. This had been the plan all along. Mab was always going to bring the dark fae back, right here, but she'd needed the polestar to do it. The map, the lifewells, the prisons—it all led to this place. Thousands of years of unrest, thousands of years of Faerie's decay, was about to end—if we trusted Eledan.

Eledan licked his lips, rolled up his sleeves, setting the green light writhing, and brought his forearms up between us. Dark vine-like warfae marks slithered across his skin —*moving*. They were the key, and we stood on the final door.

I knew what to do.

I tossed my coat off, loosened my shirt, and rolled up my sleeves, exposing my marks to Faerie's air and Eledan's life magic. His green threads lassoed around me, coiling up my exposed arms and slipping beneath my shirt, exposing the marks. Where they touched, trickling buzzing energy fizzled my skin like a low electric current.

I let it happen. Before now, I would have pushed Eledan's magic away, pushed anything Faerie back, but I was part of Faerie. We were all Faerie's children, and only now did I feel as though I belonged.

I locked stares with Eledan. The marks on my arms and neck plucked free and intertwined with those reaching from Eledan's skin. His eyes shone with liquid green life magic, and maybe mine did too. I felt the Nightshade wings unfurl, their translucent weight a steady push against my shoulders.

Oberon had made me his tek-whisperer. Faerie had made me part of her polestar. The dark fae had made me their Nightshade. The people of Halow made me their Messenger. All for this moment.

If Eledan had only told me sooner... but would I have been ready to hear my destiny before now? *Discovery is worthless without the journey.*

The sound of his tek-heart beat inside my mind, keeping pace with the throbbing power beating through my veins. He was the key. I was the lock. I hated him, had dreamed about killing him a thousand different ways, but I understood him too. This had always been our future.

The platform trembled. Light blasted over us and up,

surging free. For a moment, I couldn't see or breathe. Eledan's magic—Mab's magic—became my entire world, and then the darkness flowed closer. I knew them all, each and every single dark fae. Their darkness reached for mine, and I *pulled*, opening their way home.

There was no concept of time or anything outside their arrival, just the thundering, roaring surge of unseelie beings flowing in and pouring forth. By Faerie, it felt so right, like setting a million souls free.

More and more they pushed through, and the sense of rightness swelled, lifting the light from my veins. Dark and light. *Embrace both and you will prevail.* Ailish, despite her treachery, had spoken the truth.

The light, the dark, the power, ended.

Senses numbed, I heard Sota calling my name, but he sounded so far away that it couldn't be real. Why couldn't I feel anything?

Kellee's face filled my vision. His eyes blazed and sharp teeth glinted. I couldn't tell if he was angry or afraid.

".... here!" He pulled. His claws dug into my upper arms. "The Hunt... Kesh."

He pulled again, and the sharp jabs of pain plucked away the numbness, making me whole again. Kellee dragged me stumbling down the steps. A roaring had grown out of nothing, but it wasn't in my head. All around, moving shadows painted the trees and flowers. The sky churned with dark fae and a thick, blackening cloud with two enormous moon-like eyes.

"Wait..." I pulled an arm free and tried to turn.

Eledan was still on the platform, on his knees. He had his hands locked in his hair, his face screwed up in agony. He fell forward, tears streaking his face.

"Wait, Kellee. Eledan needs help—"

But Kellee pulled, ignoring my pleas.

Sota fired into the sky.

His shots struck the suffocating blackness and punched inside, brightly glowing before the Hunt snuffed it out.

"Wait!"

Kellee pulled. Ahead, the *Excalibur*'s huge bulk waited, his doors open.

I mentally reached for the dark fae, hooking in and yanking those nearby under my control. *"Protect Eledan!"*

The dark fae took flight like a cloud of a million bats. They swarmed in and rose up in a great wall, blocking the Hunt.

It wouldn't be enough to hold it back.

"The book..." I whirled on Kellee and tore my arm free of his grip. "Bring the book now!"

His wide eyes were the last thing I saw before I dashed back toward the platform.

"Kesh, no!"

Shadows surged alongside me. Kellee's wraiths. He'd sent them to my side.

By the time I'd climbed back onto the platform, the dark fae's screams rivaled those of the Hunt, and the shadows became solid figures, each one creating a wall around the platform. "Eledan..."

He panted, hunched over on his knees. His eyes were squeezed closed, like he didn't want to see or couldn't. He clutched his chest—over his heart. This wasn't how it was supposed to be. The life magic was his magic. It shouldn't hurt him.

"Eledan?"

The air tasted like death.

The platform shook.

We would die here if I couldn't get him up and moving.

"Eledan, please…" When I touched his shoulder, his whole body trembled.

"It is… the worst of me." He spat the words, eyes still closed and head locked in his hands. "I did not… mean for this… to happen."

"I know…" I dug my fingers into his shoulder, holding him firm so he knew he wasn't alone. "I know you didn't want this."

"I just… I wanted Faerie… to see… me."

"She does."

His mouth twisted. "Not… like this." He opened his eyes, and they shone with unshed tears. "Not like this, Kesh. I am truly sorry, for everything."

"Eledan, please. We must move."

He shook his head. "I was so very wrong. I believed revenge was all I wanted… To make them see me, as you wanted them to see you. But my true desires are much simpler. I didn't want their love, in the end. I just wanted… yours."

The plea in his eyes almost broke me open, but now was not the time for this. "Eledan, I…" *I can't love you.* But I could lie? The words almost came, but something stopped me. No more lies, not even to appease his madness.

"I know." He looked down. "I can… make it right." He tore his hand from his chest and nestled there, locked in his fingers, lay his caged tek-heart. The pain on his face faded. He looked at his heart like he didn't recognize it as his. Then his fingers parted, and the metal cage fell to the platform with a tinny rattle. The heart inside beat in a stuttered, irregular rhythm, each thud potentially its last. But he was immortal… wasn't he? Removing his heart hadn't killed him before.

"I made it right…" he whispered. "A death for a life." Color bleached from his lips. His eyes dulled from blue to gray. He looked at me, and for the first time, I saw him as he had been before: a fae desperate to be seen, to be loved; a fae so alone in the world that he'd created monsters to force Faerie to see him.

Eledan was dying.

I pulled him into my arms, pulled him so close there was nothing between us but his tremors and mine. He melted against me. His soft, shallow breaths fluttered against my cheek.

"You can make worlds..." he whispered, "and break worlds. Kesh, *live* and make the worlds better than I ever could." The words left his lips, and when I expected to feel his breath on my cheek again, it didn't come. His tremors faded. His weight lessened, and the solid crush of his body against mine dissolved into lifting, shifting clouds of glittering dust. The dust fell through my fingers and wisped away like smoke... like a dream I couldn't hold on to and would never get back.

Live.

I wanted to tell him more and make him feel that whatever he'd done, it was all right, that together we'd make it right. But the cold, dead heart trapped in its metal tek-cage told me he was not coming back. Not this time.

I clutched it in my grip and squeezed—crushed it so hard that the tek split open, and inside, the hardened dead thing that had once been Eledan's heart shattered into a thousand pieces. Jagged pieces of tek stuck in my palm. Blood welled, but among the broken bits hid a small, glowing stone no bigger than its acorn cousin: one-quarter of the polestar. I stared at the fragment and watched, numb, as the cuts on my hand sealed and the bleeding stopped.

I'd healed.

Live.

I remembered. Below Arcon, when I'd felt more alive

than ever, when he'd brought me back... I'd felt different. I still felt different.

How do you live knowing you die a little more every day?

His melancholy.

The real reason for our return to Arcon.

All life required a cost.

Eledan had traded his for mine.

I closed a fist around the piece of polestar and stood. Above, the sky was a swirl of dark fae and tangible, lashing darkness. The Hunt hadn't won. Eledan had removed himself from its grasp. The dark fae were home. Faerie was once again complete. I had the book and the polestar.

It was time to end this.

Wispy, watery tendrils appeared a few feet ahead. They grew and knotted together, forming a translucent body. I realized too late what I was seeing.

Ailish rushed in. The iron collar clicked into place around my neck.

ellee

No, no, no! Not again.

The wraiths withdrew, and where Kesh had kneeled, the platform was empty. Both her and Eledan had vanished.

"No!" Sota breathed, staggering forward. He paused, getting that long look in his eyes that said he was figuring something out. "She's not here. SHE'S NOT HERE, Kellee!" He whirled. "I can't sense her anywhere nearby. She's... gone. She's gone!"

That fucking fae bastard. I'd known he'd pull a stunt like this.

The Hunt loomed above, cushioned behind an enormous bank of dark fae. But those dark fae weren't enough to stop it. Only the book under my arm could do that, and now Kesh was gone...

"Get back to the ship."

"We have to find her."

"Sota. Fall back now!"

Sirius met us at the ramp, his face like thunder when he realized neither Kesh nor Eledan followed our retreat. "Where are they?"

"Close the doors."

The doors rumbled closed, and the ship's lights flickered from green to red, signaling the ride was about to get rough.

"Where are they, Marshal?" Sirius demanded, stalking close behind me.

The ship lurched, throwing us against the walls. "As best I can tell, Eledan took her."

"Then he took her to the Wild Ones..." the guardian snarled.

As the ship leveled, I strode onward through the corridor, with Sota armed at my side. "Will they be in Safira?"

"It's likely," Sirius confirmed, following behind.

"Then that's where we're going."

"We don't have the numbers to fight them," he warned.

I'd seen the dark fae flood the air. I'd felt the wraiths pour in. "Once we didn't. Now I'm bringing my army to their damn doors, and nothing will stand in my way."

"And how do you intend to get there?"

The *Excalibur*'s corridors throbbed around us: tek and magic woven together in harmony, creating the deadliest warcruiser in all four systems. We had the weapons we needed to go to war right at our fingertips.

My gaze fell to the guardian.

"No human vessel can travel to Safira," he said. "Safira has never granted Oberon's warcruisers access."

Never was a lie. This ship could do it because it had the best fucking pilot Faerie had ever produced. "Buckle up, Buttercup. This ride's about to get rough."

TALEN ENTERED the command deck and slowed at the sight of all the living, breathing organic constructs, complete with silvery tek-veins and magic that had made my senses itch while I'd been waiting for him.

"Where is she?" His cold, rigid look spoke of centuries spent among the fae courts. He and Kesh had argued, that much was clear, but he'd do everything in his power to save her.

"Safira."

He stopped near the foot of the steps leading to the raised deck and braced a hand against the rail. "You want me to order this ship into Safira," he guessed. "The *Excalibur* isn't ready for a journey like that. His navigation is limited. The chances are slim he'd even arrive in the correct location. One wrong calculation and he could deliver us into the heart of Faerie or worse. It's too dangerous."

"Don't tell me that." I descended the steps and looked my friend in the eye. "There's a way. There's always a way. This is Kesh. Eledan has her. We brought her back once, against all the odds. We can do it again."

"Without mature navigation, Kellee, it's almost impossible. As immortal as we are, we would not survive an impact such as you're suggesting. We'll be no good to Kesh then."

"Almost impossible?"

He breathed in and held that breath, fearing the words he spoke next. "No starship can travel blind unless it has a pilot who already knows the final destination."

To get us inside Safira with enough firepower to frighten the Wild Ones into submission, he'd need to bond with the ship. *Shit.* A newborn ship that had never had a pilot and was half tek—it could kill him.

Since Kesh broke their bond, he was free to pilot, but bonding with a ship was a permanent arrangement. There was no knowing what this tek-and-magic hybrid would do to Talen. Kesh would not want this.

"Not that way." I sighed. At every turn, there was an obstacle in our way. "Dammit, Talen. We need a break. We have the weapons we need right in front of us and we're still losing."

He nodded, understanding, and looked around him as though seeking the answers among the knots and tangles of tek and vegetation. "We could go in alone with Sirius's help... as we did before."

"They'll be expecting us," Sirius said. He and Sota entered, with Hulia close behind.

"We're getting my girl back, right?" Hulia asked, her gaze falling expectantly to me for answers I didn't have.

Sirius crossed the floor and eyed up Talen. "We need to end the battle before it begins. This ship can do that."

Talen winced. "The ship also needs a guiding pilot. Without one, he's volatile and dangerous. I tried to tell Kesh, but she has strong feelings on this."

I could imagine how that conversation had gone. Kesh already felt as though she'd lost him once. She couldn't lose him again. It would cut her too deep. "We can find another way..."

He lowered his gaze and ground his jaw. "I'm resistant to tek. I'm the only fae pilot who can bond with this ship. Once I have him under control, we will gain a formidable weapon in this war that could help subdue the Hunt." The more he talked, the more determined he sounded, and the more the words made perfect sense. "At the least, any warcruisers the sidhe lords employ against us will fail. With this ship at our control, we'll command the sky."

Not all weapons must be used... but it sure made fighting a war much easier if you had a weapon the other side feared.

But Talen would lose his freedom, which he'd only recently discovered. Since he'd spent much of his life behind bars as my prisoner, I wasn't the best person to argue with him on this.

Talen waited for one of us to argue, and when we didn't, he added, "What is the use of having the best pilot on the Messenger crew if I cannot fulfill that destiny?"

Sota stepped forward. He struggled with his words, doubting himself. "Is there no other way?"

"None that feel as right as this." By cyn, Talen was going to do this.

"You don't know how this ship will react to you," Sota said.

He smiled at our tek-friend. "That is the way of all pilots." Shrugging off his coat and under-jacket, he revealed the play of concentric circle marks etched into his arms. I'd seen him strung up as part of a ship before, when Sjora had tried to force him to pilot for her. Everything about that had felt wrong, but this was different; he'd chosen this.

Sota took Talen's coat and jacket, his gaze lingering so long on Talen's face that Talen said, "This is not an end."

"If Kesh were here, she'd stop this."

"I know... but what we want and what we must do are sometimes two different things."

Sota sighed out hard. "She'll kick our asses when she learns what happened."

He chuckled. "She'll understand—eventually." As he headed to the center of the deck, I stepped in and caught his arm, drawing him back around. His gaze met mine, acceptance nestled and resignation there, the same look he'd given me all those years we'd had bars between us. This was happening. Nothing I could say would change his mind.

"Pilots are meant to fly, Marshal," he said.

I released my grip and nodded, finding anything else I could say had lodged in my throat.

Talen found the original captain's chair beneath all the overgrown vines, tore them off, and lowered himself comfortably into its embrace. The silvery veins that had been working their way through the ship snaked up his legs. He wet his lips, placed both hands on the chair arms and leaned back. The thin silver veins thickened, turning into long, needle-sharp probes. When those needles pierced his skin and slithered inside, I winced. He didn't. The veins thickened into arteries, rooting to the chair in the same way Eledan had been rooted to Arcon. Nothing about this seemed natural, but then, nothing about Faerie felt natural to me either. I almost couldn't watch, but if he could sacrifice his freedom for us, then I was damn well watching the ship adopt my friend until it was done.

Silver fingers filtered through his hair and plunged into his neck, above the rise of his collarbone. His lashes fluttered. Silver flooded his eyes, blinding him like I'd seen happen a hundred times, but this time, it would be permanent.

Sota's fingers found mine, seeking comfort.

The ship jolted, as though shoved in mid-air. The lights blinked out.

"What—" Sota began.

The lights flicked back on, blazing a brilliant silver. The entire deck shone. Even the glass was streaked with veins of shimmering silver, like dragonfly wings. Power nipped at my senses. The ship's power and Talen's, combined as one.

"Ready?" Talen asked, his voice a strange echo of its former self. His fingers flexed on the chair arms, and light rippled through the silvery veins across the floor, strumming through the ship, making it hum a pleasant note.

I took a seat, careful to flick the vines away and watch for their creeping touches. Sota, Sirius, and Hulia took up their own seats and strapped in.

"As ready as we'll ever be."

Sota grinned back.

"Let's go get our girl." Hulia thumped her seat.

Talen smiled, and the ship's humming grew, its engines powering up.

Safira was in for one hell of a surprise.

CHAPTER 39

Kesh

Cold iron had never felt heavier.

When the rush of water settled, I blinked into Safira's obscenely bright colors and a hundred different but horribly beautiful sidhe faces, none I recognized. It was only a matter of time before the courts acted on what they'd see as a saru stealing power over them. I'd been expecting it, but with a crisis around every corner, I hadn't seen the sidhe lords' revenge coming.

Something dull and hard struck my lower back, driving me to my knees. I grabbed my whip and set the tails loose, but while I lashed out at one or two onlookers, others plunged in and tore the whip from my grip.

Smooth but hard fae hands grabbed my arms and yanked them behind my back, bringing my wrists together. Barbed vines sank into my skin and tightened. All this happened while the collar clamped off my burgeoning power. Ever since

Eledan had woken me inside Arcon, that power had been growing, but now it was gone. The collar had choked it off, like a tourniquet. I had no magic to reach for.

Hands bound and whip gone, I snapped my teeth at the fae, like the wild thing they thought me to be. I wanted to crawl into a ball and hide. Everything I'd earned, everything I'd fought for, felt too big to carry or dream of. On my knees and powerless, subjected to the fae, I was a nothing girl again. Damn them all.

"The mortal saru who wanted to be queen." A sidhe lord laughed. His tinkling laughter tickled the air, joined by a dozen others. Say what you would about unseelie, but at least they wore their ugly on the outside.

A nameless fae guard hauled me to my feet and shoved me through the jeering crowd. The pretty sidhe weren't the only ones here. Wild Ones were peppered throughout the crowd, eager to see the Nightshade, or whatever I was to them, brought to her knees. After my run-in with Dagnu, I'd left them as their equal, but the sidhe had torn me down.

The crowd parted, creating a clearing in the center of their village. There stood a huge vertical oak column. The guard shoved me against it. More sidhe swept in, tying my wrists behind the column so tightly the wood grated my spine.

The small, winding streets brimmed with hundreds of fae. Some leaned from overhanging balconies to get a better view. Agitated wisps buzzed overhead, making colors dance. So many fae, so many colors, and the sickening taste of their magic rammed its way down my throat. Had Eledan died so I could be humiliated in front of a crowd while the Hunt grew ever stronger?

Ailish came through her people like a watery phantom.

"One last show from the Wraithmaker," she announced to the crowd's glee.

There had to be a way out of this. I tried to swallow around the tightness of the collar.

I hadn't come this far to die at the hands of a mob and a mad Water Witch. Eledan hadn't died and given up his immortal life so she could use me. Kellee, Talen, Sota, and Sirius—they hadn't joined this fight to see it end uselessly here.

"What do you want?" I asked, holding a snarl.

Her hand burned cold against my chin. Her fingernails dug in. "Now that the Mad Prince is dead, your soul—the polestar—belongs to the Wild Ones."

I still had Eledan's polestar piece safely in my pocket, but the iron collar prevented me from accessing the power running through my veins. "Not true." I tore my head free from her grip. "His deal died with him. You don't own me."

She laughed. "You are saru. Of course you're owned."

"Why are you doing this? You told me we were all Faerie's children. You said I would save Faerie."

"You are, just not in the way you expected. I told you what you needed to hear."

"We need to stop the Hunt."

"The Hunt is chaos. Faerie began in chaos. She will be returned to chaos."

"And Sol? Halow? What of them?"

"Ours to reclaim."

Her sidhe crowed and her Wild Ones alike jeered and voiced their agreement.

Was there any good on Faerie? Talen believed there was. Sirius did too. I trusted them. And hadn't Faerie chosen me, a mortal saru, to harbor the polestar? Surely Faerie knew how this should go, and it wasn't so we could war with Sol all over again.

Despite the dire circumstances, a smile found its way to my lips. "You won't win this."

"How do you figure that?"

With hundreds of pairs of eyes on me, I raised my voice so they all heard, and so Faerie's breeze could carry the words far. "I have the Dark Legion. I have the last vakaru war chief. I have a guardian and a wardrone with a grudge. I have the saru, and I have a lord who became the first Nightshade. The Dreamweaver, a fae you all fear, sacrificed his life so I may live." My voice cracked at the reminder of Eledan's sacrifice. He'd given me more than his life; he'd given me his immortality, something none here knew. "So ask yourselves, how long will it be before this parade of fools brings the weight of the dark legion down upon you?"

Her grin reminded me of a curved, serrated blade. "With that collar around your neck, you have nothing."

She must still fear me, or I'd be dead already. "What do you have but some angry sidhe lords who are annoyed because their saru have left them?"

"I have Faerie, and that is all a fae needs."

I laughed and enjoyed the freeing sensation. "No, you don't. You told me Faerie loves all Her children, and that includes the saru and the humans of Sol and Halow. Billions of lives gone. Faerie's children murdered. That was not Her wish. Sirius, one of the oldest fae, turned to me, and Faerie approves. Talen, from a time when unseelie and seelie were one stands beside me, and Faerie approves. The last vakaru, left alive by Oberon, commands the wraiths of his murdered kin, and *Faerie approves*!"

Murmurs rippled through the crowd, turning over their

uncertainty. Ailish's grip on the sidhe lords was tenuous, like her grip on the truth.

"I have the polestar in my soul, put there by Faerie to end this turmoil." The wisps bobbing above the crowd glowed brighter. Strings of pulsing faerie-lights shone in every color. There were no stars in Safira, because all the light was down with us, and that light knew me; it knew my words, and it approved. The Wild Ones stirred, no longer sure of Ailish and her ways. Maybe I wasn't queen just because Eledan had made it happen, they wondered. Maybe it was always meant to be this way.

I tugged on the wrist bindings. If Faerie truly were on my side, now would be the time for Her to help.

I know you and I haven't seen eye to eye, but I need you now, I silently told Her.

Ailish saw her crowd falling apart, but the sidhe lords would not be deterred. One nodded her on. I didn't know him, but it didn't matter. They all believed I was owned and unworthy.

I pulled against the vines. *C'mon, Faerie, cut me some slack here. You made me the polestar, now help me end this for you.*

Ailish produced a bone-handled iron dagger from the folds of her silk dress. "It is a shame Eledan will not be here to see you fall." She drifted closer. Colored light licked off the blade. "He was a talented creature we misguided."

For all his mistakes, he'd died so that I got to live, and I wasn't about to let his sacrifice end here.

You neglected your prince, your child. Do not neglect his final act. Help me, Faerie. Help your children do the right thing.

"Where is your precious Dark Legion now?" Ailish's cool, hard fingers dug into my cheeks again. Her face pushed close, revealing both sides to her, the side I'd believed and the burnt ugliness that had festered in Faerie for millennia.

"At least Oberon believed what he was doing was right. You're just a mad witch clawing at power she can never own—"

The blade punched into my chest, stealing my breath and spreading its ice-like cold through my veins. This couldn't be right. It wasn't supposed to happen like this.

I'd been so sure I'd get free or Talen and Kellee would come... It didn't seem possible that the dagger's plunge was real. I had known I'd die—I had known I'd leave Talen, Kellee, Sirius, and Sota behind—but not before it was over. It wasn't right. *This* wasn't right. I hadn't come this far for it to end now.

I clutched Eledan's piece of polestar, willing it to do something, but the fragment that had fueled his heart for so long hummed uselessly in my fist. I searched the crowd for a face I knew, for anyone who might help me, but the sidhe had crowded in, creating a wall of sinister glares.

How could it all be for nothing? Whatever I'd become, the truth of me, Kesh Lasota didn't fucking die here.

"When you die, as you will in these next, precious moments, you'll turn to dust, and among your ashes, dear child"—her fingers sank into my hair and clutched the back of my head—"I'll find the polestar. When your legion come for you, so distraught they will be to learn of your demise that I'll take the remaining polestar fragments from them. Its power will finally be mine, and the Wild Ones will reign, lawless and chaotic, once more."

Invisible ice had a hold of my legs and waist. Higher, it coiled, so cold I couldn't breathe through it. I'd fought my entire life. There had to be a way to fight this too.

"Give in, child. Embrace death."

"You're... wrong."

She stroked my face and smiled like I imagined a mother might.

By Faerie, this is not how it ends!

More ice needled across my skin, plucking and pinching over my chest, where my heart stuttered its final beats. The sound of pixies chirping faded. The whole world fell quiet, and then the light faded as each wisp blinked out, one after another. Ailish's face fogged and blurred until there was nothing but darkness and the quiet of two beating hearts: mine, and the warm, pulsating beat of Eledan's fragment locked in my fist. It wasn't fading. I looked down. The fragment glowed through my fingers, the only bright thing I could see. Safira had gone. The fae had all gone. There was nothing but the quiet and that fragment feeding warmth up my arm. A dream... or something more?

A soft breeze touched my neck, no heavier that a wisp's wings.

"*A death for a life,*" Eledan whispered, but I could not see him or anything beyond the glowing fragment locked in my hand. *"A heart for a heart. A death for a life. What cannot be taken must be freely given."* He paused, and his sigh warmed my cold skin. *"Perhaps a forgotten prince may be forgiven."*

Light.

Everywhere.

It burned through skin and bone, and scorched my soul. I screamed, but my voice was too small to hear inside the blazing brightness.

I fell into the light, and I remembered Eledan once telling me, *"A monster among your kind, and a monster among ours. It must be a lonely life, Wraithmaker."*

Not lonely, just without a place. Until now.

ellee

THE SHIP JERKED out of motion, and the vines, which had tangled across my chest during travel, almost severed me in half from the force of the sudden deceleration. I clung to consciousness enough to know the wash of bright light pouring in through the ship's windows was not normal. Where it touched the floor, small curls of smoke drifted into the air.

Talen, fully latched into the ship's systems by hundreds of silvery veins, jerked in the chair and threw his head back, agony tearing through him.

I freed a handful of claws, cut my restraints, and lunged for him. I hadn't guarded him for hundreds of years for him to die now, bound to the chair by tek-and-organic veins, his eyes wide, silver, and unseeing, but there wasn't a damn thing I could do to fix whatever was wrong with him.

"What's happening?" Sota was out of his chair and

heading toward the light-flooded windows, but the moment he touched its glow, he stopped. The light, where it touched his boot and leg, began to melt both.

"Get out of the light, you idiot!"

"But it doesn't hurt," he remarked.

Sirius hissed something alien and fae. "This is Safira..." He approached the light, his aura pumped up on Faerie's magic, setting him ablaze. "But something is very wrong."

Something was wrong, all right. Talen hissed every breath through his teeth. I reached out to touch his hand, clamped on the flightchair's arm, but the tek tying him down writhed and sank deeper into his veins, forcing me back.

"This was a fucking terrible idea, Talen! If you die, you fae son of a bitch, I don't care where your wretched soul goes, I'm coming after you so you can explain what happened to Kesh. Do you hear me?"

His chest heaved.

I considered cutting him free, but crudely severing a ship's bond with its pilot would kill them both.

"*Pole... star.*" He pushed the word out.

"Is that what that light is?" Hulia asked. "It's stunning."

One problem at a time. "Dammit, Sirius, can you help him?"

The guardian tore himself away from observing the light. "Light from the polestar is flooding the ship's external sensors. Talen is just experiencing too much stimuli. He'll recover."

My heart plummeted through my gut. "If that's the polestar out there, then where's Kesh?"

"It's not the entire polestar." Sirius dug the acorn and the thimble out of his pocket, both glowing in his palm. "Not yet—"

"*Take the pieces to her!*" Talen struggled to speak, and just as

Sirius looked down at the pieces in his hands, a blast of light stole the guardian's fire-laden presence away, transporting him right off the ship.

"You finally got rid of him, right?" I asked Talen.

A hint of a smile lifted his lips.

"Kesh is alive?" I asked.

His lashes fluttered but didn't fully blink over his silver eyes. "Yes." I could only imagine the mindfuck he was dealing with, but at least he was coherent. "Then take us down there, Talen."

"Not yet."

"Why not?"

"Dark fae... coming. Hunt... coming. Need control and power above Safira." His speech came easier now, and although his eyes stayed silver, he blinked over their sheen. "We opened the door..." he said. "Now there's nowhere left for anyone to hide."

esh

THE COLLAR CLATTERED to the ground, half melted and warped. I looked at that twisted piece of metal and then at the dagger handle sticking out of my chest. I plucked the dagger free and looked at the blade. Its crude iron was a simple design that could no longer hurt me. Nothing here could hurt me. Not anymore.

Combined with Eledan's piece, I was half the polestar, and the other half was close.

Ailish's face dropped. She backed away, drifting off the ground in her eerie ghost-like way. She hadn't expected a useless nothing mortal girl to rise from the ashes as the polestar. Without Eledan's gift of immortality, maybe I wouldn't have, but I was damn well here and alive, and I had a debt of vengeance to collect.

With a flick of intent, I was beside her, having moved meters without taking a step. The wings were back, though I barely felt them. Their starry reflection shimmered in Ailish's one good eye.

"Faerie sends her regards, bitch." I slashed the blade wide, moving too quickly for her to counter. Intent became action, with nothing in between. I wanted her throat cut. The polestar in me made it happen. The iron stunned her more than damaged her. It would take more than one little dagger to kill or capture her.

A good thing, then, that a beacon of flame was making his way toward me. Sirius had the rest of the polestar on him.

"Fire Lord?" Ailish humbled herself before him. Whether she didn't know how to fight him, didn't want to, or the iron had weakened her, he flung his liquid flame at her, more powerful now than I'd ever seen from him. She screamed and kept on screaming as the blue-and-orange fire devoured her.

I didn't have it in me to care about her death.

Sirius was in front of me, presenting me with both pieces of the polestar. I knew what I looked like to him and everyone else. The sidhe lords, unable to look away, saw me as a monster, and maybe they were right. The Wild Ones saw me as an unknown touched by Faerie, and that was enough for them.

"You are... undying?" he asked, deep worry lines etched into his usually stoic face.

I nodded, still coming around to the idea. "Eledan gave me a gift."

He frowned, either struggling with the idea of my immortality or Eledan doing something good. There would be questions later, if we survived what came next.

"The Dark Legion and the Hunt are coming," he said. Kneeling, he offered up the last pieces of the polestar. "Mylana... *Kesh*, this will not be easy. As powerful as you have become, the polestar is not easily contained."

Nothing on Faerie was easy. "I know, but I have Faerie on my side."

"She spoke with you?" He didn't bother to hide the note of awe.

"In a way." I picked up the acorn, so tiny a thing to have caused so much trouble, and its counterpart, the thimble. Four pieces scattered among the stars and lost for thousands of years, and here they were, found again and in my hands. The power would be astounding. I'd be godlike.

"Kesh?"

"Hmm." The glass thimble twinkled.

"Do not let the dark or the light seduce you," he said.

I heard the words, but here was a moment, in all this madness, that demanded I take the power and make worlds and break worlds, just like Eledan had, but for real, not just in dreams. He'd said I was better. He'd told me I could make better worlds, and that was what I planned to do. I'd made mistakes. I'd taken lives. I hadn't always been good, and I hadn't always done the right thing, but I was good now. Dark and light, unseelie and seelie, were balanced in me. There would never be a better time to save the worlds.

I took the polestar pieces in my free hand. "I've got this."

Rolling, monotonous thunder sounded from above, and there, in the sky, hung the enormous hull of the *Excalibur*. His belly rippled with iridescent colors, like I'd seen on Shinj a thousand times. How was the ship here without a pilot?

Before I could ask, the thunder grew louder. The ship wasn't the source of the noise. Behind the *Excalibur*, a jagged tear opened the sky, peeling it apart, and from inside, the lashing, oily tendrils of the Hunt appeared, bigger than ever. The thing made of nightmares yanked itself through the tear and spilled its wretched form across the sky. The *Excalibur*'s silvery hull shone against its blackness.

"Who is on that ship?"

Sirius whispered, "Everyone."

The Hunt wrapped an enormous, swooping appendage around the *Excalibur*'s hull.

The wild fae erupted into screams and fled the pathways, leaving the sidhe lords caught between me and their fairytale nightmare.

The Hunt would surely crush the *Excalibur*, though his tek-bones might give him an advantage. "If Talen were to bond with the ship, they'd have a chance—"

Sirius's frown and his silence said enough. My wrecked heart sank. Talen had already bonded with the ship. That was how they were here. I'd lost him, and the last time we'd been together, we'd argued. The beautiful part-tek creature in the sky *was* Talen, and the Hunt had him in its grasp.

That changed things. Talen was a weapon, and a damn good one. All eyes turned skyward as the *Excalibur* glowed a bright, angry red. The ship's smooth hull rippled and shifted, like Sota's casing used to do before delivering a ton of "smack-down" defense. Sure enough, guns prickled his outer skin and blasted off an electric blue light. With a sky-shattering roar, the Hunt recoiled.

My insides flip-flopped.

Tek hurt the Hunt.

We had a chance!

I picked up my whip, dropped by the guards in their rush to flee, and relished the painful zing of tek and magic arching through my palm and up my arm. Like Talen, I'd been made with a foot in both worlds. The world of human-engineered technology and metals, which I'd navigated and used to my advantage, and the world of Faerie, which I'd been born into but had never been familiar with, until now.

Talen, as the *Excalibur,* let off another volley of sharp electric light, and the Hunt's pulsating mass shrank around its core, curling inward to protect itself. If we weakened it enough, it would have nowhere left to hide. Nowhere... but its home.

"Where's the book?" I asked Sirius.

"On the ship."

Of course it was.

"Can't one thing go right?" I clutched the throbbing, heated polestar pieces and backed up. "I'll draw it away from the ship. You get the book down here."

"Calla..." He hesitated, torn between following me and following my command. "You cannot stand alone against the Hunt. Are you ready?"

"I've never been ready for anything Faerie's thrown at me, but I'll survive. I always do." A different shifting darkness flooded into the sky, funneling around the Hunt. "And I'm not alone..."

Thousands of winged dark fae swarmed the ship and the Hunt. Each one was as much a part of me and Faerie as the stars were. With my whip crackling in my hand and my Nightshade wings spread, I focused my thoughts on them and commanded, *"Protect the ship. He's on our side. Distract the Hunt."*

The winged creatures pulled away from the *Excalibur*, flocking in great undulating clouds, like I'd seen Sol birds do on virtuavision. The dark fae were beautiful, and now they were home, where they belonged.

"Go," I told Sirius. "Bring the book to me at Talen's home. That's where this ends."

He tipped his head skyward, and in a blink, he vanished, snatched by the *Excalibur's* transport, leaving behind a dusting of embers.

Now I was alone among a panicked crowd. Living Faerie

throbbed beneath my boots, Her presence like a comforting hand on my shoulder.

I had the polestar pieces in my grasp. I had the power of Faerie's ultimate weapon at my fingertips and an army behind me. I was the Messenger to all, not just those on Faerie, or the saru, but to Sol and Halow, and I would not—could not fail.

alen

"It's withdrawing." Kellee announced what I already knew. The *Excalibur*'s high-energy tek-weapons dealt the Hunt considerable damage, enough for the ship to jerk at his reins and try to launch everything he had at the center of the churning nightmare. My grip on the young vessel held, but I'd been right. The *Excalibur* was like no fae or human vessel before it. As a combination of both, he had gained the firepower from the best of both races and evolved in ways I could barely understand, the same way Calicto had evolved. He was the future, tek and magic in harmony, but only if we survived.

The dark fae had pulled back, urged away from our hull by Kesh's subtle touch—a touch I'd struggled to ignore. She might never forgive my decision, but knowing what I knew now, it had been the right one.

The Hunt swelled. Purple lightning split its tumbling

clouds. The *Excalibur* charged his guns with my consent, but throwing everything we had at the Hunt too soon would reveal too much, and if it didn't work, we'd have no alternative to fall back on.

"Talen, get me down on the surface."

Kellee. Again. I would get him down there, but other paths were playing out.

Sirius, for one. Part of my mind observed him in the lower decks, collecting Eledan's book. Another branch observed Kesh below—her blinding light and hungry darkness like a beacon shining at the heart of Safira. The Hunt knew she was there, but I'd kept the *Excalibur* between them. The dark fae helped with that, and now the wraiths were close. Another force also bristled the edges of my reach. A human force. The Sol fleet. I'd hoped the niggling itch of alien tek was a glitch —some error in my bonding with the ship—but their presence had swelled outside Safira. Knowing humans as I did, they would follow the dark fae and wraiths inside the hole we'd made. Whatever plan Kesh had, she had better see it to fruition soon. I could not fight a war on two fronts.

"Talen, I have to get down there..."

Kellee's presence glowed hot red in my mind's eye. I didn't need to see with organic eyes to know where he was. The same as I knew where all the fae in Safira were and all those that were incoming, I also knew Eledan was not among them or anywhere. I nodded, struggling to concentrate on words when they were fast becoming superfluous.

"Sota..." His tek-presence glowed an electric blue. He approached, getting brighter with every step. He was more powerful here than he could imagine. "Go with Kellee to my home. Kesh is there." I didn't need to tell them to protect her. They'd die for her. "Sirius has the book. I'm sending him down now. I'll hold the Hunt back for as long as I can."

Kellee's hand fell to my shoulder, and although I didn't feel the touch on my body, I felt its comforting intent in my mind's eye.

"Don't do something stupid, fae," the marshal grumbled, his words an electronic crackle in my mind.

"Likewise, Marshal."

I sent all three down to Safira but kept Hulia on board, as my voice, should I need her, and turned my attention to the Hunt. The nightmare beast opened its enormous mouth and reached out to embrace the *Excalibur*. Funneling all weapons' targets down its throat, I smiled and sent the command. *"Fire."*

CHAPTER 43

esh

BRUISED LIGHT FLASHED across Safira's rolling dwellings and streets, and up the hill, into Talen's home, from where I observed through the huge window. Talen fired into the Hunt, but instead of recoiling, the thing swelled to an impossible size and swallowed much of the blast. Then it lashed the *Excalibur's* hull, tearing it open.

I gripped the polestar fragments, one in each hand. "No, you don't. You're never taking someone from me ever again, you son of a sluagh."

Where was Sirius with the damn book?

The *Excalibur* groaned and pitched sideways. Talen would have felt that blow as if the ship's flesh were his own. His pain threshold was high, but he couldn't hold out forever.

The ship fired a different weapon. It struck the Hunt and washed over it, sending thousands of tiny lightning strikes through its mass, like hundreds upon hundreds of falling stars.

Sirius fizzled into sight on the path leading up to the house, with Sota and Kellee beside him. Relief loosened the fear clutching my heart. Sirius had the book. He dropped it on the terrace and opened it to a random page. Eledan wasn't here to ask how this worked, but there was something of him left in me, and that something told me to draw the Hunt in close. I could only do that with the polestar's light.

Kellee saw me at the doorway and started forward. I shook my head. Whatever happened next, it could harm as well as heal.

"Where's Eledan?" he called up.

I tapped two fingers over my heart and watched his face fall. The time for explanations would come later.

"Stay back." I lifted both fists, the thimble and acorn growing too hot for me to hold much longer. "I don't know what will—"

Power.

It struck without warning and tore through my skin, surging inside and flooding into every vein, every cell, every microscopic piece that made me saru. I would not have survived had I been mortal. I wasn't sure I'd survive it now, but if there was anything I exceled at, it was defying death. By Faerie, this would not be the end of me.

CHAPTER 44

ellee

KESH BECAME a thing of light and power, a creature that made the vakaru in me want to drop to my knees and hope she either didn't see me or beg that she did. The man in me feared I was watching her die, and there was nothing I could do. The light was too thick to penetrate and too powerful to claw through, and at several dozen yards away, it burned everything exposed to it.

"She's all right..." Sota said. He stood beside me, guns armed. "She's alive inside the light."

Brighter, hotter. I couldn't stare into it any longer and turned away, shielding my face with my arm. She was a star, a beacon. I'd known it for months and known exactly what that meant.

"She's beautiful..." Sota's voice cracked, either from the magical interference or from his own emotion. He watched, his eyes able to filter out the brightness, but all I could see of him was a washed-out blur of whiteness. Heat beat against my back in long, painful waves. I wasn't leaving.

"The Hunt!" Sirius's shout penetrated the thunder above.

Darkness filled the sky. If Talen and the *Excalibur* were still up there, I couldn't see them. Even the winged dark fae had fled, although my wraiths crowded nearby, shadows upon shadows hiding from the light. Sensing I would need everything in my power to stop that thing from getting to Kesh, I let the vakaru fill me up, shedding all semblance of being anything other than unseelie.

The book lay open down the pathway, as useless and as empty as its author had been.

The Hunt blanketed us, as though the sky were black and swelling. Inside it, the faces of the dead howled and gaped, their hollow eyes turning inside out. They clawed and climbed to escape the nightmare. We could not allow this thing to escape Faerie. I loved Kesh, I loved her like I'd never loved anyone before, but staring into the heart of this thing, I understood her role and why she would give everything to stop it. She was the queen none of us had known we'd needed.

I glanced at Sota. His guns were locked and ready. His stance fierce. His eyes on his target. The wardrone would stop at nothing to protect Kesh. He lifted his guns, ready as the suffocating ocean of blackness descended over us, dragging its shadow across the land, forcing back Kesh's light. Dark and light ebbed and flowed and the earth groaned and shifted, coming to life where the two forces met.

Fear fluttered through my aged heart, a deep-seated fear I hadn't felt in centuries.

The Hunt's liquid laughter bubbled out of its depths, echoing its creator's, but this thing had gone far beyond

Eledan's design. It seemed impossible that a book alone could hold it.

"Your reign is over." Kesh said the words, but they did not sound like hers. I squinted into her glow and made out the pattern of dark wings backlit by a brightness too hot to observe. "Oberon took two weapons from Faerie, and we *will* return them."

The Hunt's laughter rolled on and on. *"The Nightshade has grown into her wings."*

"Return to the book and survive among its pages or perish forever."

A column of oily blackness descended and deposited a figure, neither male nor female but with the body of a fae—no face, no expression or detail, just the outline. It stopped at the book and looked down. *"Time, our prison. Dark, our sentence. Light, our freedom. The time has come for me to be free."*

My wraiths crept closer, their shadows inking the ground. I caught Sota's careful side-eye glance and gently nodded. We would not get a better opportunity than this, and with Kesh behind us and Talen behind it, we had to act now.

"You have your creator's arrogance," Kesh said, "but even he saw his errors in the end. Go now and remain part of Faerie, as is Her wish. She loves all her children, even you."

The Hunt's dark chuckle tried to slide beneath my skin.

"Power is meant to be wielded. That *is the way of Faerie. And I am more..."* It trailed off, and for a moment, its outline froze, cracked, and dissolved.

"Now!" I mentally sent the wraiths forward.

Sota fired his electric guns, blasting out great darts of light.

Shadows became real and fluid, each one similar to the Hunt's chosen appearance, but each one had a soul, a purpose, and had once had a life. These were my vakaru, and they'd had enough of Faerie's fuckups. They launched themselves at the Hunt, claws out and screaming. Sota fired his electromag guns, strafing the Hunt with tek-bullets. Light blasted from Kesh in a great, snapping column that tore through the dark figure, burning it away. Together, dark and light united, we were beating it.

Then two great red eyes opened in the blackness above, and the Hunt roared across the Safira rooftops and through its pathways, turning into a river of soul-eating smoke.

We'd pissed it off.

The blackness washed up the path to Talen's home, consuming the wraiths that tried to stop it, and then blasted over Sirius, quenching his blast of flame as easily as someone might snuff out a candle between their finger and thumb. In the next breath, he was gone, consumed along with the book.

Kesh's light doubled down. The column snapped and twisted, pushing back, but it wasn't enough. If the polestar wasn't enough, nothing was.

I flung out my claws and charged.

esh

IT'S NOT ENOUGH.

Every trial won, every challenge overcome to bring me to this moment, hadn't been enough.

Faerie, damn you, if this is not your wish, help us!

The Hunt swallowed Sirius, and then Kellee was gone, devoured in the Hunt's monstrous avalanche of darkness. Only Sota remained, somehow holding the Hunt back as he fired stream after stream of his tek-arsenal into it. My drone, once so small, held back a world-ending nightmare on his own.

I pulled on everything I had, reached for everything unseelie, and drew down, demanding they answer. And they did. The monsters rushed closer.

It's not enough.

The Hunt had grown too strong.

Mentally, I reached far and wide into Safira, farther into

Faerie, calling for help, for strength, for light, and heard Faerie's creatures answer. Countless bright souls, each one a piece of Faerie, answered my call. Wisps by the millions, so tiny on their own, but as they breached Safira's swollen sky, they shone with a light second only to mine. And more arrived. The saru who had been forced to fight and kill their own. Gladiators with their saru names hidden inside their souls. My family, my people. Sonya and those who had escaped their love of the fae, and others only recently freed. They answered and sent me their strength.

It's not enough.

Time was something I couldn't control, and we had already run out.

The Hunt's grasp reached around Sota. His guns smoked, his firepower immense. He screamed at the thing, and then the screams died in a static as the darkness consumed him too.

Grief added the fuel I needed to keep the light burning. If we died here, let it be for something. Let it be to save the innocent and stop the Hunt from spilling chaos across Faerie's sister worlds.

I emerged onto the terrace, aglow like a star forced into a body, wings like those that belonged to the unseelie, and a living tek-whip alive in my hand. ***"I am the Messenger and all of Faerie stands against you."***

The Hunt's laughter rolled on, as deep and far-reaching as never-ending thunder. I poured more power into the light, drawing reserves from the souls that had tried to come closer. It could not end this way.

Then the Hunt was an inch in front of me, choking off my light, and its blackness stretched into forever, like Eledan's mirror had. All of the worlds would come to this. To nothing.

"This is not Faerie's wish," I whispered, not needing to

raise my voice. The darkness was the only thing left to hear me.

A distant boom sounded. Then another. The noise was muffled, but I heard enough to know those were not Faerie noises. Another boom sounded, shuddering through the air, and the Hunt reared away, dragging its smothering weight with it.

Ships.

Not Faerie made. Sol made. The Sol Alliance emblem, which depicted their central star, blazed on their hulls. They appeared in the dark, peppering the Hunt's blackness with their tek-light. And they fired. Again. And again. And again. Great holes gaped in the Hunt's central mass, sizzling with lightning. The wounds didn't heal.

The Hunt pulled itself from Safira's paths, revealing Sirius, Sota, and Kellee sprawled on the ground. And the book, its pages open.

Kellee's clawed hand twitched.

My heart leaped. *He's not dead.*

Sirius's flame spluttered back to life.

They live!

Sota pushed up on his trembling, burned arms.

They were okay.

"Kellee..." I dropped to my knees beside him and turned him over. He winced, baring sharp teeth, then cracked a vivid green eye open. My stubborn vakaru lived! "I thought you gone."

"Now you know how I feel..." he groused.

"Holy shit... the humans found us!" Sota stumbled to his feet.

"At least they are on our side this time... for now." Sirius looked down at the book. "Kesh?"

I hauled Kellee to his feet and helped him hobble to the book.

Sirius knelt beside it. "Now that you are the polestar, touch its pages, summon the Hunt here, and end this."

"Is randomly touching fae artifacts a good idea?" Kellee asked. "Will it eat her?"

"Perhaps," Sirius replied.

Before they could argue over the best way to test Sirius's theory, I knelt in the dirt and spread my hands over the pages, like Eledan had forced me to do before. My skin crawled with an unpleasant itch, as though it were trying to unpeel itself and slither free. As I watched, the marks I'd carried for most of my life fell from my arms, from the backs of my hands, down my fingers, and into the book. Once on the pages, the marks morphed and twisted, transforming into fae words. Without Eledan, we could only hope those marks would be enough.

"What is that?" Sota asked, watching the words twist.

"It's the end..." Sirius let the words settle, and I lifted my hands.

Another boom sounded above, so loud I felt it in my bones. The Hunt screamed, and as it writhed away from the bank of Sol ships, the *Excalibur* emerged at the fleet's center, bigger, brighter, and aglow with fae colors.

A wind whipped up, carrying magic throughout Safira.

The fleet fired its tek-weapons again and again, each one landing like an iron nail through the Hunt's center. The Hunt's enormous weight lessened, and its darkness thinned, until the nightmare was little more than a normal storm being pounded into submission.

Sirius cradled the book in his arms and turned toward the sky and the battle overhead. He lifted the book and read the ancient fae words—Eledan's words, from long ago, when he'd been a young and naïve prince desperate for Faerie to notice him.

The Hunt twitched and snapped, shrinking with every blast, until finally it bucked away from the fleet and rushed toward us.

I caught Kellee's hand in mine and Sota's in the other. I knew Talen watched from above as the swirling, howling mass of nightmare turned into a thick column and plunged into the book. It howled its way deep inside.

After the last of it had vanished, Sirius slammed the book closed to a strange, calm quiet, broken only by the rumble of Sol ship engines.

It was over.

No... not over. There was one more thing to do.

Power cannot be taken. It must be gifted.

I closed my eyes, still gripping Sota's and Kellee's hands, and mentally called to the mother I'd never had.

"Faerie, I'm returning your gift. The polestar belongs in your sky, where it shall forever remain."

I expected more heat and light, but I simply felt Her gently run Her hand through my body. She was not malevolent, as I'd imagined, but a simple force made of balance and harmony, of time, dark, and light. Giving her back the polestar was the right thing to do, even if it meant leaving us vulnerable to Sol and their forces. Maybe now that Sol knew we were all Faerie's children, we could get along? At least for a little while. Either way, the polestar and the Hunt were weapons that should never be wielded again.

Power lifted from my soul. I let it slide off, like I was rising out of warm water. Above, Safira's strange sky peeled open like flower petals, presenting Faerie's night sky, and there, among a million stars, the brightest one winked at us, back where it belonged.

I would miss the polestar, but I was not sorry to see it go. I sighed, feeling more grounded and like Kesh Lasota by the minute.

"You did the right thing." Kellee's voice was soft, and the words landed gently in the strange, new quiet.

I squeezed his hand and pulled him closer, then did the same with Sota, tucking him against my side. I had done the right thing. We all had. Together, we'd ended the nightmare.

esh

HOURS LATER, when the dust had begun to settle, I ran my hand along the walls of Talen's home and watched colors pulse outward in small waves. The warmth hadn't faded, and with each new touch, my sense of comfort grew stronger. I didn't dare imagine what it meant. Perhaps this would be my home now? I'd never had a real home before.

In Talen's chamber, the view of Safira's valley drew me to the window. Tek-ships glittered in Safira's clear sky, and at their center, as though it were its own star around which all the others revolved, the *Excalibur* hovered. The humans weren't leaving, but they weren't attacking either, so maybe we had a truce to build on.

Beneath the eerie calm, the fae people slowly emerged from their homes, wary of the tek-machines hanging over them. Wherever the sidhe lords were, they'd be plotting against the humans. They likely wouldn't let this rest, but they'd have a hard time rallying any forces to war after what we'd all witnessed.

What happened now? The Hunt was gone, the polestar was back where it belonged, and Eledan was dead. Without a court, without a king, would Faerie fall into chaos? Or had balancing dark and light stopped that from happening? And me? I would live, and I had no idea what to do with an eternal life.

Sirius's presence simmered at the fringes of my awareness. He stood in the doorway, waiting for me to summon him. Would he stay with me? Would any of them? Was I still all the things to all the people, or was I something else without the polestar?

"There is much work to be done," he said, cutting short my quiet contemplation.

I rested my hands on the window ledge and soaked up the knoll's willing warmth. "I just need a moment." I needed more than a moment. I needed a lifetime to get over the past year.

Thanks to Eledan, I had a lifetime and more.

The *Excalibur*'s lights throbbed in time with the waves emanating from the knoll. Talen was watching me from above, and I took some comfort in that, even knowing he was lost to me, maybe forever. I had forever now, didn't I?

Aeon, Talen, Eledan, Shinj, billions of Halow lives, and thousands of fae—all gone. This war had cost us all so much. Those who remained would need help and guidance. The saru would need a purpose, or else they'd fall back in love with the fae. The dark fae had returned and would need their Night-shade. And now the Earthens were here.

"It's over, but I don't know where to begin fixing everything."

Sirius moved to my side. He breathed in a deep, steadying

breath, and lifting his tek-hand, he rippled his fingers, admiring the play of light across the mechanical construction. "We are at the beginning of something new, and beginnings begin with a single step."

I wanted to lean into him and let him hold me, but if I did, I might never take that first step, then the next. "The future seems so big."

"You defeated the Hunt and healed Faerie. You survived as a gladiator, and survived Oberon and his brother. You stopped Sjora and the Wild Ones. Yet making peace seems difficult, Calla?" Pride brightened his eyes.

I *had* done all those things, but not on my own.

"I can fight, but peacemaking? I do not know how to do that. Maybe I'm not the right person for what comes next?"

"I believe Faerie made the right choice in you, and I am not alone in that thought, the same as you are not alone in what comes next." He took my hands in his, gently holding them between us. "I will stand beside you, as your guardian, for as long as you'll have me."

I swallowed the knot in my throat. He and Kellee were made for bigger things than me. I'd already lost Talen... The knot tightened. I clenched my teeth and fought off the ache. It was still early. I didn't have to do everything now. I just needed to stop and take a few free breaths. I was free now, wasn't I?

Sirius's cool metal fingers slid between mine and clamped closed, offering comfort. Tek and magic in harmony was the way forward, but change wouldn't happen just because the threats had passed.

"I second that..." my lawman drawled, sauntering into the room in full-on vakaru mode, his hair free and claws gleaming. He looked as though he belonged here, among the Wild Ones and dark fae. "If you thought you could ditch me now that your crusade is over, you obviously don't know me."

Sirius released my hands and stepped back, yielding to Kellee.

Kellee dipped his head. Sirius had earned his place among us.

"Kellee..." Seeing him never failed to set my heart racing. "I can't keep you here. You're destined to be a great leader. Your wraiths are out there. They need you."

He stopped on my right and leaned against the wall, every inch the cocky marshal I'd run into in the sinks. "They need you too. You are legion, Kesh. Sirius knows the sidhe lords like no other, and you can bet they'll kick off soon. He's perfectly placed to subdue them. As for me? I'm the only lawman left, and you're going to need a sense of justice on New Faerie. The wraiths will stay, if you'll have them among your dark fae." He looked around, at us all and nodded to himself. "I see the beginnings of a ruling council that will serve *all* Faerie's children."

"You hate Faerie."

He shrugged and raised an eyebrow at Sirius, who quickly wiped off his smile. "I hated the Wraithmaker too, but as it turns out, we get along just fine. I'm sure I can make an exception for a few other fae."

I unpinned his star from my coat and handed it over. When he hesitated to take it, I grabbed his hand—avoiding his claws—and dropped the star into his palm. "If you're policing the fae, you'll need this, Grand Marshal."

Kellee's smile turned sly. "Grand, huh?" He tucked the star into a pocket and seriousness stole his smile. "The fact Eledan's not here trying to warp this into some nightmare means... what?"

I shook my head. "A death for a life."

Kellee's brow tightened. "He gave you his?"

"Magic cannot be taken. It must be gifted... and he gave me his when he took me into the well below Arcon." I hadn't known it at the time, but looking back, his melancholy made it obvious. "I wouldn't have survived the polestar without his sacrifice."

"Well, shit, that makes it a hell of a lot harder to hate him."

Eledan had left his mark on all our lives. The back of my neck prickled at the thought that without him, I might never have met Kellee. His machinations had caused countless deaths, but his last act had finally been selfless. I could never love him, but I could respect him for changing his nature.

"If we're pledging our allegiance to Kesh, sign me up." Sota breezed into the room. He eyed the guardian, prompting Sirius to arch an eyebrow, and then beamed at me. "You're going to need a bodyguard who can kick fae and human ass with style and without prejudice."

"That role's taken, Sparky." Kellee stretched his claws.

"With *style*, vakaru. You look like someone's rabid hound." Sota planted a hand on his hip. "Appearance is important while negotiating with humans. Plus, they blame you for killing hundreds of them."

"Thousands, actually, and Sota has a point," Sirius said, startling everyone by agreeing with Sota.

Kellee rolled his eyes. "I liked Sota better when he was a murder ball."

As they bantered, my heart swelled. Maybe we would be okay. I wasn't alone, and with everyone working toward a cause, we had a better chance than anyone of making peace stick.

My gaze was drawn once more to the sky and the ships

waiting there. A piece of us was missing. His absence felt like a hole in my heart that might never heal.

Sota caught the direction of my gaze and said, "We should hail the Sol fleet before they fire on us and start a new war."

Yes, we should, but I was still reeling and needed time... just a little moment on my own to stop and breathe and live.

Sirius withdrew the book from inside his coat and gave it to me. *The Origin of the Wild Hunt* I'd expected it to be heavier, but nothing about it had changed. I dared not open it. It looked like any book, and that made it terrifying.

"We should hide it somewhere among the stars." And I knew just the pilot for the job.

ADMIRAL BRIGGS BROUGHT a small contingent of guards with him as we walked Safira's recovering pathways. Sota hung back, ready to fry his ass if he pulled any funny human business, while Kellee and Sirius had opted to spread the word that we were prepared to help Faerie and Her children adjust.

In return, Faerie was on Her best behavior, and besides a few too-curious wisps that swept too close to Briggs's guards' itchy trigger fingers, the negotiations had succeeded. Briggs would return to Sol with a signed decree that stated, while Faerie was in this new transition, we would maintain peace. It was the best I could honor, considering Faerie had never had a ruling democratic council before and the fae seldom accepted change.

Exhausted, and with the adrenaline of the last few days leaving my veins, I wanted to curl up in a bed and sleep for a week, but I had one more thing to do. Talen would leave with the Briggs's fleet to represent Faerie. I just had to ask him if he would be our emissary and if he'd take the book and hide it. This meant I had to go see him as a pilot.

I wasn't ready.

I'd never be ready.

The first and last time I'd seen a pilot, he'd begged me to kill him. I couldn't watch the same torture happen to Talen, but I owed him a visit. Without his sacrifice, the Hunt would not have been weakened. He had won us the war, and it had only cost him his freedom.

The ship transported me up, and I arrived in the corridors outside of the command deck, with Hulia smiling sadly. Talen could have transported me so I'd appear right in front of him, but he'd given me the choice to enter or walk away. Or maybe he'd wanted me to see a friendly face.

Hulia threw her arms around me and pulled me in close. "It's all right. He's not hurting. He's content."

I wanted to cry in her arms, but I somehow pushed the swell of emotion down. Stepping back, I straightened my whip at my side and sighed. "I wanted to speak with you about the saru. Can you help a friend of mine, Sonya, suggest to them that there's a new home waiting for them on Calicto, if they want it? Calicto needs guardians, and the saru need to get away from Faerie if they're to ever be free."

"Of course, *sugah*." She beamed and stepped away from the door.

Walking through felt harder than anything I'd faced, knowing that what I found inside would break my heart, but I couldn't rest until I'd thanked him for doing what I couldn't allow. He had a million worlds to visit. He was free now, as it should be.

"All right," I told him.

The door opened, revealing a command deck filled with brightly colored flora. The smell of night lilies and jasmine soothed my rattled thoughts. Whatever else he had become, he was still Talen inside.

Vines and roots slithered out of my way, offering me a path. This wasn't like the other ships I'd seen or been inside. Silver tek wove among the organic growth in a marvel of evolution. Talen was the future, but it still hurt to know he had a higher purpose. The Messenger wouldn't be the same without him.

The path presented a meandering way to the flightchair and the figure absorbed within. I lifted my gaze and blinked through tears I had no hope of holding back. Of course, he was beautiful. A vision of a fae, wrapped in the *Excalibur's* embrace. There was no violet in his sightless silver eyes and no slight smile upon his lips.

I'd told myself I wouldn't cry.

And I'd failed within seconds.

This was what he'd wanted. He'd chosen this. I would respect that. I didn't own him. I didn't own any of them. They'd always been free to follow me, but Talen... I'd loved his honest, gentle heart and kind words. He'd encouraged me when I was low. He'd loved me when I thought I wasn't worthy. He'd never hurt me and never would. Talen was a better person than any of us.

He heard me now and saw me. He probably knew how I felt better than I did. Shinj had always sensed our emotions.

"This is..." My voice failed. I cleared my throat and tried again, wiping away the tears to pretend I was holding it together. "I don't know if anyone told you, but Eledan gave me his immortal life. He gave me a gift I'll forever be grateful for." An immortal life I couldn't spend with Talen. Fate was cruel.

His expression stayed blank, and my heart fractured.

"I understand why you did this, and I don't blame you.

Well, maybe a little, but I'm only saru..." Nothing. I was talking to a wall. "You are remarkable, Talen. I will miss you more than you'll ever know."

He'd become so integrated into the ship he probably couldn't talk, but I wanted to hear his voice, one last time. I wanted to feel his touch on my face and his kiss on my lips, and I never would. He was further from me than he'd been behind the glass cage I'd met him in.

More tears fell. I angrily brushed them away. "We did it, because of you and this ship, because of your sacrifice. Thank you. It's not enough, I know, but thank you, from all of us." The bioluminescent lights glowed a warm green. A good color. He was content. That was all I could ask for, I supposed. It didn't seem fair. He'd feared that this mission would kill me. I should have died, but here I was with countless lifetimes ahead of me, and none I could spend with him.

"I just... I wanted to say... I love you, and I wish—I wish we'd had more time."

His silver lashes fluttered. He blinked. It was a small sign, but seeing him move told me he was still in there. I wanted to go to him, but if I did, I'd want to touch him, and I wasn't sure my heart could take it.

He blinked again. His right arm moved, dislodging a bundle of tek-vines. The silver threads unraveled and coiled away, freeing his arm, and then more dislodged, unplucking themselves from beneath his skin. Where those threads detached, he healed. The thicker arteries at his chest snapped free, and Talen gasped, becoming animated. I watched, fixed to the spot, caught between wanting to rush to him and help him and not wanting to upset what was happening. The ship was letting him go.

His lashes fluttered again. Silver bled away, and the fierce rings of violet burned through.

Oh, by cyn, dare I hope he was coming back?

He pulled an arm free, then the other, and shoved from the chair, tugging his right leg against the vines that hadn't yet released him.

I couldn't wait any longer. I rushed to him and threw my arms around him. He trembled. My fierce, devastating fae *trembled* in my arms.

"Kesh." His fingers sank into my hair. He pulled me close —so close he surrounded me, tucking me into him.

"I thought I'd lost you..." The damn tears were back, wrecking my voice.

"Never." He staggered, free of the ship's grasp.

I hugged him close and breathed him in, filling myself with Talen. "I'm dreaming?"

"No, this is real." He caught my face in his hands. The frown messed up his features, and what looked like pure determination had his eyes wide and emotive. "I love you too, Kesh. I've loved you since I met you, my star."

He kissed me, messy and desperate. Breathless, I kissed him back. I was never letting him go again. "How?"

"Evolution..." He wiped my tears away. A secret smile touched his lips. "Tek and magic. The rules have changed. I can bond when needed and walk away when not. You changed the rules, Kesh."

It seemed impossible, even as I had him in my arms, warm and solid and so very Talen. "You're really free?"

"We all are." He kissed me again, with a smile mixed in, then withdrew and said, "You are remarkable."

I grinned, feeling as though my life was finally my own, and echoed, "We all are."

We really would be okay. The saru, the humans, the dark fae, everyone. We could make it happen, together, just as he'd always believed. The Messenger really had made a difference.

Looping my arm around his waist, I helped him away from the flightchair. We had come a long way together, and we had a long way to go. Maybe the biggest challenges still lay ahead, but with my guardian, my vakaru, my silver fae, and my wardrone beside me, we would prevail.

The dream began like any other on New Faerie, full of wants and color and light. I danced among the fae, the saru, and a few intrepid Sol humans. The jolly Wild Ones played their music. Their laughter tinkled, and from high above, the stars observed, captivated by life. Kellee was here, dancing with the others, his long hair braided and beaded as it had been on Valand. Sirius made the light from the campfire frolic among us, directing it with his hands as though he were a maestro directing an orchestra, and Sota showed the young fae his array of gleaming tek-weapons, igniting their squeals.

I danced and whirled, as free and unburdened as the wisps that twirled overhead. The music became my heartbeat and my body the music. Hand to hand, we danced, skipping and clapping, switching partners around and around.

This was freedom. It was love and life and everything I'd never known but now had lifetimes to experience.

A warm hand caught mine. Another slipped around my waist. I fell laughing into the familiar grip and rocked with him, ignoring the warning niggle at the back of my mind. Nothing could hurt me here. Nothing could hurt me again.

We danced, and when warm, fat raindrops fell from Faerie's sky, I lifted my face and let the rain kiss my cheeks. A soft, teasing kiss brushed the column of my neck, and the fae whose arms I had fallen into said, *"You danced with the Dreamweaver and carved out his heart, but there is no death in dreams, my queen, where we shall never part."*

I woke with a gasp, jolting up in bed, the words still alive and real in my head. Their touch fluttered against my neck. I rubbed the strange sensation away and searched the knoll's shadowy room.

Kellee stirred on my left and rolled over, blindly reaching. "Okay?" he mumbled.

On my right, Talen blinked awake, instantly alert. "Kesh, what is it?" He shifted to sit up, but I laid my head back down, pillowed against Kellee's chest.

"Just a dream..."

Talen wasn't buying it, so I added the kind of sly smile I knew he couldn't resist and pulled him close, hooking him by the leg to reel him in. Even with them so close I wasn't sure where they ended and I began, the dream words slipped through. Sleep crept closer, and I wondered if my reply had been a lie and if anything would ever be "just a dream" again.

The End

Did you enjoy the Messenger Chronicles? Please leave a review here. All reviews help books find new readers, keeping the authors you love, writing the stories you love.

Don't forget to sign up to Pippa's newsletter. She'll email you most months with news, competitions, art and more...

The Veil Series

Wings of Hope - The Veil Series Prequel Novella

Beyond The Veil (#1) (FREE everywhere)

Devil May Care (#2)

Darkest Before Dawn (#3)

Drowning In The Dark (#4)

Ties That Bind (#5)

Get your free e-copy of 'Wings Of Hope' by signing up to Pippa's mailing list, here.

Chaos Rises

Chaos Rises (#1)

Chaos Unleashed (#2)

Chaos Falls (#3)

Soul Eater

Hidden Blade (#1)

Witches' Bane (#2)

See No Evil (#3)

Scorpion Trap (#4)

Serpent's Game (#5)

Edge of Forever (#6)

The 1000 Revolution

#1: Betrayal

#2: Escape

#3: Trapped

#4: Trust

#5: Deliverance (coming in 2019)

New Adult Urban Fantasy

City Of Fae, London Fae #1

City of Shadows, London Fae #2

Writing dark LGBT fantasy as Ariana Nash

Sealed with a Kiss, 0.5 Silk & Steel

(free to Ariana Nash subscribers)

Silk & Steel, Silk & Steel #1